THE SHOFAR
AND THE
ECHOES OF TIME

A TIME TRAVEL NOVEL

BY JOSHUA KREITHEN MD

Cover by Joshua Kreithen MD
Artwork by Jacob Kreithen
Edited by Leslie Kreithen

First paperback edition published 2018

ISBN-13: 978-0692144220 (Shofar & the Echoes of Time, The)
ISBN-10: 0692144226

To Missy,
Skylar,
Ginger,
Madison
and Gavin

THE SHOFAR AND THE ECHOES OF TIME

THE SHOFAR CHRONICLES
BOOK 1

CONTENTS

CHAPTER 1

THE NAZIS

Amsterdam August 4th, 1944

It's a dark and rainy night. Suddenly a bolt of lightning streaks across the turbulent sky high above the occupied city. The thunder is deafening. A lone figure in a grey trench coat runs across a cobblestone street just as another flash of lighting illuminates the Nazi flag waving violently in the strong wind on top of the Gestapo headquarters on Euterpe Street. More thunder rolls through, shaking the buildings below. The running man, stopped by the guards in front of the building, shows his identification papers. The guards allow him to enter.

After a few moments, the double doors burst open and dozens of heavily armed Gestapo police run into the street and begin to file into the back of two transport trucks parked next to the headquarters. Lightning bolts and thunder continue as the storm becomes more intense. The rain and wind are torrential. Finally, the Nazi trucks are full, and the two truck drivers come out and get in the front cabins.

The Gestapo Police Chief Legers calmly walks out of the building alone, looks up into the sky and slowly puts on his black leather gloves. A streak of lightning flashes above the building, revealing Legers' severely scarred face. He has gleaming blue eyes and short blonde hair. His black cap is decorated with an eagle and a skull with crossbones. He makes a sinister smile and begins to laugh loudly. He runs from the covered porch through the heavy rain and gets into the first truck. He yells "Gehen!" at the driver, and the two trucks begin to accelerate down the street towards the city center.

It's late at night. The rain and lightning continue. There's no other vehicle traffic. The trucks pass by the massive Rijksmuseum and cross over the Singelgracht canal. Both trucks are driving fast. Several pedestrians wear raincoats and hold umbrellas; and a few bicyclists almost get run over. Legers orders to the driver to turn on the police lights and siren. The other truck follows suit as well. The loud sirens are piercing. After crossing a few more canals, the first truck with the Police Chief makes a left onto Prinsengracht Street and heads northwest. The second truck continues straight on Nieuwe Spigelstraat.

The first truck continues along Prinsengracht Street for several blocks and abruptly stops in front of one of the row houses along the canal. The address plaque says 263. It stops raining just as the police siren and lights are turned off. All along the street frightened residents look out from their dark windows at the Nazi truck. The Police Chief gets out first and looks up at the house. Next the driver gets out, runs to the rear of the truck and opens the back door. The Gestapo police begin to jump out, and Legers points to the top floor of the four-story row house and yells "Sie sind auf dem Dachboden, hol sie!" The Nazis smash the front door down.

The second truck continues north through the city along the narrow streets. Just as the rain stops, they pass an empty Rembrandt Square. There are Nazi flags and posters all over the once festive square. In the far corner of the square on some tall wood posts are three bodies hanging on nooses with burlap over their faces. On their ragged shirts are the yellow Star of David emblem with the word "Jude" embroidered in the center. The truck turns and then stops in front of one of the nearby row houses. The blaring siren and police lights are turned off.

Above in the attic of the house are several families of Jews who have been hiding from the Nazis for over 4 years, ever since the German occupation on May 10th, 1940. They hear the police sirens coming from afar, and their fears came true as the sirens came closer. Now, evil and fate stares them directly in the face.

Yeshua, a 13-year-old boy with red hair... cautiously peaks out the attic window and looks down. "They are here Mama, they are below," he whispers to his mother, a thin frail woman huddled in the corner of the room with her husband and his two other siblings. There are a total of 12 souls in the room, all frightened to death. Yeshua knows why the Nazis are here; everyone in the room knows why they have been hiding here for so long! Could the rumors be true of what the Nazis do to the Jews after capture? Downstairs, they hear pounding on the front door and the yells "Erschließen! Erschließen!!!"

Everyone hears the front door being smashed in and then some screams followed by machine gun fire. Yeshua looks around the room. Some of the people are crying, some look white as ghosts. The older men get on their knees and start to pray. They chant *"Sh'ma Yisrael Adonai Eloheinu Adonai Echad."* Yeshua looks around the room for some way to escape. It's a small, triangular attic space. There's an undersized door on one side, and a tiny window overlooking the street five stories down on the other side. It's dark. The only light comes in from the streetlights outside through the window. The Nazis below are searching the entire house and coming up the stairs.

Yeshua's heart starts to race faster. In his mind, he is more angry than frightened. He thinks to himself "I must escape from this horror." Yet, where is he to go? How can he get out? He hears the Nazis come closer up the stairs. They are very close now. Everyone in the room feels pure doom. The footsteps on the stairs get closer and closer. Then, a knock on the door. "Offne die Tur!" The man yells... "Offne die Tur!" Then, a moment of silence. Yeshua steps slowly closer to the window. All eyes are on the door. The Gestapo begins to kick the door down and smashes through quickly. Although it's quite dark, Yeshua sees the German policeman clearly as they make instant eye contact. Holding a Luger semi-automatic pistol and pointing it directly at Yeshua, he yells "Im Namen Hitlers werden Sie alle verhaftet!"

Several of the other Jews in the room begin to cry and panic. Yeshua sees the Nazi's attention diverted for a moment, and then he makes his move. He turns around and runs towards the window. Time feels like it is standing still as Yeshua leaps forward and shatters the window into thousands of pieces as he breaks through. Arms outstretched, Yeshua flies into the air, if only for a moment he is free. The heavy thunderstorm has finally passed, and the full moon shines from above. He looks upwards into the heavens and wishes he could just fly to the moon, far away from this nightmare. Yet, after a moment, gravity takes hold of the young Yeshua. He starts to fall downwards. He sees the Nazi truck below. The wet cobblestone street reflects the moonlight back at him as he descends faster. He thinks to himself "I am free" just before he hits the ground...

CHAPTER 2

THE ROMANS

Beersheba Orphanage, Israel 2013

"Wake up, wake up! It's time to wake up!" Young Mohammed says as he shakes Yeshua awake.

"My dear Bedouin friend, I just had the most horrible nightmare," says Yeshua half asleep, covering his face with his pillow.

"Happy Birthday! It's your Bar Mitzvah day, Yeshua! It's Saturday. Are you excited?" yells Mohammed as he begins to shake the small cot upon which his best friend is sleeping.

"Ok, Ok... Oy Vey! I'm getting up. Is it time to leave yet?" says Yeshua.

"Yes! The sun is rising now. The bus leaves for Masada in 30 minutes. Let's get ready! I'm so happy and excited for you," exclaims Mohammed.

Yeshua has been preparing for this day for many, many months. He has been practicing reading the Torah, the Hebrew Holy Book, in this ancient rite of Jewish adulthood. He has memorized singing the prayers and a special verse of the Torah for this auspicious day. By tradition... after today, he will be a man.

Yeshua puts on his best clothes; grabs his satchel and the two boys leave the orphanage and walk down to the bus station a few blocks away. It's dry and hot in Beersheba, a small city near the Negev desert in southern Israel. The boys purchase two tickets and enter the old bus.

It's a bumpy 45-minute drive through the arid desert to the fortress of Masada at the forefront of the Moav

Mountains. The bus arrives near the cable car entrance on the east side of the Masada and the boys depart. They purchase two tickets at the visitor's center and enter the massive cable car that will bring them to the top.

Including Yeshua and Mohammed, there are 18 people in the cable car. As it ascends to the top, an old man with a long white beard wearing a tour guide uniform begins to talk to his group in English. The two boys listen in…

"My dear friends. Thank you for coming and welcome to Masada. Masada means 'strong foundation or support' in Hebrew, and this fortress palace was built by King Herod in the first century BCE. Because of its strategic defensive position on this giant elevated plateau thousands of feet above the Dead Sea, King Herod thought that this structure was impenetrable. During the turbulent times of King Herod, the Roman invaders occupied Israel, and there were many bloody revolts by the Jews for their freedom. In 70 CE the Romans finally destroyed the Second Great Temple in Jerusalem, and a group of Jewish rebels made their last stand here against the Roman legions. In 73 CE the Roman governor Lucius Flavius Silva came here with almost 15,000 men and laid siege on the fortress. They built a giant earthen ramp on the west side of the Masada with slave labor, and then…"

The cable car shuddered as it reached the upper station and came to a full stop. Yeshua looked out to the vast space eastward and saw the Dead Sea and Jordan in the far distance. He felt dizzy from being up so high in the air.

The tour guide said, "I will continue the story inside Masada. Follow me!"

Everyone left the cable car except Yeshua and Mohammed. Young Yeshua heard a loud buzzing sound in his right ear. He grabbed his ear with his hand and winced.

"What's a matter?" said a very concerned Mohammed.

"I don't know," replied Yeshua, "Something doesn't feel right."

"Where are we supposed to go now?" asked Mohammed.

The buzzing sound and discomfort in Yeshua's ear finally stopped.

Feeling much better, Yeshua said, "We are supposed to go to the Synagogue here for my Bar Mitzvah service!"

The two boys left the cable car station and walked up to the Masada entrance. Although Yeshua had never been here before, it all seemed so familiar to him. There was a giant stonewall around the entire perimeter of the fortress. He looked down at the zigzag hiking trail that came up the mountain thousands of feet below from the east side.

As they passed through the East gate, they were amazed at the massive scale of the architectural ruins inside. Yeshua did not need to look at a map. He knew exactly where he needed to go. He walked due west, past the storehouses and administrative buildings.

Yeshua found the ancient Synagogue in the northwest part of the plateau along the western wall and walked through the entrance. Gathered around the five inner stone columns stood six young boys, three girls and the Rabbi.

In the center of the room was a makeshift platform and table (Bima). There was no roof... the sky above was blue and cloudless. A warm desert breeze came from the west.

Behind the old Rabbi, resting on the stonewall, was the decorated Torah scroll. The morning sun continued to rise over the eastern mountains and prisms of light radiated through the dusty room.

Along the edge of the other three walls were five elevated stone steps upon which a couple dozen people were sitting facing towards the center. Yeshua realized they all were the family and friends of the other children who were about to become Bar and Bat Mitzvah.

It was time. Yeshua opened his satchel and took out his grandfather's old white prayer shawl (Tallit) and wrapped it around his shoulders. The other young boys and men, as well as some of the women in the audience, also wore their Tallit.

Yeshua then took out two blue skullcaps (kippot) and placed one on his head. He handed the other to Mohammed who smiled as he placed it on his head. Mohammed sat down on the stone steps. He looked at Yeshua and gave him a thumbs-up.

"Let us begin," declared the old Rabbi. Yeshua thought he very much looked like Gandalf from Lord of the Rings. All the children sat down on the folding chairs among the ancient stone columns. The Rabbi gently grasped his long white beard with his left hand and spoke.

"Welcome and Shabbat Shalom. My name is Rabbi Yohanan. We have all travelled from afar and are here at this sacred site to honor an unbroken chain of thousands of years of Jewish tradition. Today, here at Masada, these children will become adults in the eyes of God and our communities. They will read from the Torah and be blessed beyond measure."

The Rabbi looked up at the sky for a moment and paused.

"Almost two thousand years ago, the full destructive might of the Romans Empire came upon this very place in an attempt to defeat us. Yet, here we are… alive and well… two thousand years later. And where are the Romans? What has become of them? They are all long gone, only to be found in the pages of history books. As Jews, we have endured every genocide, every slaughter, every persecution to be here alive and present today. We will now initiate these young men and women into their sacred birthright."

Suddenly overhead, two Israeli F-35 fighter jets flew over Masada moving rapidly northwards. As they passed, a loud boom echoed in the valley as the jets bursts through the sound barrier. Behind the jets, a flash of compressed air formed into cylindrical swirling white waves of energy. Yeshua looked up at the sky in awe.

The Rabbi held his speech for a few moments until the reverberations gradually fell back to calm silence.

"Before we begin the Torah service, I want all of you to realize that this is much more than a religious ritual. Throughout the ages, the collective wisdom, experience and history of our ancestors now fill this space with us."

"Think about what it means to be a Jew. What are our collective values? Why are we here? What is our purpose?"

Yeshua reflected deeply on the Rabbi's words. He then recollected the horrible dream about the Nazis he had last night. He thought about the Romans. Then he remembered the history about the Assyrians, the Babylonians, the Egyptians and the Greeks. He realized that almost every world empire and culture in history that had tried to destroy the Jews were now completely gone. Yet the Jews still remain, miraculously surviving every era of time. He thought deeply about the repetitive pattern throughout history with the Jews and persecution.

The Rabbi continued. "There are three guiding principles upon which our future generations should pursue and follow. To the young men and women in front of me... as you live your lives, do your best to focus your consciousness on these positive behaviors. Also, at the same time, realize that it is much more important as to what you actually do in this world, rather than what you believe."

"The first value is 'Gemilut Hasadim', which means acts of kindness. Be kind and compassionate. Care for others. Not just towards Jews, but for all of humanity and creatures of this Earth. Be humble. Love thy neighbor as thyself. Even in a moment of anger... do your best to remove hate from your mind and act with benevolence. Take the high road whenever possible."

"The second is 'Tzedakah'. Help others! Be charitable. Feed the hungry. Clothe the naked. Heal the sick. Devote yourself to acts of higher service."

"The third is 'Tikkun Olam.' We are here, as Jews, to help repair this Earth. This world is very broken, like fragmented shards of splintered glass... and it is imperative that we heal it with our actions and good deeds. Be a light unto this world my friends!"

The Rabbi then started the Sabbath service. A variety of blessings, prayers, psalms were conducted, as well as some silent mediation. Then it was time for the Torah service. The Torah scroll was held high up in the air, marched around the room, then placed on the table in front of the Rabbi. Each child came up to read a portion of the scroll with the appropriate before and after blessings.

Finally, it was Yeshua's turn. He was called up to the platform. He sang the Aliyah blessing and then sang his Torah portion in Hebrew to the congregation.

His portion was from the Book of Genesis, Chapter 6 Verse 4 which in English translates to:

And it came to pass when man commenced to multiply upon the face of the earth, and daughters were born to them, that the Benei Elokim saw the daughters of man when they were beautifying themselves, and they took for themselves wives from whomever they chose. And the Lord said, "Let My spirit not quarrel forever concerning man, because he is also flesh, and his days shall be a hundred and twenty years."

The Nephilim were on the earth in those days, and also afterward, when the Benei Elokim would come to the daughters of man, and they would bear for them; they are the mighty men, who were of old, the men of renown.

Yeshua finished singing the verses perfectly and felt elated and euphoric. He sang the closing prayer, and the Rabbi placed his right hand on his shoulder in congratulations. Yeshua looked over to a smiling Mohammed and he saluted him with a fist pump from where he was sitting across the Synagogue. There was pure joy... he did it.

After finishing, Yeshua sat back down on his chair in the center of the room. He couldn't remember being this happy. All the months of preparation had come to fulfillment. The Torah service ended, and then the final prayers and songs were chanted as the service came an end.

The Rabbi then said "Congratulations on becoming B'nai Mitzvah! May you be a source of pride and inspiration to your friends, families and your communities. I wish you all the very best as well as health, joy and good fortune for all your days. L'chaim!"

The children were then surrounded by their friends and families. There were many hugs, smiles and high-fives that morning in Masada. The ceremonial wine and the challah bread were brought out into the celebration. Yeshua and Mohammed made a lot new wonderful friends that day.

As noon approached, the desert heat became oppressive. Yeshua was getting thirsty and decided to drink a glass of wine. After a few moments, he started to get somewhat dizzy. He heard that annoying buzzing sound in his right ear again, and decided to walk out from the Synagogue into the open Masada plateau for a breath of fresh air. The buzzing became louder, and then he grabbed his ear in discomfort.

The sound then dramatically changed. It seemed to get louder and louder, coming from a location near Masada's outer walls, just south of the Synagogue. It sounded more like a shrilling trumpet. Yeshua thought it might be the sound of a shofar, a ram's horn.

Yeshua had heard the blowing of the shofar during the Rosh Hashanah New Year's service and was very familiar with the sound. Now, he was absolutely sure it was a shofar.

Yeshua decided to investigate and started walking in the direction of the shofar's blowing sounds. Suddenly, the sound of three or four more shofar horns joined in unison. He unexpectedly felt very dizzy, and then his vision became blurry.

Ba-ba-baaaaaaaaaaaaaa…

Ba-ba-baaaaaaaaaaaaaaaa…

Ba-ba-baaaaaaaaaaaaaaaa…

Yeshua began to stumble and almost lost consciousness as the shofars became louder and louder. Then, the shofar sounds abruptly stopped.

He smelled smoke, looked around, and felt shocked to see many of Masada's buildings on fire. Red and black plumes of smoke billowed up into the air.

Although his vision was very blurry, Yeshua saw that something was very different about Masada. The buildings and structures were no longer ruins. Almost everything looked original. There were roofs on the stone buildings. The columns and arches decorating the structures were intact and painted with fancy patterns. From where he stood, there were now elaborate geometric patterns in the mosaic tile on the floor path instead of gravel and sand.

Yeshua was quite confused as to what was happening. Even though his vision was still cloudy, he looked ahead and saw something incredible. Just to the south of the heavily fortified double stonewalls was a giant towering wood building located just outside the fortress. There were men in strange uniforms climbing from the tall wood structure into Masada.

Curious yet cautious, Yeshua creeped closer to get a better look and walked up a nearby staircase onto the main fortification's top wall without being seen by any of the strange men dressed in silver, leather and red outfits. Wearing gold helmets leather strapped sandals, many held ornate round shields. Some had swords, others had long spears.

Looking over the wall down into the valley to the west, he was completely astonished to see thousands of men in uniforms coming up the steep ramp towards the mountaintop. He saw the complete wooden structure, a giant siege tower with a battering ram sitting atop the earthen ramp right next to the outer wall of Masada.

They were invading the fortress. It was the Romans! Somehow, Yeshua was watching the end of the siege of Masada from almost 2,000 years ago. Far down below at the base of the giant earthwork ramp he could see the walled Roman encampment, the size of a small city, busy with activity among the tents and buildings.

Yeshua looked back at the siege tower as scores of Roman soldiers climbed up to the top and navigated over the walls into Masada. Yeshua's vision now had returned completely back to normal. He glanced around the vast

Masada plateau and noticed there no people inside except for the dozens of Romans who had just scaled the walls.

"Wait a sec," thought Yeshua to himself... "Why is Masada empty?" There was absolutely no one else there. There were no Jews trying to stop and fight the Romans. Why weren't they battling the Romans?

After a few more minutes, several hundred Romans came inside, searching the seemingly empty fortress.

Yeshua noticed that inside Masada, a few dozen yards away from the siege tower, a group of Romans were dressed differently wearing more decorative uniforms than the others. One of the Romans in the center of the group had an incredibly ornate chest plate and a very fancy gold helmet with a giant red mohawk on the top.

Standing next to him, another fancy looking Roman wearing a red mohawk helmet held a tall pole at least ten feet high with a beautiful large golden eagle statue on the very top. Under the eagle was a decorative gold rectangular box with the letters "SPQR" written inside. Under the top box was a gold circular emblem with an image of an elderly man's head wearing a wreath in the center. Written around the man's head in gold letters were the large words "TIBERIUS CAESAR IMP." Under middle circle was another rectangular shape within the words LEGIO X written in gold.

Yeshua moved closer to see what was happening. Unseen, he hid near the wall close to a group of important looking Romans. He heard someone crying; it sounded like a young girl.

Coming out from one of the nearby buildings on fire, led by a Roman soldier, were two women and five children in chains and shackles. As they got closer, Yeshua saw that the Roman soldier's face was badly scarred. He looked very familiar to Yeshua, and then it clicked... that was the face of the Nazi Gestapo Police Chief! He looked just like him. A sense of dread came over Yeshua.

And then, even more surprise. The oldest boy in the group of captives had red hair. He looked just like Yeshua. He had the same eyes, the same facial structure. Was he actually looking at himself, 2,000 years ago?

The Jewish prisoners were led up to the group of important Romans. The man with the scarred face yelled in Latin, although Yeshua could understand what he said. "Everyone kneel down now! Everyone get on the ground." The young girls were crying.

"Sergeant Legers," said the man wearing the fanciest uniform. "Where are the rest of the prisoners?"

He replied "General Silva. There are no more prisoners. They all took their lives before we arrived here today."

The General looked shocked and angry. "What say you? All dead?"

"Yes sir," said Legers "They are no more. This child says he has a message for you. Stand up boy!" He yelled at boy who looked just like Yeshua.

The child got up off his knees. He looked directly into the eyes of General Lucius Flavius Silva.

Yeshua stared at his doppelganger. He was full of emotion. Then he saw a bearded middle-aged man standing next to General Flavius wearing robes instead of a soldier's uniform. Just as the boy began to speak, the man pulled out a quill and ink and started to write on a piece of parchment.

The boy said, "Our leader, Elazar ben Yair told me to give you this message Sir." He paused for a moment, looking exhausted and dehydrated. His lips were dry and cracked.

"Give him some water," said General Flavius. One of the soldiers gave the young boy a leather skin who then took a sip of water.

The boy said, "Since we long ago resolved never to be servants to the Romans, nor to any other than to God Himself, Who alone is the true and just Lord of mankind, the time is now come that obliges us to make that resolution true in practice...We were the very first that revolted, and we are the last to fight against them; and I cannot but esteem it as a favor that God has granted us, that it is still in our power to die bravely, and in a state of freedom."

All the Romans looked at the child in silence for a few moments. Behind them, the buildings burned. Several vultures now hovered in circles high above the in the sky.

"That is all, child?" said Flavius.

"Yes Sir," said the boy softly.

"Should we just kill them now?" said Sergeant Legers.

General Flavius looked at Legers in disgust.

"No. There has been enough death here today. We are done. It is time to leave this dreaded place. Send these prisoners back to Rome as proof of our victory. Hail Caesar!"

All the surrounding Romans follow suit and yelled "Hail Caesar!"

Suddenly someone grabbed Yeshua on his back. He turned around in horror as he thought he was going to be captured by the Romans.

"Yeshua, where have you been all day? I've been looking for you everywhere," said Mohammed.

Stunned, Yeshua looked around, he was back to the 2013 Masada. It was almost sundown as the sun was setting in the western sky. "What the hell just happened?" thought Yeshua.

CHAPTER 3

THE NEPHILIM

"We have to leave now! The last bus back to Beersheba leaves very soon," said a nearly panicked Mohammed.

The two boys ran due east across the Masada plateau, back to the cable car entrance. Luckily, the cable car was there at the top waiting for them. They got inside with a few other tourists and started their descent.

"What happened to you?" asked Mohammed. "Where were you? I looked everywhere. You were gone for hours. I thought you fell off the mountain or worse!"

To the west, there was an exceptionally beautiful sunset with orange, pink and purple clouds among glorious massive rays of orange and yellow light radiating up towards the heavens. As the cable car descended the decline, Yeshua described in detail to Mohammed the entire epic story of his experience with the Roman time warp.

"Wow! All that from drinking one glass of wine?" They giggled and laughed together for a few moments.

"And the young Jewish boy looked exactly like you?" asked Mohammed.

"Yes. It was like I was looking at myself. My doppelganger," replied Yeshua.

"Incredible! How is that even possible?" asked Mohammed.

Yeshua just shrugged. It had been quite a day. He was exhausted mentally and physically. He just wanted to go back to home and get into his comfortable bed.

The cable car arrived at its final destination, and the two boys departed. They walked over to the bus depot and found their return bus to Beersheba. Aside from the bus driver, there was no one else on the bus.

They climbed up the steps and handed the bus driver their return tickets who asked, "Where are your parents?"

"We're orphans Sir," said Mohammed. "We're going back to the Beersheba orphanage."

The bus driver replied "You kids need to be with a parent or an adult. Sorry. That's the rules."

Yeshua then said "I had my Bar Mitzvah today here at Masada. I am a man."

The bus driver looked at him with a peculiar expression and then said, "Ok, get in. It's going to be a bumpy drive."

The two best friends walked to back of the empty bus and sat down on the last row of seats. The bus left the station and headed south towards Zohar Fortress.

"Yeshua," said Mohammed. "What did you read from your Holy Book today? What did it mean?"

"That's a great question. I've been trying to figure it out myself," said Yeshua. "It talks about Angels coming to earth and making babies with some beautiful human women. Their children are called Nephilim, and they were supposedly huge giants with great powers."

"Like superheroes? Like Thor?" asked a very excited Mohammed.

"Yes, something like that," answered Yeshua. "It's all so very interesting. It certainly would make a great movie. I did a Google search and found out there's something called the Book of Enoch that describes what happened with the Angels and the Nephilim in more detail. It's from one of the ancient Dead Sea Scrolls that were found in some caves not far from here."

"So, these stories are true? There are giant superheroes in your Holy Book?" said Mohammed.

"Well, I don't think they were actual superheroes," said Yeshua. "It seems like they were more like super-villains. Supposedly things got really, really horrific during that time. Like lots of evil and bad stuff. Apparently they really angered God, and as a punishment a Great Flood was sent that destroyed almost everything."

"Holy smokes!" said Mohammed.

"Well, more like Holy Water. It rained for 40 days and nights to cleanse the world, and apparently only Noah and his family were the only humans to survive," said Yeshua.

"So, all the Nephilim were destroyed in the flood?" asked Mohammed.

"Well, actually, No. Later in the Torah, after the Hebrews had escaped Egyptian slavery, they wandered in the desert for 40 years. As they got closer to returning to Israel, they sent out some spies to see if the coast was clear. But they ran into some Giant Nephilim, and they got pretty freaked out."

"Wow!" said Mohammed. "So, are there still Nephilim around today?"

"I don't know," replied Yeshua. "There sure is a lot of evil left in the world, so maybe."

"And are there good Nephilim too?" asked Mohammed.

Just then, the bus stopped suddenly. It was nighttime now as the bus approached the outskirts of Beersheba.

Shining in the bus headlights ahead were two masked men holding their arms up in the air. They were yelling in Arabic. Without warning, one of the masked men threw a leather bag into the bus through an empty window. The driver of the bus quickly opened the front door and ran out into the street.

Yeshua saw the bag being thrown into the bus. Everything seemed to go in slow motion. Sitting in the back seat by the aisle, he turned to open the emergency back door, but it was locked.

"Get down!" he screamed at Mohammed.

He covered his body over Mohammed's as the bomb blew up the bus.

CHAPTER 4

GOD

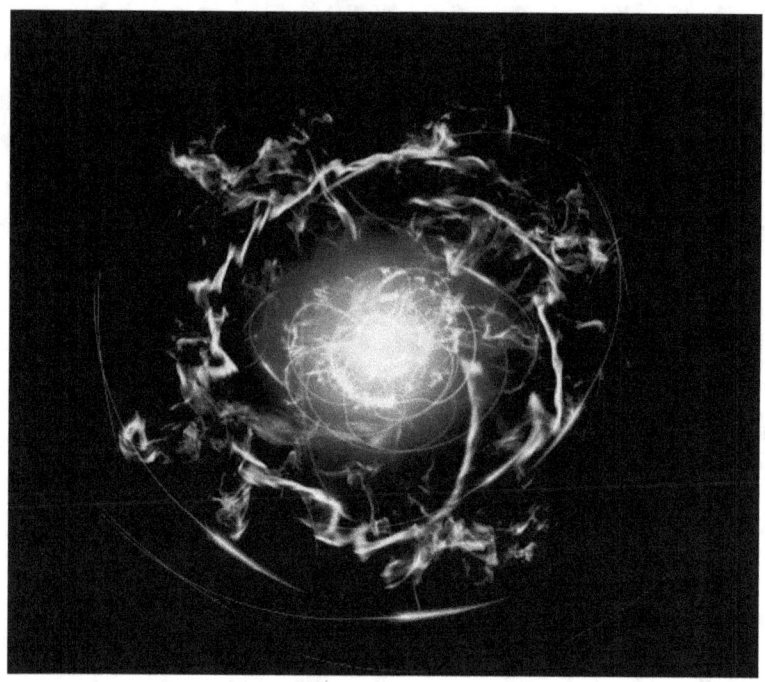

Everything was black. Or maybe everything was nothing. There was no thing. Yeshua couldn't see anything, or even feel anything. "Where am I?" he thought.

Then he felt a slight sensation. It felt like... warm water gently sprinkling on his face. It felt really good. Then it felt like more like a steady drizzle. He could feel beads of water dripping down his face.

He went to wipe the water from his wet brow, and then miraculously he could see! To his amazement, he was standing near the stage inside a giant outdoor concert stadium. There were thousands of people around him facing forward and dancing. They all seemed completely mesmerized and enjoying the musical concert in front of them.

Upon the stage, super bright lights flashed on a tall man standing in the center of the raised concert platform. He was bathed in golden light; and Yeshua couldn't clearly see his face. He was playing a guitar, and it sounded just incredible. The lights shimmered on the guitar, and each musical note beamed as both sound and light waves went out onto the crowd of happy concertgoers.

The wonderful music seemed so familiar to Yeshua; however, he couldn't recognize the exact song. He felt the musical vibrations move right through him, and his entire body tingled. Everyone around Yeshua seemed very familiar to him, yet he could not think of anyone's specific name.

It started to rain harder, but no one around him seemed be bothered by the heavy rain; however, Yeshua decided to try to find somewhere dry and out of the rain. He turned around and made his way through the crowds of familiar people. He headed upwards towards the top of the stadium, looking for cover. He went up many aisles and rows, yet he couldn't find anywhere dry. At some point, he no longer cared about the rain.

Yeshua turned around to look back at the stage. Somehow, he found himself at the very top row all the way in the rear of the stadium. He saw the massive sea of people in front of him. There must have been at least 100,000 souls watching this hypnotic concert.

From his viewpoint high above, the stage looked very small. The shining guitarist continued to make wonderful music that radiated out to the crowd. Above the stage an enormous metallic array projected a fantastic laser light show. The laser beams of incredible colors and geometric shapes oscillated in a magical and synchronized way with the music. Yeshua had never seen (or heard) anything so beautiful in his life. The wondrous geometric rays of light that emanated from the stage scintillated over the huge stadium above the crowd.

Then, something seemed to shift. The laser show changed, and all the beams harmonized in unison into a giant translucent sphere. The massive orb high above the crowd illuminated the entire stadium in golden light. The resonant music became louder, and Yeshua felt incredible reverberations throughout his entire being.

He looked up into the sky in awe. The gigantic sphere was now rotating and swirling, like a planet around the sun. There were whirls of morphing colorful patterns that phased in and out of different intensities along the outer edge of the luminous ball. What an incredible show!

Suddenly the dark clouds above the stadium began to swirl in unison with the giant spinning glowing sphere. In the night sky, a wide vortex of flowing clouds rotated clockwise around the orb, shaped like a hurricane. Yeshua was transfixed on the massive twirling glowing globe above him. The sphere seemed to get even larger and then supercharge as blue and yellow electrical bolts began to shoot and dance from the edges of the rotating orb, like a plasma lamp that reacts to your fingertips when you touch it.

Completely mesmerized, Yeshua looked down at the stage far across the stadium for a moment. He was beyond belief as he noticed the giant orb did not seem to be coupled with the laser light show beams anymore. The orb seemed to hover above the concert by itself! Then, the sphere began to oscillate larger and smaller, almost like a heart pulses with beats.

Yeshua looked around him and saw that no one else was looking at the giant floating electrical orb above the stadium. Everyone was focused on the music. Many people were dancing ecstatically. He thought to himself... was it possible that he was the only one seeing it? He looked back up at the sphere, and felt deeply spiritually connected to it. He felt almost as if it was reading his mind. Yeshua then reflected back on the incredible events of the last day... the dream about the Nazis, his Bar Mitzvah at Masada, the Roman history flashback, and now this mystical and surreal concert.

"What is this Orb?" he thought to himself.

There was a moment of silence.

"I am God," said the Orb back to him, telepathically. As Yeshua heard these words reverberate in his mind, the Orb expanded with lighting bolts jetting out in every direction into the sky.

Yeshua was astounded. He was in presence of God. Words cannot describe adequately the feelings and emotions that he experienced at that moment. He felt incredibly blessed, filled with so much love. There was no fear, only bliss and wonderment. God was communicating with him through this miraculous spinning Orb.

Time seemed to ebb and flow as the Orb hovered and spun above the massive stadium. Yeshua decided to pray and give gratitude to the Divine Being above him. "Thank you, God, Thank you," he prayed. He had so much gratitude. "Thank you, for everything. Thank you." The Orb began to spin faster. The colors and energy seemed to intensify and magnify more and more as Yeshua prayed.

Then, after some time had passed, another powerful thought came from the Orb into Yeshua's mind.

"Ask me a question," said God.

Yeshua immediately paused his prayers. "What should I ask?" Yeshua thought to himself. "If I could ask one question to God, what would it be?"

He began to go within and meditate about God's request. Then, the question crystallized in his mind.

"What is the meaning of life?" thought/asked young Yeshua.

Right after he thought/said the question, the energy of the Orb changed dramatically. It rose up several hundred feet into the clouds and became much larger. More lightning and electricity shot out as it spun faster and faster. The vast vortex of clouds revolving around the Orb now started to get sucked into the center of the sphere like a black hole.

Yeshua was startled for a moment. He sat down on the bench under him and looked up at the unbelievably supernatural phenomenon above him. It seemed like God was processing his question above as the Orb spun out of control.

After what seem like a long time, the Orb stopped in midair. Everything stopped. Yeshua stood back up, and waited to receive the answer.

God said, "The MEANING of LIFE... is the DIFFERENCE between ONE and ZERO."

Then the Orb lifted upwards high into the sky and disappeared.

"The meaning of life... is the difference between One and Zero?" Yeshua repeated in his mind. "What does that even mean?" he thought. As a 13-year-old boy, he had no idea what it meant. However, many years later, he looked back at this moment and everything made complete sense.

After the Orb left Yeshua, time shifted once again. He was deep in contemplation about what had just happened to him when suddenly all the overhead lights turned on. He looked out into the vast coliseum and everyone was gone! The concert was over. He was sitting at the top of the stadium in the last row. Everyone had left, and he hadn't even noticed. He just sat there in bewilderment.

CHAPTER 5

THE SHOFAR

Yeshua felt something in his hands. He looked down and saw that be held a Shofar. An ornately decorated leather strap connected to both ends of the long, curvy ram's horn.

"Yeshua, Yeshua! Are you awake?" shouted Mohammed.

Yeshua looked around the room. He was in a hospital bed. His best friend sat next to him. He noticed he had an IV in his left arm that was attached to a bag of fluid that hung on a pole above his bed.

"Wow. Am I dreaming again, Mohammed?" asked very disoriented Yeshua.

"You've been in a deep coma for seven days. You saved my life when the bomb blew up the bus. The doctors didn't know if you would ever wake up!"

Mohammed started crying. He embraced Yeshua.

"I'm so happy you're alive!"

"You'll never believe what happened to me," said Yeshua. He then told Mohammed the entire story about the concert, meeting God and the question about the meaning of life.

"Amazing!" said Mohammed. "I think you had a near death experience. I saw a TV show once about many people who had similar stories. It's like you went to heaven, then came back! God sent you back!"

"And then God told you the meaning of life is the difference between one and zero?" asked Mohammed.

"Yes," replied Yeshua.

"Hmmm. Fascinating. I wonder if it means something about computers? Like all digital information is stored as ones and zeros. Maybe we are in some kind of holographic computer simulation?" asked Mohammed.

"I don't know, perhaps. Anything is possible," said Yeshua.

"Hey, how did this big shofar get in my hands?"

"The Rabbi from your Bar Mitzvah brought it here while you were in the coma. He came and said some prayers, then he placed it in your hands," said Mohammed.

"Gosh, I was in a coma for seven days?" asked Yeshua.

"Yes. I stayed here the whole time praying to Allah that you would wake up," replied Mohammed.

"I can't believe it," exclaimed Yeshua. "It only feels like a few hours ago we were on the bus back to Beersheba. Were you injured in the bus explosion too?"

"It's a miracle," said Mohammed. "I wasn't injured at all. You jumped on top of me as the bomb exploded and saved me from certain death."

Yeshua looked down at his body. He didn't see any burns or trauma. He felt fine, save for being a little weak and groggy.

"Except for being in a coma, did I have any other injuries?" asked Yeshua.

"No. The doctors said it was another miracle. They can't explain it. The entire bus was blown to smithereens.

We survived. Except you were in coma. Thank God you are okay!"

"Yes my dear friend! Thank God!" Yeshua said as he smiled.

"Mohammed, did Rabbi Yohanan say anything else about this Shofar while he was here?" asked Yeshua as he held it up in the air with both hands. It seemed to shine and glow in the hospital room light.

Mohammed replied "Ah, yes he did. He said that Shofar is very special. It would help you heal. He said that you should always keep it close. Oh, and he also told me that you shouldn't blow the Shofar until you turn eighteen years old."

"Eighteen, huh? That's my lucky number! In Hebrew, it means 'Chai', it means 'Life'. I was born on the 18th too. So, wow, I have to wait five years to blow this thing? That's a very long time from now. Speaking of a long time, I'm starving. I feel like I haven't eaten in a week!" said Yeshua.

"You actually haven't!" joked Mohammed.

The two best friends started to giggle, then laugh uncontrollably.

"Let's go find some somewhere to eat," declared Yeshua.

He got out of bed slowly and put his feet on the ground for the first time in seven days. He felt very weak. Mohammed supported him up by putting his arm around his shoulders, although quickly Yeshua groaned and sat back down on the bed.

"I have an idea. I'll be right back," said Mohammed. He left the room. After a few minutes he came back with a wheelchair. He was accompanied by a young, pretty nurse with long blonde hair. They both helped Yeshua into the wheelchair, and then she placed his IV bag on the metal pole attached to the back of the chair. Yeshua reached over and grabbed his Shofar from his bed and put it on his lap.

Yeshua looked up at the angelic nurse and felt some butterflies in his stomach. He looked for her name badge on her chest and then whispered "Hi…"

"Miriam. Nurse Miriam," she said. There seemed to be a warm, soft glow around her. They both smiled at each other. Yeshua noticed she wore a necklace with a silver cross pendant. However, it was different than any cross he had ever seen before. It looked like two figure eights intersecting each other.

"Miriam took care of you here almost the entire time. She nursed you back to health," said Mohammed.

"I'm so glad you have arisen Yeshua," said Miriam.

"Thank you so much! Thank you. I am forever grateful! Soooo… where is the cafeteria?" asked Yeshua "I'm starving!"

Nurse Miriam walked over to the doorway and pointed with her outstretched hand to the right. "It's down this hallway, past the maternity ward and then make a left into the Atrium."

Mohammed pushed Yeshua in wheelchair towards the door and then out into the hallway. They turned right and went down a long corridor and then through some double doors.

Yeshua suddenly heard a high pitch buzzing sound in his left ear. He grabbed his ear with his hand. Mohammed looked down at him while pushing the wheelchair and asked "Are you okay?"

Just as he was about to respond, they both heard the sound of a crying baby. As they passed the nursery area of the maternity ward, they saw glass wall and on their left that separated the newborn room. There were ten little cribs inside, and three of them had tiny children wrapped in blankets. One of the newborns was crying loudly.

The buzzing sound in Yeshua's ear stopped.

"What hospital are we in?" asked Yeshua.

"We are in Soroka Medical Center in Beersheba. Why do you ask my friend?" said Mohammed. He stopped pushing the wheelchair in front of the nursery.

"Amazing! I was born here almost exactly thirteen years ago. I was precisely right here the day I was born," said Yeshua.

"That's really cool!" said Mohammed. "Do you think it is a coincidence or a synchronicity?"

"I don't know. What's the difference?" asked Yeshua.

"Well, a coincidence is when something happens that seems to be totally random or just accidental. Like meeting three people in a row with the same name. But a synchronicity is much deeper. It's when coincidences or events happen over and over again that aren't random or based only on luck. Like finding dimes or pennies all the time. It's like the Universe is trying to tell you something," explained Mohammed.

"So, I must be having a synchronicity right now," said Yeshua.

"Really? Awesome! How so?" asked Mohammed.

"Well, before my parents died…. I remember my Father telling me a story about the day I was born. He said right after I was delivered, they cleaned me up and took me to the nursery. The one we are standing in front of right now. They put me in the crib wrapped in a blanket, just like that baby right there. Then as my Father looked at me through the glass, he said he saw something incredible. He said above me, a shadowy figure appeared and seemed to hover over me."

"Whoa. That's incredible!" interjected Mohammed.

Yeshua continued. "Then he said the phantom apparition split into two figures, then the two split into four, and so on until there were 16 figures. They were all hovering over me in a semi-circle."

"Could he see their faces?" asked Mohammed.

"I don't think so," answered Yeshua. "He said they were dark, cloudy and translucent, like some kind of ghosts. Although, he said he was not afraid at all. He somehow knew they were not bad, and they were not there to hurt me. Then, my Father told me a woman came up to him and said 'What a beautiful baby!' and he looked at her and said 'Thank you'. When he looked back at me, the floating figures were gone."

"Wow Yeshua. You sure have had a lot of crazy stuff happen to you! What do you think those shadow figures were?" asked Mohammed.

"Well, my Father said he thinks they were my ancestors coming to visit me on my birthday," said Yeshua. He started to get emotional and cry.

"What's a matter, my friend?" asked Mohammed as he started to push the wheelchair down the hall towards the Atrium.

"I miss my parents, so much!" cried Yeshua.

"I never asked you this out of respect. What happened to your parents?" said Mohammed.

"When I was five years old, they were both killed by a Palestinian suicide attack. My family was living in Gaza in a settlement at the time. The Israeli government was forcing all the settlers to evacuate, and right before they were supposed to leave a man wearing a bomb came into our house and blew himself up. My parents, siblings and my aunt and uncle's family were all in the house. Everyone died but me. They found me alive in the rubble, then I eventually ended up in the Beersheba Orphanage," said Yeshua.

"Oh my God," said Mohammed. "I'm so sorry. You don't have any other family that would adopt you?"

"No. Sadly, there is no one else is here. I think I might have some relatives in America, but no one knows for sure. How about you? How did you end up in the orphanage?" asked Yeshua.

"Well, here's what I know. I don't remember much. They told me that an old Bedouin woman dropped me off at the Beersheba orphanage when I was a small child, around the age of five as well. She said that they had lived in the village of Dahaniya near Gaza and they were being relocated to a town called Arad, not far from Masada. My people were seen as traitors by Hamas, and my parents were murdered by the Palestinian Hamas because they were suspected of being traitors and informants to the Israelis. Apparently, I had no other family," explained Mohammed.

"Oy vey!" said Yeshua as he placed his hands over his forehead. "Both our parents were killed by the Palestinians. Why do you think they hate us so much?"

"It's a sorry state of affairs, my friend," exclaimed Mohammed. "Your people are seen as illegal occupiers and oppressors by many of the Arabs here, even back to biblical times. The Palestinian Hamas terrorists in Gaza and the Iranians are hell bent on your destruction. I learned that there was a big war way back in 1967. Almost all the surrounding Arab countries attacked Israel, but by some miracle your country won decisively and took over a lot of land, including Gaza, the Golan Heights in Syria, a huge part of the Egyptian Sinai peninsula and what you call the West Bank as well as the Holy City of Jerusalem. The Israelis eventually gave back the Sinai land to the Egyptians and signed a peace treaty. Your people even gave the Gaza Strip back to the Palestinians. Yet, they still hate you. Now, there's almost two million Palestinians trapped in a little sliver of land, and they are becoming more and more desperate."

"Dear Lord, why can't we all be friends?" asked Yeshua.

"I wish we could Yeshua, I wish we could. Maybe, someday," replied Mohammed.

The two friends then entered the Hospital cafeteria for a very well-deserved meal.

CHAPTER 6

THE WELL

5 years later
2018
Beersheba, Israel

It was the year of Yeshua and Mohammed's 18th birthdays. According to custom, both he and Mohammed enrolled into the Israeli armed forces. On Yeshua's birthday that fall, just before entering their military duty, the friends travelled to the nearby biblical archeological ruins of Tel Be'er Sheba National Park.

"We're almost there!" gasped Yeshua as he peddled harder on his mountain bike, with his long, helical shaped Shofar slung across his back.

"Why couldn't we just take the bus?" asked a very tired Mohammed bicycling behind his best friend.

"No more buses, okay? I don't do buses!" exclaimed a nearly out of breath Yeshua.

They were riding off road, through the desert valleys eastwards from the city towards their destination on a dry, hot and dusty morning.

The two young men finally rode past the entrance of the lush Genesis Gardens, then biked up towards the base of the massive walled city, constructed on a large hill thousands of years ago. They parked their bikes and walked up the incline towards the threshold of the ruins.

At the entrance of the site was a stone well just outside the old city's gates. Constructed over the well was a basic wooden roof enclosure. Connected next to the well was small stone cistern that contained some water in the bottom of its basin.

A tour guide stood in front of the well and spoke to a small group of foreign looking tourists.

"Shalom and welcome to Tel Be'er Sheba. Beersheba means 'Well of Seven' or 'Well of the Oath' in Hebrew. These ruins are tremendously significant and rich in history. This site was recognized as an UNESCO World Heritage Site in 2007. Archeologists have evidence that this location was inhabited over 6,000 years ago, and then for some mysterious reason, it was abandoned for almost 2,000 years. Beersheba is mentioned in the Bible 33 times and it's very possible that this well in front of you, or maybe another one nearby, may be the actual location mentioned in the Hebrew Torah and described as Abraham's well. This area was assigned to the tribe of Simeon in the Book of Joshua and was heavily built up during the Iron Age between the eleventh and eighth centuries BCE. We think King Saul may actually have fortified this town when fighting the Amalekites. It's also likely that around 700 BCE the town was completely destroyed by the Assyrians then later rebuilt and destroyed again around 587 BCE by the Babylonians. Needless to say, the residents of this place had to be prepared to defend themselves from hostile invaders and long sieges. The most valuable resource here on the outskirts of the desert is water, and the designers of this city had an ingenious way to collect water in a large, deep cistern that I'll show you on the tour. Let's enter this way through the front gate."

The tour guide motioned for his group to follow him into the vast, sprawling stone complex. They all trekked forward into the fortress, yet Yeshua just stood there staring at the well. He walked over the edge of the well and looked down into the dark abyss. He was mesmerized by the well and almost appeared to be in a trance.

"Yeshua, are you okay?" asked Mohammed.

"I'm hearing some high pitch buzzing in my left ear," said Yeshua as he swung his Shofar from around his back into his hands.

"Is that good or bad?" inquired Mohammed.

"Well, I've learned that when I hear buzzing in my right ear it's usually a warning sign that something bad is going to happen or has already happened. When my I hear buzzing in my left ear it's usually a sign that something good is about to happen. Either way, it's always a signal I should take extra notice as to what is going on around me. I can't explain why, it just is," said Yeshua.

"Oh great! Then something very good is about to happen?" questioned Mohammed.

"Yes. I believe so," said Yeshua. He paused. "I've been waiting to do this for a very long, long time."

Shofar in hand, Yeshua brought the mouthpiece up to his lips and he blew hard into it with all his might. The horn beamed out a really big, long blast.

Then, everything changed. Yeshua began to lose consciousness and started to black out. He dropped his Shofar as he fell forward. Just as he was about to plunge into the deep well, Mohammed grabbed him from behind and pulled him back. His weight was too much to hold up, and both young men crumbled to the dusty ground next to the well.

"Yeshua, Yeshua! Wake up!" screamed Mohammed as he shook his best friend's inanimate body with both hands. There was no response. His eyes were closed, but thankfully he was still breathing shallowly. Mohammed pulled him up off the floor and placed his back against the stonewall of the well. He checked his pulse and was relieved that he was alive.

"Oh no," wept Mohammed. "My dear friend, what has happened to you?" He looked around for help and there was no one nearby, so he grabbed his cell phone out of his pocket and dialed an ambulance by calling 102 and asking for emergency medical services to be dispatched to the site. Mohammed decided to check Yeshua's eyes, and pried open his eyelids with his fingers. To his surprise, his pupils were completely dilated. He could see none of his hazel colored iris. They were completely black.

Meanwhile, Yeshua was experiencing nothing. He felt nothing. There was only darkness. He was completely out of his body, like in a dream. He remembered blowing the shofar and then diving into blackness. He thought... "Where is my body? Am I falling down the well?" He tried to concentrate and will himself to return back into his body; however, he could not. Wherever this place was, he was mystified.

It felt like he was moving through the darkness, like floating. He could sense some movement forward, yet he was definitely not aware of his physical body. He could not feel his hands. Then, he saw something up ahead. Out of the darkness came an array of lights. First it was dim, and then, as he got closer, he could see that he was flying through some kind of strange tunnel formed of repeating concentric circles. The lights got brighter, and he saw a magnificent display of multicolored circular patterns rotate around him as he seemed to glide through a magical infinite space.

A bewildered Yeshua asked, "What am I doing here? What is this place?" The kaleidoscopic patterns morphed and shifted around him as he seemed to fly even faster and deeper into the tunnel. He tried to look down at himself and did not see his body. He was in awe.

Then, from the most distant point of the tunnel, in the center of the entire construct, he saw a tiny spark of bright radiating light becoming slowly larger as it moved towards him from the opposite end of the tunnel. As the light became larger and closer, he could see that it was a glowing Orb. He was flying towards it, and it was flying towards him. As it advanced in his direction, Yeshua could see that it was oscillating and rotating. There were some kind of figures or forms within the Orb.

He thought to himself "Could this be the Orb from the concert when I was 13? Could this be God again?"

As the brilliant energy Orb got even closer, Yeshua took more notice of the figures within the light. They looked like human faces, spinning around the outside of the revolving globe. Then the Orb was almost right in front of him. He was still flying through the enormous tunnel as the concentric circles of rotating colors and patterns continued to pass by seemingly at almost light speed.

The huge shining Orb now hovered directly before him, almost occupying his entire field of vision. He recognized the faces spinning within the luminous ball of light.

Moses…

Jesus…

Muhammed…

Buddha…

Gandhi…

Albert Einstein…

Martin Luther King, Jr…

There were a few other faces within Orb that looked very familiar; however, he wasn't quite sure of their names.

Yeshua felt a wonderful, blissful, warm sensation come over him. He could feel the light of the orb radiate through him. It was ecstatic. As he bathed in the boundless energy of the Orb, Yeshua wondered why he had been brought to this mystical place. He thought about a possible reason for this encounter. Why was he here?

These were the prophets and messengers of God in front of him who must have a message for him.

He directed his full cognition towards the Orb. "I am ready to receive your message," thought Yeshua.

Orb seemed to energize and spin faster, just like the God Orb did when Yeshua was 13. The faces morphed in and out of focus as the speed of the orb increased. Then the Orb slowed down. Yeshua could see their faces more clearly as they spun around and morphed into each other.

They spoke in unison…

"All is One."

And then repeated again…

"All is One."

Yeshua could see their lips moving as they spoke, their words reverberating and echoing all around him. The Orb's energy intensified as electrical bolts shot out from its surface. Then suddenly, the Orb dissolved and disappeared right in front of Yeshua. Just before it completely faded away, the faces in the Orb softly said...

"Share this."

"Share this..."

Everything then shifted once again for Yeshua. He seemed to reach the end of the tunnel of concentric kaleidoscopic circles, and he literally "passed through" the light at the end of the tunnel.

He found himself back at the well on top of the hill. Surprisingly, it was not the exact place he had remembered. There was no walled city next to the well. There was only desert around him as far as the eye could see. The sun was setting in the west and beautiful golden rays of light shone up into the sky.

Yeshua looked down at the well and saw that it was just a small hole in the ground with no surrounding stonework. Lying on the ground next to the well, he saw an old wooden bucket tied to a long-braided rope. He went to grab the bucket for some water and was shocked to discover that he had no hands! He still wasn't in his body! It was like he was in a dream. He could look around, yet he was still out of his body.

Then, in the far distance to the west he heard someone crying. It sounded like a woman. He looked down the hill and could not see her, so he decided to investigate. As he had no legs, he concentrated intensely and willed himself to float in the direction of the weeping woman.

At the bottom of the hill, Yeshua came across a young man lying under a shrub. He wore a tan burlap shirt, shorts and leather sandals. He looked to be about thirteen or fourteen years old and was almost dead. His lips were very cracked and dry, and he was moaning softly in angst. Yeshua came up close to him and saw that was still breathing. He looked just like his friend Mohammed as a child.

It was getting darker as sun had set beneath the horizon to the west. Yeshua heard more crying in the distance, at least an arrow shot away. He left the boy and went in that direction until he found the woman in the middle of the dry desert valley. She was weeping on the ground, kneeling face down, wrapped in dark robes and a headscarf. Lying next to her was an empty water skin. She had run out of water in the desert; Yeshua thought that the young man he found under the shrub must be her son, dying of thirst. She was searching for water to save her child.

Yeshua tried to form words to talk to her but he had no mouth to speak from. He was there in spirit but not in body. He wanted nothing more but to help this poor woman and her son.

He came up close to her head and sent her a telepathic message. He told her to get up, go back over to her son, and that he would show them the well to get some water.

She immediately stood up, looked up into the sky and raised her arms upwards. She spoke some words in a language that Yeshua did not understand. However, he knew she was praising God.

Yeshua followed her as she walked back through the desert to her son. She knelt down next to him under the shrub only to discover that he was almost dead from dehydration. He was moaning and gasping. She tried to lift him up, but she was too weak.

It was getting darker now. Dusk was ending, and night was quickly approaching. The dim light from the sunset faded in the distant sky. The new crescent moon rose up from the east and directly next to the moon was the bright planet Venus.

Yeshua telepathically whispered in the woman's ear again. Time was running out. She put her arms under her son and tried to lift him up again. Yeshua focused all his energy and pushed with all his might to help raise the child. They got him up into a standing position and Yeshua assisted both of them up to the top of the hill.

Yeshua brought them to the well. They gently placed the boy down on the ground and the woman prayed and thanked God again; then she grabbed the bucket and slowly lowered it down into the well with the rope. As he lay on the ground, the boy's right foot dangled down the edge of the well.

The rope wasn't long enough! She was holding the end of the rope, but it didn't reach the water. Yeshua heard the woman scream in desperation. There was no way for her to get the water. She dropped the rope and bucket into the well in frustration, and after several seconds it splashed at the bottom, probably a hundred or more feet down.

In that moment of certain defeat, Yeshua had an idea. A fantastic idea. Although he still did not 'occupy' his body, he literally dove his spirit down into the well. Like the tunnel trip he had just taken to get to this place, he travelled down to the bottom of the well into the water. He did not make a splash... he just went into the depths of the water. There was no light and it was pitch black, yet he could see. Then he concentrated very hard. With all his might, he pushed the water upwards, up the well.

It worked! The water rushed up the well, a hundred feet or more, and splashed out into the ground around the woman and her child. She took her empty water skin, filled it with the overflowing well water and gave some of it to her child to drink.

Yeshua felt water splashing on his face.

"Wake up Yeshua. Wake up!" yelled Mohammed. He stood over Yeshua holding an empty water bottle. He had just poured the contents of the bottle unto his best friend's face. Yeshua was sitting on the ground with his back leaning against the stone well next to the entrance of Tel Be'er Sheba. His Shofar was in his hands. He was soaking wet.

"Dear God. What happened?" asked Yeshua.

"I don't know. You tell me! You blew the Shofar a few minutes ago, and then you passed out. I called an ambulance, and they're on the way. Why did you go into another coma? Your eyes were totally black! I thought you said something good was going to happen?" said a very upset Mohammed.

"I'm okay. Whoa! It was just a few minutes that I was unconscious?" asked a perplexed Yeshua. It seemed like he had been gone for hours.

Mohammed made a phone call on his cell. He told the ambulance dispatcher that everything was fine and that the ambulance didn't have to come. He told them that his friend had fainted from dehydration and was okay now. He hung up his phone.

"Yes. It was just a few minutes you were out, until I poured the water onto your stiff-necked head. I was freaking out! What happened?" asked Mohammed.

"Well... Ha-ha. Get it? Well? Ha-ha-ha-ha." Yeshua tried to make a joke. Mohammed looked back at him sternly. "Not. Funny," he said.

"Okay. You just won't believe what happened to me," said Yeshua, still sitting against the stonewall of the well. He then proceeded to tell his friend the entire epic story in detail about the mystical tunnel, the Orb with the Prophets, the message about "All is One" and the saga in the desert with the woman with her dying son who looked just like Mohammed.

After he was done listening to the story, Mohammed sat down next to Yeshua by the well. He looked absolutely dumbfounded. He just stared out into space, in a daze.

"Mohammed. Are you okay?" asked Yeshua.

"Ya Allah! The woman and the boy, did they say their names? And are you saying that everything happened right by this well although there was no fortress city next to it?" asked Mohammed.

"Hmmm. I don't think they said their names. The boy was almost dead from dehydration and the woman spoke a language I didn't understand. I don't think they even saw me, it's like I was a ghost or something. And there was no town here, it was just all barren hilly desert except for the old well; however, there were no stones around it. It was just a hole in the ground," said Yeshua.

"My friend, do you remember the story of Hagar from your Torah book?" asked a very serious looking Mohammed.

"Ummm. I think so," said Yeshua. "I'll try to remember. I think she was the maidservant of the biblical Patriarch Abraham, and she had a child with him named Ishmael because his wife.... Ummm... Sarah. Yes, Sarah. She was super old and couldn't get pregnant. But then after Ishmael was born Sarah did get pregnant with Abraham and they had a child named Isaac. Then... wait a sec. Oh, right.... Sarah was very jealous and made Abraham kick out Hagar and Ishmael into the desert. And then an Angel showed Hagar the well when she ran out of water and... Oh my God...."

Yeshua paused and looked shocked. He looked down at his Shofar.

"Do you think it was Hagar and Ishmael that I found in the desert? I led them to the well? How is that even possible? And the boy... he looked just like you. Whoaaaa! Is this Shofar some kind of time machine? And did it turn me into an Angel?" asked Yeshua.

"Are you sure it was this exact spot? Could it have been a different well?" asked Mohammed.

"I'm not sure. It seemed to be right here, although I suppose it could have been anywhere. We were in the desert. There were a lot of hills. It could have been a different location, I guess. Why do you ask?" questioned Yeshua.

"In Mecca, Saudi Arabia, in my people's holiest city, is a place called the Zamzam Well. It is within the Great Mosque of Mecca, the Masjid al-Haram. Millions of pilgrims journey every year there to complete special holy rituals and drink from the Well during the Hajj, which is our sacred duty as Muslims much like your Bar Mitzvah. In the center of the Mosque is the holiest site in Islam, the Kaaba. It was built by Abraham and Ishmael. The Kaaba is a sacred cube shaped building and is considered to be the center of the world with a gate to Heaven above it. During each pilgrimage, which I plan to do someday, each worshiper walks seven times around the Kaaba. Also, there's a holy ritual in which we travel back and forth between two hills called Safa and Marwa seven times to represent the search Hagar made looking for water for Ishmael. The Zamzam Well is where the Angel Gabriel made the water flow up to save them from dehydration," explained Mohammed.

"Wait a second," said Yeshua. "So, Abraham... the Father of my people is the same Father of your people? Isaac and Ishmael were brothers? And Abraham built your holiest site?" asked Yeshua.

"Yes, my friend. We are brothers," said Mohammed.

"Then why... why do most Muslims hate the Jews so much? Why do they want us to be destroyed?" asked Yeshua.

"Honestly, I'm not really sure," said Mohammed. "Maybe, sibling rivalry? Maybe power and politics? Or perhaps someone or something is playing us against each other for nefarious purposes. I just don't know. Hopefully someday there will be a way to find forgiveness and peace between our peoples. We are family, really. Brothers. We come from the same father. Perhaps it will be possible."

"And your Allah..." said Yeshua. "Isn't Allah the same as our Hebrew God? And isn't Allah the Creator of the Universe the same as 'God the Father' of the Christians?"

"I believe so. There is no God but Allah," said Mohammed. "Even in my Holy Book, the Qur'an, it says 'Our God and your God are One.' We are all children of Allah."

"All is one! Yes!!!" cheered Yeshua as his stood up. The echoes of his words reverberated off the walls of the ancient city and down bellow into the valley. "That's what the Prophets said to me in my vision. Mohammed, Moses and Jesus... they were all there together as one. Then they told me to share my story."

"Yes, my friend. All is one. We all come from the same Creator, and Abraham is the father of all our peoples. Maybe if we could stop killing each other over our differences, the world would be a much better place," said Mohammed.

"Hmmm. You said differences. Remember when I was 13, after the bomb blew up and God came to me in a vision and said, 'The meaning of life is the DIFFERENCE between One and Zero,' said Yeshua.

"Yes. I remember that well. That statement has many meanings. Everything is connected, and everything happens for a reason. We can choose to focus on our differences and continue to hate and destroy each other, or we can focus on what we share in common and that which brings us together," said Mohammed.

"Indeed!" said Yeshua. "That's the difference between One and Zero. We are all one, and let's not let our differences reduce us to nothing."

"Well said my friend, you should be a Prophet!" said Mohammed.

The two young men laughed as they walked into the ruins of Tel Be'er Sheba.

CHAPTER 7

GRADUATION

Beersheba, Israel

On graduation day at Makif Gimel High School, Yeshua and Mohammed sat in the large auditorium next to each other wearing light blue robes and caps, surrounded by all the other students. The school principal called each student by name up to the podium and handed all the proud and accomplished young men and women their diplomas. Mohammed was called up as 'Mohammed Al Heuwaitat'. Yeshua walked up when his named was called 'Yeshua Rabin'. He received his diploma in his left hand and shook the school principal's right hand who nodded at him and smiled.   After everyone's name was called the school principal stood up at the podium and spoke into the microphone.

"Congratulations on this momentous occasion my esteemed students. You have all reached an important milestone on your journeys. After today, most of you will join the armed forces in defense of our nation. I wish you all the very best and may you be successful and safe during your upcoming endeavors. We live in a challenging time, and there will be many dangers and potential conflicts that each of you will encounter. You are all prepared to go out into the world and truly make a difference. We hope you have learned your lessons well and pass each and every one of your future tests. Be proud of who you are and what you have done here. Mazel Tov!"

The principal paused as the students clapped and cheered.

He then continued. "I have a very special guest today here for you on your graduation. His name is Chaim Katz, and he is one of the last known survivors of the Warsaw

Ghetto uprising from World War II. He has a very important message to tell you."

The principal walked over to the chairs behind him and helped a very elderly man up out of his chair and escorted him over to the podium. He was a short, very frail, wrinkled man with short white hair who wore bifocal glasses.

"My name is Chaim Katz," said the old man into the microphone. "I was born in 1930 in Warsaw, Poland. My parents owned a tailor shop. I had three siblings and many aunts, uncles and cousins. I remember being very happy until the Nazis came and invaded our city in 1939. They put all the Jews in a ghetto the following year. Over 400,000 Jews were trapped behind walls and chain linked fences. Many of us starved to death. Then, in 1942, the Nazis started to round us up and deport us on trains. They told us we were be resettled to the east, but in actuality they were sending us to our deaths at the Treblinka extermination camp. My parents and siblings and most of my relatives were sent away on trains."

The man stopped talking for a moment and became teary-eyed. The principal, standing behind him, handed him a handkerchief. He blotted his tears and continued.

"When the Nazis finally came to take my family, I ran away and hid in the sewers. I lived off of crumbs and rainwater for months and eventually I joined a group of resistance fighters. They told me what the Nazis were doing... that their final solution plan was to the kill all the Jews and steal their possessions to help fund their war to take over the world. We were not going to surrender ourselves to these murderers!"

The old man slammed his fist down onto the podium. Yeshua thought about the Nazi dream he had when he was 13. He remembered how the Nazis were coming to get him and his family in Amsterdam and that he jumped out the window rather than be captured.

"We were going to fight!" exclaimed the old man.

"In April of 1943 the Nazis entered the Ghetto to round up the rest of the surviving Jews and deport them. I was 13 years old. We were armed with guns, knives and Molotov cocktails. We would not surrender. Although we took heavy casualties, we surprised them and pushed them into a retreat. They were shocked how some starving Jews could push back the Nazi army. We even took over control of the Ghetto for a short time. Even their commander, Von Sammern-Frankenegg was relieved of duty and court-marshaled for his defeat in the Ghetto. But our victory was short lived. The Nazis came back in full force and annihilated the entire Ghetto, block by block. We were destroyed. Almost all of my comrades were killed. I was captured and put on a train to the death camp. Miraculously, a Polish man helped me escape. I spent the following two years with the Polish resistance. Many brave Poles died by my side resisting and sabotaging the Nazis. Eventually, the Russians came and liberated Poland from the Nazis. I later learned that my entire family had perished. After the war, I came here to Israel and immediately upon declaration of our country's formation... almost every surrounding Arab country attacked us. This time, we were better prepared. We would not be defeated and slaughtered again. We fought them back and won. And still, many of the Arabs do not recognize our right to exist. They chant 'Death to Israel'. And I say, we will never forget. We will never forget Warsaw.

We will never forget the extermination camps. And will never let our people be murdered again."

The old man paused. He looked very tired.

"So, my message to you is this: Defend our people with all your heart, with all your might and with all your soul. Don't let them succeed in what Hitler failed to do. And perhaps, by some miracle, God willing... we can find peace with our enemies. Amen."

Everyone in the room repeated "Amen."

Then, there was an eerie silence in the auditorium. The principal helped Chaim back to his chair, then returned to the podium.

"Students of Makif Gimel High School. Congratulations! You are graduated! L'chaim!"

Everyone threw their caps up into the air in celebration. Yeshua and Mohammed exchanged high fives and celebrated with their student friends.

After the ceremony was over, Yeshua walked outside. It was nighttime which confused Yeshua somewhat because the graduation was held at noon. "Where has the time gone?" he thought. Then, his left ear started buzzing. Across the school grounds, an unusual looking man with a long brown beard wearing old brown robes was talking loudly into a loudspeaker on the top of the school steps. A small group of people gathered around him. The crowd became larger as many of the graduation students and families as well as other pedestrians joined the enlarging group from the surrounding streets. Yeshua couldn't really understand what he was saying, it sounded like it was perhaps ancient Aramaic. Yeshua walked over to the crowd and stood there, listening to the robed man's speech. Although he couldn't understand the words, he felt a message. He felt like he was receiving a set of instructions to follow. After a few minutes, a couple thousand people were listening to this charismatic man speak. Yeshua looked around him and there were people congregated as far as his eyes could see.

A woman walked through the crowd, right up to Yeshua. The buzzing in his ear stopped. She had blond hair and was very beautiful. Yeshua recognized her immediately as Miriam, the nurse from the hospital who had taken care of him when he was in a coma. She wore a short, white, flowing dress with embroidered flowers. She came right up next to him, very close to his body. He smelled lavender. He looked down at her necklace with the figure of eight intersecting cross. She smiled, raised her right hand and gently touched her index and middle fingers on the middle of his forehead. He closed his eyes. Then she grasped his hands with her hands. She unfurled his hands into a cupping position and then placed a small stone object into his hands. He looked down at the rectangular piece of stone that looked like a small tablet and had some words written on it in an ancient language that he could not understand. He gently placed the stone in the pocket of his long blue robes that he was still wearing.

He looked back up and Miriam was gone! He searched around the huge crowd for her, but she wasn't there. Suddenly the robed man stopped speaking into the loudspeaker and walked away. Everyone in the crowd started to disperse in all directions. Yeshua thought he saw

Miriam down the street to the east in the distance. He quickly walked in her direction, hoping to find her.

The strong winds kicked up as Yeshua walked through the city streets. He passed by shops and apartment buildings. He walked towards an intersection. The streets were filled with pedestrians who wandered in every direction. He could still see the woman with blonde hair far ahead of him in distance.

Trying to move faster to catch up to her, he almost collided with a woman pushing a baby stroller. She wore black robes and a niqab that covered her face except for her eyes. He almost ran over the baby carriage, and fell to the ground trying to avoid an impact. The woman stopped pushing the baby carriage, and went to help Yeshua up, but at the last moment she pulled back and wouldn't touch him. Yeshua stood up on his own and looked at the woman and saw that she had dark black eyes. There was no color in her iris, just black. Then the woman went back to her baby carriage and pushed it down the street towards the west, in the opposite direction that Yeshua had been going.

Yeshua checked to see if the stone tablet was still in his pocket, and it was gone! He panicked and searched all his pockets. Then he saw the tablet lying on the grass next to him and he picked it up. He placed it in his front chest shirt pocket under his blue robe. He looked down the street towards the east and didn't see Miriam at all now. In fact, all the people walking on the streets were gone. He was alone on the sidewalk. There were no cars; the city seemed empty; the only sound was the strong wind blowing towards the south.

He turned at the intersection and headed south. The streetlights illuminated the night as Yeshua travelled along the barren sidewalk. Then, he noticed some movement coming from his peripheral vision. There seemed to be some dark, shadowy figures following him in the alleyways adjacent to the street that he was walking down. When he turned his head to get a better look, they disappeared.

After a short walk through the empty city, Yeshua came upon a circular stone building with large double red wooden doors. He walked into the middle of the street in the front of the building and stopped. Surrounding him just out of his view in the shadows were the dark moving figures that had been following him. There were dozens of them just out of his sight, watching him. At first Yeshua thought the building in front of him was a church; however, as he walked closer to the structure there was a sign on the wall next to the doors that said "Abraham's Well."

The wind suddenly stopped. Yeshua heard that familiar buzzing sound in his right ear. It was quite loud, and he grabbed his ear in an attempt to quiet the sound. He slowly walked up to the giant double red doors. As he got closer to the building, the ear buzzing got louder, and he felt heat coming from the stone tablet next to his chest. He looked down and saw that it glowed and pulsed in his shirt pocket under his robes.

He went to reach for the ornate brass door handle of the building, and then both doors burst open and Yeshua stumbled backwards and fell down onto the gray brick sidewalk. White smoky fog poured out unto the street from the open doors. He felt stunned and disoriented.

As he gathered himself, he looked up at the open doorway and was shocked to see two giant men emerge from the white mist, one ten feet tall, the other about twelve feet tall. They looked almost identical, with short curly light brown hair and fair complexions. Their eyes were pitch black, and Yeshua saw one man looking down at him in anger. From their large flowing tan robes, Yeshua saw folded feathery wings coming from their backs. There was a faint glow around their heads. They were Angels!

After a few moments of silence and bewilderment, Yeshua stood up. He noticed the shorter Angel had a scar on the right side of his face. He looked very familiar. A sense of dread came over Yeshua.

Yeshua looked behind the Angels through the doorway and was astonished at what he saw. Inside the building was a large tan stucco two story courtyard supported by tall columns. Although it was dark and foggy inside, he saw a huge stone well in the far corner of the space. The room was illuminated by hundreds of candles. He saw a large circular iron grate against the wall next to the well that covered it. More sinister looking large giant Angels climbed out of the well. A dozen or so stood around the well.

Then, the angrier looking Angel stood in the door well in front of Yeshua, turned to the other one, and said...

"Let's kill him right now."

He started to move towards Yeshua, but the second taller Angel blocked him from moving forward with his long, outstretched arm and said, "Wait!"

He turned to Yeshua and said, "Why are you here?"

Behind the Angels, Yeshua saw that more and more of these giant beings were climbing out of the well. He put his hand into his chest pocket and grabbed the glowing stone tablet.

"I am here... to save the world..." said Yeshua, as he took out the radiant tablet. Glorious beams of light shot out of the stone fragment in every direction. Yeshua looked down and started to read the illuminated words aloud that were written Aramaic. Somehow, he could read the words now.

As he spoke, all the giant Angels around the well started to scream. The two Angels in front of him looked at him in horror and began to scream as well. Bright, intense light beamed from the tablet in Yeshua's hands and filled the room. The building started to rumble as if there was an earthquake. Everyone screamed...

Chapter 8

Hatzerim

Beersheba Orphanage

"Yeshua, wake up! Wake up! You're screaming!" said Mohammed as he shook Yeshua awake. "You're having another nightmare!"

Yeshua opened his eyes. He was screaming. He looked at Mohammed and stopped.

"Dear God. It was just a dream. It seemed so real," said Yeshua.

"Oh boy. What happened this time?" asked Mohammed.

"Ummmm. Speaking of time. What time is it?" asked Yeshua.

"It's 5:30AM," said Mohammed.

"Well, let's finish packing and get ready for our first day of basic training. We have to get to the Hatzerim Air Base by 7am," said Yeshua.

As the two young men gathered their belongings, Yeshua told Mohammed the entire dream about the graduation, the man in the robes with the loudspeaker, Miriam, the stone tablet and the showdown with the giant Angels.

Finally, they were ready to go, duffle bags in hand. They said goodbye to their orphanage headmaster and thanked him for taking such good care of them for so many years. They did not know when then would be back again, but they promised to return someday to visit.

The two young men left the orphanage and walked down the dark street to the nearby bus station. The sun was rising in the east.

"I don't like buses," said a very uneasy Yeshua.

"Don't worry. It's just a short ride to the Air Base," said Mohammed.

A few dozen young men and women with duffle bags waited at the bus station to be transported to the Air Base for their basic training assignment, many accompanied by families and friends.

A few moments later a large military bus pulled into the bus depot and stopped. The door opened. Most of the young men and women hugged their parents, boyfriends and girlfriends goodbye. It was an emotional scene, and many tears were shed that morning.

Yeshua and Mohammed entered the bus first. They walked all the way to the back and sat in the last row. Yeshua's hands trembled. He looked white as a ghost. The rest of the bus filled up with the passengers, and the driver closed the door. The bus left the depot, heading west. All the people at the bus station waved as the bus drove off into the distance.

"Do you hear any buzzing sounds in your right ear?" asked Mohammed.

"No," said Yeshua as he shook his head.

"Marvelous news! Alhamdulillah! Then we should be fine, yes? No danger here, correct?" said Mohammed as he smiled.

"I guess so, yes," said a tired looking Yeshua. "Mohammed, I have an important question to ask you."

"Okay... sure, what's your question? Ask me anything," said Mohammed curiously.

"Well, being Jewish... I had to enlist in the military. It's my duty. But you... you are a Bedouin Arab, why did you volunteer? You didn't have to do this," asked Yeshua.

"That's easy my friend. Who is supposed to look after you when you go into one of your crazy comas?" said a grinning Mohammed.

"Well, thank you. I have your back too. I sure hope they don't split us up when we get there, Baruch Hashem," said Yeshua.

"What does that mean exactly?" asked Mohammed.

"Baruch Hashem? It means 'God willing' in Hebrew. I hope God keeps us together. I don't know what I would do without you."

The bus passed the Israeli Air Force Museum and a few minutes later it arrived at the entrance to the vast Hatzerim Air Base, located just west of Beersheba on the outskirts of the Negev Desert. Everyone departed from the bus and filed into the parking lot. There were hundreds of young men and woman there who had recently departed their buses and stood in large groups.

Yeshua and Mohammed waited by their bus with the others, then an older man in soldier's uniform came over and said, "Ladies and gentlemen, please get out your identification cards and assignment letters." Everyone started to hastily search through their belongings looking for their letters.

Yeshua thought about the day when he was formally summoned for military duty, about a year ago. It was called Tzav Rishon. It was an all day, extremely stressful four part intensive test and scored examination. Both he and Mohammed had gone to the local recruitment center together. The day began with a lengthy personal interview. He was asked about his school grades, personal history, all the details of his murdered family, why he was in the orphanage, and his reasons for wanting to go into the military. It seemed more like an interrogation. Afterwards, they tested him in Hebrew proficiency and then had a full physical and medical exam. The next part of the grueling day was a psycho-technical exam that he took on a computer. He felt like he totally aced that part. At the end of the day, he met with an army social worker and then a psychologist. There were so many questions about his goals for his service and his dedication to Israel. He remembered saying "I am willing to make the ultimate sacrifice for my country."

A few weeks later he was e-mailed the results of the tests, which he printed out and gave to the soldier who now stood next to the bus. The soldier looked at the letter and he said, "Go to Building Eight," and pointed over his right shoulder behind him. After the soldier read Mohammed's letter, he also said, "Go to Building Eight." The two young men were so relieved that they were staying together.

Yeshua and Mohammed walked down the broad sidewalk towards Building Eight. There were now hundreds of young men and women walking from the bus parking lot over to several large buildings deeper into the grounds of the Air Base.

The two young men entered Building Eight through a shiny metal door and were surprised to see that the room they entered was quite small. Several young men and women wearing white tee shirts and camouflage long pants sat on uncomfortable looking folding chairs against the walls of the room. In the middle of the room behind a small wooden desk sat a young, pretty woman wearing an officer's uniform. She had short brown hair, light olive skin and blue eyes. She wore a red beret, and there was a small medal emblem on her beret that looked like a scimitar sword surrounded by two bird wings.

The woman glanced up and down at Yeshua and Mohammed, sizing them up. She said, "Papers and identification, please." They handed over their papers to her and then waited in silence as she read them. She then stopped reading the papers and looked up at them.

"Welcome to Hatzerim Air Base. My name is Lieutenant Colonel Ariella Eliora. Very impressive gentlemen. You both scored a ninety seven on your exams. Well done. You are exactly where you are supposed to be."

Yeshua and Mohammed looked at each other and smiled.

She grabbed two wrapped packages from a box next to her and slid them on the desk towards them.

"Go into the changing room next door and put these clothes on. Grab some boots and put them on. Leave your duffle bags in the room and come back here and sit down. Your belongings will be delivered to you to your final destination," she said.

"Yes Sir," said Yeshua. His face immediately turned red. "I mean, yes ma'am."

"You can address me as Lieutenant Colonel," she said with a very serious face.

"Yes, Lieutenant Colonel!" said both young men in unison.

They walked across the room, opened the door to the adjacent room, and entered and closed the door behind them. There were a few long tables in the windowless room. Several duffle bags were on one table, and on another table there were many various sized black combat boots.

"I can't believe you called her 'Sir'!" said Mohammed. "Our first day here and you are already not making friends in high places."

"Yeah, my bad!" said Yeshua as he looked for the right sized boots. He found the correct size and double checked to make sure his most valuable possession, his shofar, was still in his duffle bag. They removed their civilian clothes and changed into their new white tee shirts and camouflage pants and put on their combat boots.

The two young men left their duffle bags on the table with the others and walked back into the reception room and sat down. Yeshua counted a total of ten conscripts including themselves sitting on the chairs, seven men and three women. Yeshua could see that although everyone had their best 'game-face' on, he could feel a lot of nervousness within the room.

After a few minutes, Lieutenant Colonel finished her paperwork at her desk and stood up and walked to a door in the back of the room.

"It's time to go. Follow me. Those who dare... wins," she said as she opened the door.

A strong wind blew into the room from the open door. Yeshua heard an incredibly loud roaring sound coming from outside. It was the sound of a helicopter. They all filed outside the building one by one. Sitting on the tarmac nearby was a giant green Israeli Air Force Sikorsky CH-53 helicopter. Its six massive rotor blades were spinning at a super speed. On the side of the helicopter was a blue Jewish star surrounded by a white circle. The side door was open, and an armed soldier motioned the young men and women to come over to the helicopter. The Lieutenant Colonel walked over to the helipad while holding her beret on her head with her left hand. They all followed her in line to the helicopter and each one was handed a green aviation helmet as they got inside. They all put their helmets on and sat down. The Lieutenant Colonel sat down in the co-pilot's seat up front, next to the pilot who was already sitting there. She gave a thumbs up, and the soldier that greeted everyone closed the door and sat down. The soldier held a black automatic Uzi machine gun.

Yeshua was elated. He had never been in a helicopter before. He had seen many helicopters in the air looking from the ground up; however, this was beyond exciting. The helicopter lifted upwards and headed towards the northwest, several hundred feet into the air. Yeshua looked out of the window and saw his home city of Beersheba get smaller and smaller to the southeast. This was actually his first time flying. He was amazed at the view outside. Everything looked wonderful and very different from this perspective. It was a spectacular view looking down at the Israeli countryside.

The helicopter lifted up higher and Yeshua looked to the northeast.

After a few minutes of blissful enjoyment, Yeshua's right ear started buzzing loudly. It was much louder than the noisy sound of the helicopter blades rotating. Something bad was about to happen. Something very bad. After looking inside the helicopter and then outside into the air, he visually scanned all around the ground far below for danger through the window next to him. Then, he looked to the south and saw a flash of light on the ground. It came from the Gaza strip. Then he saw a smoke trail and something shiny that was heading in the direction of the helicopter. Someone just launched a missile at the helicopter!

Normally, the advanced radar system of the CH-53 Helicopter is designed to detect hostile incoming missiles that would trigger an alarm. Next an automatic anti-missile system would activate and target the missile, shooting it down. That didn't happen. Something failed.

Yeshua saw the missile getting closer. He unbuckled his seatbelt and stood up. Although he didn't know how to use his helmet's communication system, he started to move towards the front cabin to alert the Lieutenant Colonel about the incoming missile. As he got to the front the helicopter, the armed soldier who sat in the back grabbed and stopped him. When Yeshua pointed to the missile getting closer through the window, the soldier's eyes got very big. He activated the communication walkie-talkie in his helmet and said "Evasive action! Incoming at seven o'clock!"

The helicopter pilot looked to his left and saw the fast-moving missile coming. It was very close now. A smoke trail streamed behind it. The Lieutenant Colonel saw the missile and attempted to manually activate the defense system on the control panel, but it seemed to malfunction. Something was jamming their electronics. The missile flew closer and was about to hit the left side of the helicopter. Yeshua and the others looked out the windows as they prepared to meet their death.

The Lieutenant Colonel turned on her headset and said "Mayday, mayday ground control! Incoming air attack from north Gaza over Yad Mordehai. Request support! Mayday!"

At the last moment, the helicopter pilot veered hard to the left and descended as quickly as he could. Since Yeshua was standing by the cockpit, he fell hard against the window on the left side of the helicopter as it went into its evasive maneuver. The missile came within inches from his face. Miraculously, the missile whizzed by and narrowly missed impact with the helicopter. Yeshua could very clearly see the green, white and red Iranian flag painted on the missile.

The helicopter leveled out after its short descent downwards. Yeshua regained his balance and stood back up. He looked out the right window and saw to his horror the missile turned and made a huge arc and re-directed itself back towards the helicopter. Yeshua tapped on the back of the Lieutenant Colonel who turned to look at him. Yeshua pointed in the direction of the oncoming missile. She then pointed out the returning missile to the pilot.

The Lieutenant Colonel spoke into her headset to the pilot "Turn in the direction of the missile and hold your ground!" He faced the helicopter directly in front of the oncoming missile. She went back to the controls and tried to activate the weapons system to shoot down the missile, but nothing was working. She pounded her fist on the control panel in frustration.

"Sergeant, give me your weapon!" she screamed into her headset as she unbuckled herself and stood up, then turned around and walked into the cabin. The Sergeant handed her his Uzi machine gun. She walked back to the copilot chair and stood there for a moment and looked out the window. The missile was getting much closer. Collision was imminent within seconds. Then, the Lieutenant Colonel placed her right foot on the chair seat and bent her knee. She held the gun with both hands and steadied her right elbow on her knee. Yeshua looked from the back of the helicopter and saw the missile about to make impact. He braced himself against the back of the cockpit.

The Lieutenant Colonel took aim and pulled the trigger of her gun. Bullets shattered the helicopter glass and shards flew everywhere, almost seemingly in slow motion. The missile was about to hit the helicopter then BOOOOOOOM!!! It exploded right in front of them. There was a massive burst of flames, smoke and shrapnel that reached just a few feet away from the front of the helicopter. Somehow she made an incredible bull's-eye and shot down the missile with her gun. For a split second, Yeshua thought he saw some kind of huge demonic face in the huge explosion.

Wind, broken glass and a few small pieces of shrapnel blew violently inside the helicopter through the shattered window. Yeshua turned around to look for Mohammed and check to see if he was okay. He sat in his seat, looking completely stunned. A few of the other conscripts were hunched over and puking. Everyone looked shocked. Yeshua calmly walked back over to his seat and sat down. He buckled himself back into the seat harness.

"What the flip just happened?" said the pilot into his headset.

"I don't know for sure. It seems like they launched a new kind of missile that jammed our radar and defense systems. Thank God we didn't lose control of the helicopter," said the Lieutenant Colonel.

"Should we proceed to our original destination or abort?" asked the pilot.

"Yes, let's hit the beach. And by the way Captain, nice flying!" she said.

"Thank you! And nice shooting Lieutenant Colonel! You have great aim!" he replied.

Just then, two Israeli F-15 warplanes flew in formation over the helicopter and turned south. Yeshua looked out of the window as the jets soared overhead. He saw both of the planes fire missiles southward towards the Gaza. The planes then rapidly flew upwards into a higher elevation. Yeshua saw a huge explosion on the ground at the same location where the ground-to-air missile was launched at the helicopter from within the Gaza strip.

CHAPTER 9

YOM SAYAROT

As the helicopter continued to fly to the northwest, Yeshua could see the Mediterranean Sea get larger and larger as they got closer. They were getting near the coastal city of Ashkelon. Once the helicopter started its descent, Yeshua looked down and saw the beach. He thought to himself "The Lieutenant Colonel wasn't kidding! We are going to the beach!" Below he saw about a half dozen other large helicopters that were already on the ground in a rural area just off the beach. Next to the landing area was a large semi-circular outdoor amphitheater located adjacent to a heavily wooded area. Although they looked like little white ants from his view, Yeshua saw that the amphitheater was partially filled with military conscripts wearing white tee shirts.

Yeshua had come to this place before, on a school trip. It is the Ashkelon National Park. He remembered having fun on the beach with his classmates, and then they had a good tour of the archeological ruins along the cliffs. He remembered about the huge ancient fortress here and the several epics battles between the Christian Crusaders and the Muslims a very long time ago. He also remembered seeing in the ruins some large statues of Angels with wings in the ruins.

When the helicopter landed, the Lieutenant Colonel and the pilot took off their helmets and got out first. The soldier in the back of the helicopter turned on his communication walkie-talkie on his helmet and said into everyone's built in helmet headphones, "Is everyone okay? Does anyone need medical assistance? Give me a thumbs up if you are okay."

All the conscripts in the helicopter gave a thumbs up. Miraculously, everyone was uninjured from the explosion and shattered glass. The soldier said, "I am Sergeant Berg. Everyone take off your helmets and leave them here in the helicopter. Please follow me to the amphitheater for further instructions." They all followed his instructions and deboarded the helicopter.

As soon as Mohammed left the helicopter, he got down on his hands and knees and kissed the ground. He got back up and said to Yeshua "I know you don't like buses… however, I don't like helicopters now!" They both started laughing.

They all followed Sergeant Berg single file from the landing area on a narrow dirt trail over to the back entrance of the amphitheater. As they walked, two more helicopters landed nearby. There were dozens of military trucks parked along the outer edge of the landing site. Yeshua saw the Lieutenant Colonel and the pilot over by the trucks and they were talking to an important looking military officer.

Yeshua had a déjà vu moment as they reached the crest of the hill at the back of the amphitheater. He remembered being there before, on his school trip many years ago. The large, sprawling half circle stadium filled with concentric stone sitting steps had a stunningly beautiful view of the Mediterranean. Behind the large, white elevated stage was a scenic backdrop of tall palm trees planted in a lush tropical garden. Yeshua remembered this place was supposedly built by the Romans or Greeks at least two thousand years ago.

He visually imagined all the seats filled with Greeks wearing togas being entertained on the stage by actors and actresses wearing silly masks. Then he visualized executions of Hebrew Rabbis, rebels and heretics here during the

Roman-Jewish wars. Now, two millennia later, the seats were filled with young Israeli future soldiers wearing white tee shirts and camouflage pants on their first official day of military duty. He estimated there were at least one hundred young men and women. Sergeant Berg walked them over to the front right corner of the stadium and instructed everyone to sit down. Then the Sergeant left them, and he walked away.

Yeshua and Mohammed sat together of course. They were inseparable.

"What do you think will happen next?" asked Yeshua.

"I don't know. Maybe they will do some comedy routines for us up on the stage?" joked Mohammed. They both laughed.

After a few minutes, the Lieutenant Colonel walked by herself onto the front platform. Her red beret seemed to shimmer in the bright Israeli sunlight. All the conversations in the entire amphitheater stopped, and there was total silence.

"Welcome soldiers. Welcome to beach day!" she said.

Laughter broke out in the large crowd of young men and women. Yeshua and Mohammed looked at each other and smiled. A little humor always breaks the tension. She did not need a microphone; her voice projected out loudly into the circular amphitheater.

"My name is Lieutenant Colonel Eliora. I'm sure all of you are wondering why we brought you here today on your first day of military training. From the thousands of applicants that we evaluated this year, you are the chosen ones. You are the best, the smartest, the strongest and the brightest. You are here today to be tested for acceptance in the elite Sayeret Matkal Special Forces unit. Training for this unit is the most grueling and harsh of any of Israeli Defense Forces. If you excel in the challenges today, you will immediately move onto the Gibbush selection camp that lasts approximately one week. Before we get started, if anyone does not want to voluntarily move forward with possible enrollment into our unit, please leave this amphitheater now. There's a transport vehicle waiting behind you beyond the grass field. You will be transferred to a regular IDF assignment for the rest of your military service."

She pointed to the back of the large grass field behind everyone. At least 20 of the conscripts stood up and began walking out of the stadium. As they were leaving, Yeshua remembered hearing about the Sayeret Matkal unit when he was a young boy. They are a Special Forces unit in charge of deep reconnaissance, counterterrorism and hostage rescue. For many years the elite group was top secret. The most famous mission of Sayeret was called 'Operation Entebbe' when approximately 100 commandos rescued 100 Israeli hostages in Uganda in 1976. The leader of the raid, Yonatan Netanyahu, was killed during the assault. He was the older brother of Benjamin Netanyahu, the current Prime Minister of Israel.

The Lieutenant Colonel waited until all the dropouts left the stadium, then she said loudly "I stand here today on the coast of Ashkelon, and listen very carefully... the echoes of time are speaking to us!"

She paused, and the word "us" reverberated and echoed several times in the perfect acoustics of the amphitheater. She waited a moment until the echoes faded back into silence. From the west, everyone could hear the soft sound of waves rolling onto the beach and a few seagulls that chattering in the sky above.

"This place has paid its price in blood many times. The archaeologists dated this area inhabited over 10,000 years ago by nomadic hunters. During the times of the Pharaohs there was a large ancient Canaanite walled city here with at least 15,000 people. Approximately 3,000 years ago, the aggressive sea-faring Philistines took over this city forcefully. Then Nebuchadnezzar and his Babylonians horde destroyed Ashkelon in 604 BCE as well as our Great Temple in Jerusalem and took our people into exile in Persia. Ashkelon was later rebuilt only to be conquered by Alexander the Great and the Greeks in the 4th century. Next, the Romans took it over and occupied the entire land of Israel. King Herod built monumental buildings here during the Roman times. After the Roman Empire fell, the Byzantines and then the Egyptian Fatimids ruled this strategic site. The Christian crusaders fought many battles here in the 1100's and eventually it was conquered by Saladin and his Islamist army. A few hundred years later, it was controlled by the Ottoman Empire until the modern era. After World War I, these lands were under the jurisdiction of the British Empire. As a consequence of World War II, and the extermination of six million Jews by the Nazis, Israel was finally granted its Independence in 1948. And this year, 2018... we celebrate our 70th year of democratic independence!"

All the conscripts stood up and started to cheer, yell, clap and whistle. The Lieutenant Colonel smiled. The elated energy in the amphitheater was very powerful. After a few moments, everyone sat down, and silence once again filled the stadium, except for the sounds of the ocean nearby.

"Almost immediately upon declaration of our statehood, virtually all our surrounding neighboring Arab countries attacked us. They tried to destroy us, yet we fought them back, and we finally took control of this land after almost two thousand years. Now we are here with the responsibility to defend this beach and all of our land from future invaders."

She paused for a moment. It was a lot to contemplate mentally. Yeshua was taken aback from all the epic historical events and battles that had transpired here on this little slice of land along the beach.

"Each of you will be tested today, and each test will be scored based on your performance. Only the top 36 of you will make it to the next phase of training. You will team up in pairs. For the first objective, go back to the landing area and find the helicopter you arrived in and get inside. Then you will be flown out to the Mediterranean Ocean to the designated drop zone. Jump in the water and swim back to the beach where you see the Israeli flag flying. Once on the beach, pick up a medical stretcher with your partner and run with it north to the Ashkelon Recreation Village Parking Lot. There you will receive your next set of instructions. Consider this a competitive race. The first three teams to the finish line are the winners. Now go!"

The word "Go!" echoed loudly in the amphitheater. Quickly, everyone started to leave the stadium and run up the steps back towards the helicopters. The conscripts were choosing their partners and paring up as they left.

Yeshua said to Mohammed as they ran up the steps "I wonder who I should pair up? Any thoughts?"

Mohammed said "Very funny, my friend. You are a comedian. Do you remember how to swim?"

"I do. It's been a while since we swam in the Dead Sea during summer camp. It was so salty we just floated. I think it might be a little harder to swim in the Ocean," said Yeshua.

When they reached the landing area, most of the helicopters were had already starting up their rotors. Yeshua counted 11 helicopters. Dust and wind blew all over the grassy field. All the conscripts were boarding their helicopters. But when Yeshua and Mohammed got to their helicopter with the broken front window, they found it unoccupied.

"Holy Smokes!" yelled Mohammed. "We need to find a new helicopter fast!"

They ran to the nearest helicopter, and jumped inside just as it was about to take off. There was an armed soldier inside who closed the side door after they entered. Yeshua looked down at the ground as they lifted up and he and saw about a dozen conscripts were boarding an almost full transport bus. They were already giving up and too unnerved to join Sayeret Matkal.

The helicopters flew together in close formation over the beach and then westward out to the beautiful turquoise colored Mediterranean Sea. Yeshua looked down at the beach as they passed it. He saw a large Israeli flag flying on a giant flagpole along the water's edge surrounded by dozens of empty orange rectangular stretchers. He then looked out of the helicopter's front window and saw a giant orange buoy floating due west along the water's horizon. He estimated that it was approximately 1.5 kilometers (about a mile) out to sea. It was too loud to try to talk or hear on the helicopter, as they didn't have their aviation helmets. Yeshua gave Mohammed a thumbs up who gave one back.

The helicopters soon arrived at the location over the large orange buoy. Yeshua looked out of his window and saw below, around the buoy, that there were three large amphibious green military motorized rafts with soldiers in each one. He figured they were rescue crews in case any of the conscripts started to drown in the water.

The helicopters descended and hovered close over the sea surface. Violent ripples and waves of water radiated out from the high winds generated from the helicopters. The soldier in the back of Yeshua and Mohammed's helicopter opened the main side door and pointed down. Everyone in the helicopter started to jump in the water and swim east towards land.

Yeshua looked back at the Israeli flag eastward and saw that it was really far away on the beach. It would be a long swim. Both he and Mohammed jumped out of the helicopter at the same time. They made a giant splash. Yeshua was shocked at how cold the water was. He got some seawater in his nose when he landed and started to cough. There were now dozens of swimming conscripts surrounding him in the water. He looked around and somehow he had lost track of Mohammed. Where was he? Yeshua waded in the water for a few moments until got his bearings. He started swimming freestyle towards the beach. Hopefully, he thought... he would find Mohammed on the way.

Once all the conscripts were in the water, the helicopters lifted upwards and headed back towards the coastline. The intense winds died down, and the waters became much calmer. Yeshua paused from swimming for a moment to look around again for Mohammed. He was nowhere in sight. He looked back in the direction of the orange buoy and saw that several of the swimmers were being helped out of the water by the military raft crews. They must have been drowning.

Yeshua starting swimming again. At this point, most of the conscripts were far ahead of him in the waters. He wasn't a very good swimmer, yet he did his best. It was hard to swim with his heavy combat boots on. He really did not enjoy swimming, and he was already quite exhausted from this insane day, yet he kept up a good pace, and he soon found himself in the mid-pack of the conscripts. He saw the beach getting closer and closer; the blue Jewish Star of the Israeli flag became clearly visible.

He was almost at the beach when his right ear started buzzing loudly. As so many times before, he knew that he was getting a warning. He paused swimming for a moment, and he treaded water and looked around. Still no Mohammed. Where could he be? Yeshua was very tired and tried to catch his breath. It certainly felt good to rest for just for a moment as he treaded water. He could see a lot of the conscripts were already on the beach and running in pairs with their empty stretchers towards the north.

Suddenly, Yeshua saw two swimmers pass him by a few feet away. He looked in horror as one of them inadvertently kicked the other one directly in his head while he was swimming. Then there was blood in the water. The young man was knocked unconscious and started to sink and drown. Yeshua immediately swam over to him to help him. He grabbed him under his shoulders and held his bloody face up out of the water. He was still breathing and just appeared just to be knocked out. Yeshua looked around for the rescue boats but didn't see them anywhere.

Yeshua swam the best he could with the young man in his arms towards the beach. He was already exhausted from swimming so far, and his efforts were beyond strenuous. Finally, he arrived in the shallows and could feel the sand under his feet. He continued to pull the unconscious young man towards the beach as the strong waves broke over them, knocking them both down. Yeshua hit the sand under the water and started to choke on the saltwater. He was almost out of energy. Another big wave crashed over him and pushed his entire body downwards. He lost grasp of the young man he was trying to rescue.

"Yeshua! Yeshua! Are you okay?" screamed Mohammed as ran out from the shoreline. From under the water, Yeshua heard his name being called. His friend was coming to save them. Mohammed grabbed Yeshua and the other young man from underneath the water. He pulled them both back to the beach to dry land.

"Thank you. Thank you..." said Yeshua. He just lay there in the sand, exhausted. Mohammed checked the young man's pulse with the bloody face and leaned down to make sure he was breathing. He was alive.

There was no one else on the beach. All the stretchers were gone.

"We've lost the contest Yeshua!" said an upset Mohammed. "I was the first swimmer out of the water. The first one! I waited and waited for you. I watched all of the others come out from the ocean and grab their stretchers and run up the beach towards the finish line."

Mohammed pointed with his right index finger northwards up the beach towards the rocky coastline. On the edge of a nearby cliff were the giant ruins of an ancient stone Crusader wall.

"And there you are… trying to save the world again. You are quite the mensch!" said Mohammed.

Yeshua had finally caught his breath and he slowly sat up and looked at Mohammed.

"How do you know what a mensch is?" he asked.

"I know lots of Yiddish. I love that Jerry Seinfeld show! You are a good and noble person my friend," said Mohammed.

"As are you," said Yeshua.

Yeshua stood up. He was soaking wet. Without saying anything, the two best friends grabbed the unconscious conscript lying on the sand by his arms and legs and gently placed him on the last remaining stretcher. He had a deep gash on his forehead all the way down to his bone, and he was still bleeding. Mohammed took off his white tee shirt, made a tourniquet, and wrapped it around the young man's bloody head.

Yeshua looked upwards and saw some vultures flying and circling high in the sky. He wondered how many times those vulture's ancestors had seen blood and came to this beach in the past, looking to scavenge a meal.

They lifted up the stretcher and placed the four wooden handles onto their shoulders. Mohammed was in the front and said, "Are you ready for this? Do you have enough strength?"

Yeshua replied, "Yes. Let's do this. Although, I wonder where his partner is?"

It was around noon. The hot middle eastern sun shone down directly over the beach. They slowly walked northwards up the sandy, rocky beach. The beach was full of footprints from all of the combat boots of the other conscripts.

"I guess we are going to come in last in this race," said Yeshua.

"I guess so. I wonder if we will be demoted to a regular IDF unit?" asked Mohammed.

"I don't know. It's in God's hands now," replied Yeshua.

It took about 20 minutes for them to get to their destination. They walked up an incline along a path from the beach to the Ashkelon Recreation Parking Lot. Standing under the shade of the surrounding trees along the parking lot were all the other conscripts. They were all staring at them in silence as they walked up from the beach.

Sergeant Berg walked out to meet Yeshua and Mohammed at the parking lot entrance. He told them to put the stretcher down as he handed both of them bottles of water and a few meal rations. He gave Mohammed a new white tee shirt. They both saluted Sergeant Berg and said, "Thank you, sir!" then they walked over to a shady spot under a nearby tree and sat down. Mohammed put on his new dry tee shirt, and they both drank some water and ate some food. It had been quite a day so far.

An ambulance drove over and parked next to the stretcher holding the unconscious young man with the bloody face. The paramedics got out and placed the injured conscript onto a new stretcher and put him into the back of the vehicle. Inside, they started an IV and hooked him to the monitor. They closed the back door and the ambulance left.

Yeshua looked around the edge of the parking lot. He counted about sixty or so conscripts remaining among the trees. He gave a gratitude prayer as he drank his water and ate his food. He could feel his strength returning.

A large green military truck drove into the parking lot and stopped in front of the grove of trees. The Lieutenant Colonel came out of the front passenger door. All of the conscripts got up and stood in attention.

"Well done!" she said. "Almost all of you made it through your first challenge. I want to congratulate the three winning teams. Please come forward when I call your names."

She paused and then said, "Team Cohen-Perez step forward."

A young man and woman stepped out from the under the shade of the trees onto the hot, black asphalt. Everyone else started to clap, cheer and whistle.

"Team Levy-Freidman step forward," said the Lieutenant Colonel. Two young men walked out and joined the first team on the parking lot. There were more claps, cheers and whistles.

"Team Rabin-Al Heuwaitat step forward," she said. The clapping and whistles stopped. There was silence.

Yeshua looked at Mohammed and said softy "Ummm… we won? We came in last."

They were stunned. They just looked at each other with surprised expressions.

"Team Rabin-Al Heuwaitat, please step forward!" yelled the Lieutenant Colonel.

The two young men walked from under their shady tree and stood next to the other two winning teams. No one was cheering them; there was only silence in the parking lot. The Lieutenant Colonel looked at Yeshua and Mohammed and smiled.

"There's a very importing saying you all need to know from one of the ancient Talmud teachings," she said very loudly so everyone could hear. "It says 'Whoever saves one life, saves the world entire'. Remember that, always."

She paused for a moment. Yeshua though he could see a tear forming in her eye.

"Your next challenge is another test of strength and endurance," she said. "Each of you will come to the back of this truck and receive a stone. You will all wait until everyone has their stone. Then, when I give you the signal… you will all race back down the beach with your stone and place it at the base of the Israeli flagpole. The first two stones placed there belong to the winners. You will receive your next set of instructions at the flag."

Everyone walked out from under the shady trees and gathered behind the truck. The back of the truck was open, and there were four soldiers inside who were lifting large stones that were piled from the floor to the ceiling that they handed to each conscript.

Yeshua waited patiently next to Mohammed behind the truck to receive his stone. Finally, he was in position and was handed his stone. It was very heavy, at least 40 pounds. He looked at the stone and turned it in his hands. Painted in white on the back was the number 18.

"Eighteen! My lucky number," said Yeshua. "What's your number?" he asked Mohammed.

"I'm number seven. Ha. That's my lucky number too. Seven is a very special number. Gosh, this rock is freaking heavy!" said Mohammed.

After all the conscripts had their stones, the Lieutenant Colonel pulled her black Jericho 941 semi-automatic pistol out from its holder on her belt. She raised it upwards and shot one round up into the sky. Everyone started running west in unison down the path towards the beach. Some of them cradled their stones in their arms like a baby and others held them with both hands over their heads, some on their shoulder.

Just in front of Yeshua and Mohammed, one of the conscripts running along the path lost his footing and dropped his stone as he fell down. This caused a chain reaction as his falling rock caused others behind him to trip and fall. Like a Nascar car race pile up, a dozen or so of the runners fell and lost their stones all at once.

Somehow… miraculously, Yeshua and Mohammed were able to navigate through the mess by jumping and sidestepping to avoid the chaos. Rocks and conscripts fell all around them. After dodging the near disaster, they both reached the wide beach. There were about ten runners in front of them rushing quickly southwards down the beach along the sand by edge of the cliffs.

Yeshua looked down at his hands and saw blood. The course stone had scraped some of the skin off both his palms. It hurt badly. The stone seemed to be getting heavier.

Suddenly, Yeshua looked to his right side as Mohammed took off in a burst of speed. He had never seen someone move so fast. Mohammed uncradled his stone from between his arms and moved it above his head. He ran down to the edge of the water as he yelled out a shrilling scream at the top of his voice. Yeshua wondered why he decided to run all the way down the wide beach to the wet sand rather than run on the dry sand that was closer to the cliffs.

Yeshua decided to run after Mohammed across the wide beach, even though it made them both lose some ground in the race as the others who were running closer to the cliffs ran further ahead. Once down to the water's edge, Yeshua held his stone over his head and ran as fast as he could. He was very pleased to find that it much easier to run on the compact wet sand rather than the dryer loose sand by the cliffs.

Ahead, Yeshua saw Mohammed run faster than any human he had ever seen. It was late afternoon now, nearing high tide. It was perhaps an illusion, but it looked like Mohammed was running on water as the waves crashed upon the shore next to him. Then, Yeshua looked along the cliffs and saw the other runners on the beach who were running just slightly ahead of him. He had gained a lot of ground by running on the compact wet sand.

Mohammed was well advanced from everyone and reached the flag first. He won! Yeshua saw him put his stone down against the pole and he lifted both his arms into the air as he let out another shrilling yell. Yeshua dug down deep for a second wind and he ran as hard as he could. He closed his eyes and screamed a yell like Mohammed as loud as he could.

The large Israeli flag was in the middle of the beach, halfway between the cliffs and the edge of the water. Yeshua was getting very close to the flag and started to the run from the edge of the water towards the flag. Two of other runners who had been running closer to the cliff were now running right next to him, and all three of them were neck and neck. Just slightly behind them were about 20 of the other runners.

Yeshua could feel himself near exhaustion and out of breath. He started to lose some ground to the other runners who were just a couple dozen of yards away from the flagpole.

Surprisingly, Yeshua saw some small objects on the ground. He noticed about 50 or so small shovels partially buried in wide concentric circles in the sand all around the flagpole. Then suddenly, his foot caught one of the shovels.

He began to lose his balance and fall. Ahhhh! He was so close to the flagpole.

With all his might, he threw his stone towards the flagpole as he tripped and fell to the sand. The stone left his bloody hands and it flew threw the air. Seemingly in slow motion, Yeshua's stone landed at the bottom of the pole next to Mohammed's number seven stone just a millisecond before the other two runners arrived at the flag and threw their stones down.

Mohammed was laughing loudly next to the flagpole. The two other runners were Cohen and Levy, winners of the first challenge.

"You are stoned my friends," said a smiling Mohammed to Cohen and Levy. "We've won the race."

A few moments later, most of the other runners came up the beach and placed their stones against the flagpole in a big pile. Everyone was out of breath and looked exhausted, expect for Mohammed.

Yeshua lay on the ground. He was totally worn out. Mohammed walked over to him and offered his outstretched hand. "Get up soldier. We won. We did it!"

Yeshua grabbed Mohammed's hand and pulled himself up. Mohammed looked down at his hand and saw blood on it.

"My friend, there's blood on your hands," said Mohammed.

"It's just a scratch from the stone. I'll be fine. Mohammed…. how did you run so fast? How did you know to run down to the wet sand?" asked Yeshua.

"We Bedouins… we have to know how to run fast. How do you think we have survived thousands of years in the hostile dessert?" explained Mohammed.

"Well said. Well said," said Yeshua. "I think we are doing really good here today. I wonder what the next challenge will be?"

Just as Yeshua said those words, almost in synchronistic way… a green Israeli army jeep drove down from a sandy road between the adjacent cliffs onto the beach and parked close to the flagpole. Yeshua looked around and counted about 50 conscripts left. There were less than half of the conscripts remaining than those who had sat on the stone steps of amphitheater earlier in the morning. It was a day of attrition.

The Lieutenant Colonel got out of the passenger door from the Jeep and walked over to the flagpole. All the conscripts gathered around her. Sergeant Berg got out from the driver side and walked to the back of the Jeep. He grabbed two cases of bottled water and brought them over to the group and placed them on the sand by the Lieutenant Colonel. Each bottle had an interesting looking large black top.

"Strong work soldiers! I know that was not easy. In Sayeret Matkal, nothing is easy." she said. "You must be very dehydrated. Drink some water please, and hang onto your empty water bottle. These are special water bottles whose carbon filters will convert saltwater to drinkable water. Keep them with you always." Sergeant Berg passed around the bottles; everyone opened them and drank their water.

"In your last challenge of the day, find your stone in the pile here. Somewhere on the beach around us there is a shovel in the sand that has the same number on it as your stone. Find your shovel and then dig down in the sand exactly at that spot until you find water. Fill your bottles with water and then bury your stone completely in the sand. I want this beach to look like nothing happened here. When you are done, run up the road behind us with your water bottle and shovel and meet me back at the amphitheater for final assignments."

The Lieutenant Colonel and Sergeant Berg walked back to their jeep and got inside. Already, many of the conscripts were pulling out their stones from the giant pyramidal shaped pile leaning against the flagpole. Many others were scrambling around the beach looking for their designated shovels. The jeep drove away on the beach and then up towards the road in between the cliffs and then it disappeared.

Yeshua knew his stone was all the way at the bottom of the pile. He was standing next to Mohammed and said "No point in waiting here until all the stones are gone. I'm going to go look for my shovel."

"Me too!" said Mohammed.

The small shovels were arranged in three large and wide concentric circles centered around the flagpole, each spaced approximately ten to fifteen feet apart. Mohammed found his quickly as it was near the flagpole. He started digging.

It took a while for Yeshua to find his shovel. He found it along the most outer circle; it was the absolute furthest one away from the ocean. By the time he located his shovel, almost all the other conscripts had their stones and had found their shovels and were digging their holes. Instead of going back to get his stone, Yeshua immediately starting digging in the sand.

The sand was soft and loose. It was easy to dig. Yeshua quickly dug a deep hole. He glanced over towards the flagpole and saw that Mohammed had already reached water and was using his hands to pour the sandy water into the filter of his water bottle.

Yeshua keep digging. He suddenly had a memory from his early childhood. He must had been six or seven years old, and he remembered going into the large backyard of the orphanage in Beersheba and digging a deep hole and just sitting in it. He would just watch the world go by for hours by from the safety of his hole. The other boys in the orphanage would always make fun of him, for his bushy long red-orange hair and for his hole. He remembered the horrible feeling of being bullied.

Yeshua hit something hard. His shovel made a loud clunk sound. His hole was pretty deep already, at least three feet deep. Next to his hole was a large pile of sand that Yeshua had dug out. He put down his shovel, got down on his knees and reached into the bottom of the hole. He felt a stone or a rock at bottom. He grabbed his shovel again and dug out some more sand. There was a huge rock at the bottom of his hole.

"Whatcha got there?" asked Mohammed. His full water bottle was tucked into a pocket of his camouflage pants. Behind him, few of the conscripts were running up the beach towards the cliffs. Many more of them were finishing burying their stones in the sand.

"There's a freaking rock at the bottom of my ditch!" said Yeshua. Mohammed looked down into the bottom of the dark hole.

"Hmmmm. Keep digging. I have an idea. I'll be right back," said Mohammed. He walked back over towards the flagpole. Yeshua grabbed his shovel and dug out more sand from around the rock, which was large, flat and white. Yeshua couldn't seem to dig out beyond edge of the rock; it must have been really wide.

Mohammed soon came back and stood over Yeshua holding the number 18 rock on his right shoulder. Some of Yeshua's blood was still hand-printed on the large stone.

"Ok. Now stop digging and get out of the way," said Mohammed.

"What?" said Yeshua as he stopped digging and turned around to look up at Mohammed.

The sun was starting to set in the west over the vast Mediterranean Sea. There was a brilliant display of glorious incandescent colors in the sky and among the scattered cumulus clouds far off in the distance. Mohammed's body formed an almost surreal silhouette in front of the sunset from Yeshua's perspective down by his ditch. Around them, the last few conscripts were finishing burying their stones.

"Just move. Move away from your ditch. Trust me," said Mohammed. He had a crazy look in his eyes.

"Ok," said a very exhausted Yeshua. He rolled over from his ditch digging and just lay there on the sand, looking up at his best friend.

Mohammed walked over to the edge of the hole and raised the stone directly over his head. He let out another one of his shrilly super loud screams as he lunged the stone as hard as he could into the ditch. It made a loud cracking crunch sound as it took a direct hit on the stone below it.

Yeshua rolled back on the sand and looked down into the hole. His number 18 stone was shattered in pieces. Miraculously, the white rock at the bottom of the ditch had a large crack in its center.

"You did it! Brilliant! Thank you. I hope I can break through the rock now," said Yeshua. He grabbed his shovel and wedged the edge of the shovel blade into the new crevice. He pushed as hard as he could on the shovel from the lying position on the ground with his arms extended deep into hole. It wouldn't budge.

Yeshua lowered his feet into the ditch and placed them on the flat rock. There was just enough room for him to stand, three feet down. He pushed the shovel deep into the crack and grabbed the handle of the shovel as tightly as he could. He closed his eyes, and suddenly a vision came to him. It was his memory of the Well at Tel Be'er Sheeba when he dove in to help the woman and her son get a life saving drink of water. He remembered jumping into the water and pushing it upwards.

He prayed to God for a moment. He prayed for help. "Help me. Please help me," he thought. Then Yeshua focused all his energy on the water below the rock. "Come up. Come forth," he thought. Eyes closed, he pushed with all his might on the handle of the shovel. There was a cracking sound as the stone broke apart. Water gushed from the crack and filled the bottom of the hole.

"Allah 'Akbar!" yelled Mohammed. "God is great!"

Mohammed handed Yeshua his empty water bottle and he reached down to fill it in the rising waters. Once full, he climbed out of the ditch and stood up.

"Let's finish this," said Yeshua. He and Mohammed started to shovel the large pile of sand back into the ditch. They were alone in the beach. All the other conscripts had buried their stones in the sand and left for the amphitheater. All that was remaining on the beach was Yeshua's ditch and the huge Israeli flag on the tall flagpole.

In the west, the sun set along the distant horizon of the green-blue ocean. It was a stunningly beautiful view from the beach. Rays of golden light beamed from the disappearing huge orange sun and illuminated a dazzling array of surrounding glowing pink and purple clouds.

"Do you know that the sun does not set?" said Mohammed as he shoveled the sand into the ditch.

"What? Why of course it sets," said Yeshua. "Look, its setting right there over the ocean." He paused shoveling for a moment and pointed to the Sun.

"It's actually a strange optical illusion. Our Earth is rotating in orbit around the Sun at 67,000 miles per hour," replied Mohammed. "And here on Earth we are spinning at approximately 1,000 miles per hour to the east. So, it may appear as though the sun is moving and setting in the west horizon; however, it is actually US that is moving away from the sun. The sun isn't really setting, we are just flying through the Milky Way Galaxy on this big spaceship called Earth."

"Whoa. You are making me dizzy just thinking about that. How do you know so much?" asked Yeshua.

"I love to read and watch TV shows about astronomy and quantum physics," said Mohammed. "Did you know that at the center of every galaxy is a supermassive black hole, and in the center of every atom is a black hole too? It's almost the same exact design, like a vortex. And it's very possible that all the black holes in the entire universe are connected together via inter-dimensional wormholes, like tunnels that go everywhere. For example, you can have two atomic particles that are connected through something called quantum entanglement. That means that if something happens to one particle, the exact same thing happens to the other particle. Look it up… it's real! Your famous Jewish scientist Albert Einstein called it "spooky action at a distance." Now, if one particle is halfway across the universe and something happens to the other particle… they both change instantaneously. That means that all the information is transferred across the universe immediately, faster than the speed of light. The only plausible explanation is that the information is sent via a black hole wormhole tunnel between the two particles."

"That's incredible. Do you think we can travel through those worm-holes, instantly through time and space?" asked Yeshua.

"I think so my friend, yes indeed," said Mohammed.

The two young men, finally done shoveling the sand back into Yeshua's ditch, ran up the beach towards the cliffs with their full water bottles.

CHAPTER 10

NITZANIM

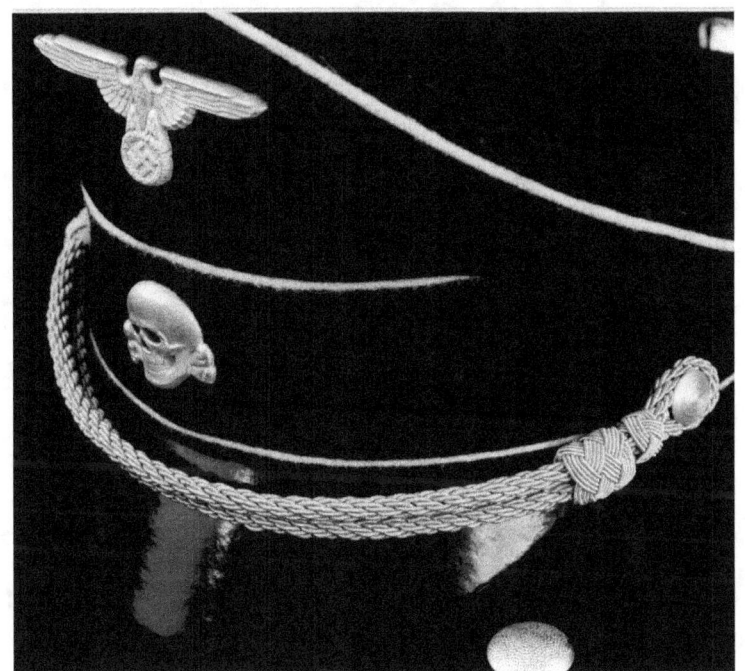

"Why did you cheat?" asked the Lieutenant Colonel.

Yeshua and Mohammed were sitting in the last row of seats in a military bus. On the way back to the amphitheater, Sergeant Berg had intercepted Yeshua and Mohammed and made them sit in the back of a bus parked near the helicopter landing area. They waited about and hour, then the Lieutenant Colonel and the high-ranking military officer she had been talking to earlier that morning came into the bus and now stood in front of them.

"Cheat? We didn't cheat, Lieutenant Colonel," said Yeshua.

"On the last challenge, Mohammed helped you bury your stone in the sand. You were supposed to do that yourself. You disobeyed the rules!" she said in a very agitated way.

Yeshua looked at Mohammed with a shocked look on his face. He didn't know what to say.

Mohammed stood up and looked at the Lieutenant Colonel directly in the eyes.

"We did not cheat Lieutenant Colonel. At the beginning of the day, your instructions to us were specific. You explicitly stated that we would team up in pairs. That means we are a team. I helped my team mate bury his stone."

"At ease, soldier," said the important looking officer. Mohammed sat down. There was silence.

"My name is General Geller. Son, how did you run so fast on the beach? Have you been taking performance enhancing drugs?"

"No sir!" said Mohammed immediately. "I've always been able to run fast. It's in my nature."

The General whispered something into the Lieutenant Colonel's ear, and then she responded back into his ear. He then looked at Yeshua.

"Son, I want to thank you for alerting your helicopter crew about the incoming missile this morning. You saved a lot of lives. I highly recommend the both of you continue to work as a team. Now you will be transferred to the Nitzanim Army Base for your one week Gibbush endurance testing. You two are the best we've seen in a long time, so good luck. I'm sure we will meet again at the appropriate time."

Yeshua and Mohammed stood up, saluted and said "Sir, yes sir!"

The General saluted them back, and he then turned around and started to walk down the center aisle towards the bus entrance. The Lieutenant Colonel smiled at Yeshua and Mohammed as she turned around and then followed the General out of the bus.

Sergeant Berg stepped up through the front entrance of the bus and sat in the driver's seat. A few moments later, about 20 very exhausted looking conscripts wearing white tee shirts entered the bus and found seats. It was dark outside. The clear night sky was full of stars.

"I think we passed all of our tests today," said Mohammed.

"Yes we did! Checkpoint. Onto the next adventure. But gosh, I hate buses," said Yeshua.

"Hate is such a strong word, my friend," replied Mohammed.

"Yes, you're right. I need to remove that word from my vocabulary. I really, really dislike buses," said a grinning Yeshua.

The bus engine turned on, and they drove out from the helicopter landing area and onto Heil HaYam Street. They turned right onto the Sderot David Ben Gurion causeway and out towards Highway 4 North.

Yeshua fell asleep with his face smooshed against the window. He was beyond exhausted. Next thing he saw was a very familiar sight. Outside the window was the dark cobblestone street in Amsterdam from his dream many years ago. He was 13 again, hiding in the attic from the Nazis surrounded by his frightened family. They all heard the police sirens in the distance. The Nazis were coming to get them, again! In the dream, Yeshua realized he was having the recurrent nightmare from his childhood. The Nazis were on their way to arrest them and deport them to extermination camps. The siren got closer and closer; then the truck appeared on the street and parked in front of their house, five floors below. The Gestapo police got out of the vehicle and broke down the front door. Downstairs were screams, then gunshots. He heard them coming up the stairs, one floor at a time. Then there was a knock on the door to the attic. "Open the door," screamed the Nazi in German. Yeshua felt dread and fear. They were trapped again... the only escape was to jump out the window.

The Nazi policeman kicked the door down and pointed his gun at Yeshua. Then, something suddenly shifted. Instead of seeing the Nazi with the gun pointed at him as he did every time when he had the recurrent dream, this time Yeshua's perspective was that he was looking at himself. He saw himself near the window, with all the frightened Jews around him. He looked down and saw that he was holding the gun, pointed at the small red headed boy near the window of the attic. After a moment of confusion, Yeshua looked down at himself and saw that he was wearing the Nazi Uniform. He was the Nazi Gestapo policeman.

"Yeshua, Yeshua… wake up! We're here!" said Mohammed.

"I'm the Nazi," said Yeshua as he stirred back awake.

"What? You're a Nazi?" asked a surprised Mohammed.

"In my dream, I was the German Nazi. I was coming to kill myself," said a very tired and groggy Yeshua.

"The Universe works in mysterious ways, my friend," said Mohammed. "There's no time to interpret your dream now as we've arrived at the Nitzanim Army Base. We have to get off the bus right now."

All the conscripts got off the bus and walked towards a large tent. It was very dark outside; the only light visible came from the opening of the tent. Yeshua looked up at the sky and saw millions of stars. He could see the faint outline of the Milky Way. A bright shooting star passed over them traveling east to west.

Once inside the tent, Sergeant Berg told them to sit down for processing. There were about 50 chairs, half of them filled with sleepy conscripts wearing white tee shirts. Everyone from the bus sat down on chairs. There were three long tables at the far end of the tent. Behind each table sat a soldier wearing an olive-green uniform. They were calling names, and conscripts were waking up to the tables and sitting down in front of the soldiers.

Almost immediately after sitting down, one of soldiers called for "Yeshua Rabin." He stood up and walked over to the table and sat down on the lone chair in front of the soldier. The man was middle age with sandy hair and a dark, sunburnt complexion. He wore glasses and was looking at some papers on the table next to a laptop.

"Private Rabin?" the soldier said.

"Yes sir!" said Yeshua.

The soldier turned the laptop around and faced it towards Yeshua. On the screen was the image of a front facing camera view, so Yeshua was looking at himself. He thought to himself that he looked very, very tired. In the center of the screen was a small yellow crosshair.

"Come closer to the laptop with your head and focus the center of your left eye in the crosshair. We will be scanning your eyes for identification purposes," said the man.

Yeshua pulled his chair as close to the table's edge as possible and leaned forward towards the laptop. His eyes magnified to a huge size within the computer screen. Once his left pupil centered on the crosshair, a red hologram laser projected from the top of the laptop and scanned both of his eyes from top to bottom, then from left to right. He could see on the screen the colors of his speckled hazel brown iris light up from the red laser. Within his iris was the faint pattern of a vortex spiral centered around his black pupil, similar to the shape of a hurricane or a galaxy.

The soldier turned the laptop back towards himself and then pushed two black objects that looked like large round coasters on the table towards Yeshua. They were connected by wires to the laptop. He started typing on the keyboard. He then grabbed a strange looking black head cap full of sensor pads and stood up and reached over the table and placed it firmly on top of Yeshua's head.

"Place your both of your hands inside these sensors on the table and position each finger firmly into the slots inside; then hold still. We are going to scan your biometrics."

Yeshua followed his orders and put his fingers inside the devices. He found the slots and placed his fingers tightly into each one.

"Hold still and stay very calm," said the man. He was typing on his laptop again. Yeshua closed his eyes and relaxed. He emptied his mind of all thoughts and slowed down his breathing. He mentally went to his 'happy place.' It was a form of self-taught meditation he had done since early childhood when life got too stressful, lonely or disappointing.

Yeshua could feel his entire body relax, and he knew he could have easily just fallen asleep right there in the chair. It had been a very intense day, and he was exhausted. He felt like he was floating in space as he deepend into his trance-like state of quiet relaxation. The hand sensor devices activated, and he experienced a warm tingling sensation go up his arms, then into his chest and up into his brain.

"How did you do that?" asked the soldier.

Yeshua opened his eyes. "How did I do what?"

"You just changed all of your vital signs. Your pulse and blood pressure went down 20 points, and your heart and brain waves went into total electromagnetic coherence. How did you do that?" asked the soldier. He took off his glasses and looked more closely at his computer screen.

"I don't know," said Yeshua. "I just closed my eyes and relaxed just like you told me to do, sir."

"Wow. Okay," he said. The soldier looked rattled. "Um. The next thing we are going to do is a lie detector test. Okay? Please keep your fingers in the devices until I say we are done. "

"Yes sir," said Yeshua.

"State your full name, country of birth, age and home address please," asked the soldier.

"My name is Yeshua Rabin. I was born in Israel. I am 18 years old. Before today, I lived in the Beersheba Orphanage."

"Do you have any connection or association with Hamas, Hezbollah, ISIS, Al Qaeda, Fatah, the Taliban or any other Islamic extremist or terrorist organizations?" asked the soldier.

Yeshua paused and thought for a moment. He grimaced. "The only connection that I have is that my parents and family were killed by a Palestinian Hamas suicide bomber."

"I'm very sorry," said the soldier. He paused for a moment and gave Yeshua an expression of sympathy.

"Have you ever used or are currently using any performance enhancing substances, steroids, prescription or illegal drugs?" he asked.

"No sir. I have not," replied Yeshua.

"Okay Private Rabin, you may now remove your hands from the detectors and please gently take off the head device and leave it on the table," said the soldier. He handed Yeshua a metal dog tag on a chain with his name on it. He placed it around his neck. Then the soldier slid Yeshua a small clear plastic glass bottle.

"Please exit the back of the tent. Take your specimen container with you. There are some latrines outside behind the tent. Fill your jar with a urine specimen, then enter the building behind the latrines for your medical examination." said the soldier.

Yeshua stood up and said, "Thank you sir." and grabbed his container. He started to walk to the back of the tent, and he saw Mohammed getting his eyes scanned two tables down. He left the tent and filled his specimen container in the privacy of a small port-o-potty. He then entered the large building next to the latrines.

There was a small waiting room in the entrance to medical building. Inside were about a dozen folding chairs positioned against the walls, and there were six conscripts sitting there and waiting. Along the far wall was a sliding glass window that was open next to a closed metal door. On the other side of the window sat an old woman with gray hair who looked like a nurse.

As soon as Yeshua walked in, the old lady said loudly "Private, come here!" He walked over to the sliding glass window. She said, "Write your name on your sample and place it here." She handed him a sharpie pen, and she pointed to a small plastic box on the counter next to her. It was filled with other several other specimen containers. He followed her directions, and then she handed him a long medical questionnaire on a clipboard. There was a pen attached to the clipboard. Yeshua sat down on an empty chair nearby and started filling out the paperwork.

The metal door opened, and another ancient looking female nurse walked out and called one of the conscript's name. When he got up, she brought him through the open door, and then the door closed. A few more conscripts came into the room, and handed in their urine samples, and sat down to fill out their questionnaires.

Yeshua finished his questionnaire quickly. He was completely healthy and marked "no" to almost every question. The metal door opened. A different older female walked out and called his name. Yeshua got up and walked over to the open door. He followed the old woman through the doorway, and the door closed behind them. Ahead was a long narrow hallway as far as his eyes could see. It almost looked like it went to infinity. There were dozens of metal doors going down both sides of the hallway. The nurse said, "Follow me," and they walked down the hallway.

After passing by a dozen or so doors, the old nurse stopped and turned. She opened a door to her right. It had the number 18 printed in white on the metal.

"Come inside," she said. "It's time to take your blood specimens for lab work."

They both entered the very small room. There was just enough space for an examination table, a chair and a small countertop with drawers underneath.

"Sit down and hold your arm out," she said. Yeshua followed her instructions. She put on some gloves, and then she placed a tourniquet around his left arm and reached into one of the drawers and pulled out a butterfly needle and seven small empty vacutainer glass tubes. She took her index finger and thumb and flicked his antecubital vein near his elbow. It was bulging now. She wiped off the skin with an alcohol pad.

Yeshua said, "Will this hurt?" He had never had his blood taken before.

"Don't worry," said the nurse. "This won't hurt me a bit."

She shoved the needle into his vein and flash of blood appeared in the tubing. Yeshua felt an intense stinging pain for a moment; then it quickly disappeared. The nurse next connected the first empty glass vial to the needle tubing which rapidly filled with blood. She took the vial out and filled another tube, then another until all seven tubes were filled with Yeshua's blood. She then took the needle out and held pressure with a small piece of gauze over his vein with one hand as she popped off the tourniquet off his right bicep with her other hand. She then put a band-aid over his vein.

"Ok, next I will administer our vaccines. Roll up your left sleeve please," said the old nurse.

Yeshua once again followed her orders. He rolled up his sleeve. She cleaned the skin over his deltoid with an alcohol pad and then pulled out a large needle and syringe from her short white lab coat pocket. She pulled off the cap and Yeshua stared down at what seemed like a very large needle. His eyes got very big.

"Hold still please," she said. She then plunged the needle deep into his arm. He winced in pain as she pushed the contents of the syringe quickly into his arm muscle. She pulled the needle out and held pressure on the area for a moment then placed another band-aid on his skin.

"Wait here until the doctor comes to do your physical examination." She paused for a moment. "Is there water in your bottle?" she asked.

Yeshua looked down at his pants and saw she was looking at his water bottle that was attached to his belt.

"No ma'am. Its empty. I'm very thirsty. And I'm very hungry too. I haven't eaten food for many hours. Do you know when we will be given some water or food?" asked Yeshua.

"I don't have any mana, but here, take this..." said the nurse. She opened one of the drawers and handed him a container of Neviot bottled water. Then she left the room and closed the door behind her.

Yeshua drank the water bottle in almost one big gulp. He was very dehydrated and hungry. He thought back and reviewed the past day's events in his mind. Had it just been one day since he and Mohammed walked to the bus station near their orphanage for their first day of military service? He was so tired and just wanted to sleep.

The door opened and the doctor walked in. He was an older man, with gray hair and a short gray beard. He had on a long white jacket and wore bifocal glasses. Around his shoulders was a black stethoscope. He held a clipboard with Yeshua's questionnaire on it.

"My name is Dr. Saul. I'm here to do your exam. I've reviewed your medical history, and it says you have no medical conditions, correct?"

"Correct," said Yeshua.

"Okay, take off your shirt please and sit on the exam table," said the doctor. Yeshua followed his instructions. The doctor grabbed a small otoscope and inspected both of Yeshua's ears.

"Do you hear any buzzing in your ears?" asked the doctor.

"No, I do not," said Yeshua. He would not tell the doctor his secret.

Dr. Saul then placed the ear buds of his stethoscope into his ears and then placed the bell pad on Yeshua's heart. He closed his eyes and listened for a few moments, then took the stethoscope off and placed it back around his shoulders.

"What's that?" said the doctor as he pointed to Yeshua's left chest.

"What's what?" replied Yeshua as he looked down at his left chest. "Oh, that. That's my birthmark." Just below his left nipple, at the bottom crease of his chest was a dark brown spot.

The doctor stepped closer to look at Yeshua chest. "That's an accessory nipple," said the doctor.

"A what?" replied Yeshua. "I have an extra nipple?"

"Yes," said the doctor. "It's uncommon. Some people have a birthmark there; it's a congenital growth. It's completely benign. Only one in about 18 people have them."

"Eighteen, huh?" responded Yeshua. "That's my lucky number!"

"It's interesting, birthmarks you know," said the doctor. He grabbed his bread. "When I was in medical school at the University of Virginia many years ago, there was a psychiatrist there named Dr. Ian Stevenson. He did a lot of research on reincarnation. He studied hundreds of children that had memories or dreams of past lives, and often they would have a birthmark that would correspond to the place of trauma from a previous life."

"What? Really?" said a surprised Yeshua. He looked shocked. "Can I tell you something in confidence? I've never told this to anyone before."

"Well, everything we do here is part of your military physical exam. However, you can tell me something off the record, okay?" said the doctor.

"Since I was five years old, I've had multiple recurrent dreams over and over again. One is that the Nazis are coming to get me in Amsterdam. Other ones are about these strange aliens or dark angels that masquerade as people and who are trying to take over the world. Another one is that I'm falling and falling and then I land on a spike or a spear.

Right into my chest. Right here." Yeshua pointed to his birthmark.

"Let me ask you a question," said the inquisitive doctor. "In your dreams, are you aware that you are dreaming?"

"Yes! Yes! How did you know that?" asked Yeshua. "I just thought I was crazy. When I'm dreaming, I often realize that I'm in a dream. Like when I am free falling for example. I know that as I'm falling, I will be landing on the spike and die. I know it's coming. Everytime. I know that after I fall onto the spike in my dream that it's a portal to another dream. It's like I have to die to go onto another dream."

"Very interesting. That's called Lucid Dreaming," said the doctor. "Perhaps Dr. Stevenson was right. Perhaps we do reincarnate."

"I've never put the dreams together with my birthmark before. Now it all seems to make much more sense. You are saying that this birthmark is a sign that I was killed with a chest wound in a previous life?" asked Yeshua.

"Well, that's Dr. Stevenson's hypothesis," said the doctor. "I don't know if there's anyway to really know for sure."

"Well, maybe we are here to 'Prove It.' It's like everything happens for a reason, like fate or destiny. Perhaps you were sent here right here right now to tell me about this past life stuff. And now, a new door of infinite possibilities has opened, yes?" said a very excited Yeshua.

"What happened to your hands?" asked the doctor. He lifted up both of Yeshua's wrists and looked at the palms of his hands. There was blood in the center of each of his palms.

"Um, during the tests earlier today we had to carry a heavy stone down the beach. The stone rubbed off some of my skin, and I bled a little bit. Don't worry, it's just a scratch."

The doctor looked more closely at his bloody hands.

"You weren't Jesus in a past life, were you?" asked the doctor with a very serious look on his face.

"No. I don't think so. I'm not the Messiah. I'm just an 18-year-old Israeli here on his first day of military duty," said Yeshua.

CHAPTER 11

GIBBUSH

Yeshua held the large gun in both hands. It looked like something out of a Star Wars movie.

"You are holding the IWI Tavor X95 fully automatic nine millimeter submachine gun. It has a 380 millimeter barrel and an integrated grenade launcher attachment," said Sergeant Berg.

Yeshua, Mohammed and eight other conscripts stood in single file in their new barracks. Each one held their new gun.

"This gun is your new best friend," yelled Sergeant Berg. He pointed to the top of his gun. "Here is the ITL multi purpose aiming reflex laser sight device. Each clip is a standard NATO magazine with thirty rounds. The safety is here." He pointed to a latch near the trigger.

"Keep your safety on at all times unless I tell you to it's time to go live. Do you understand?" yelled the Sergeant.

"Sir. Yes Sir!" said everyone in unison.

"By each of your bunks is a standard issue duffle bag and backpack with all your supplies for the next week. Inside your duffle bag is the instruction guide to your X95. You need to know this gun inside and out and how to disassemble, clean and reassemble it within 10 minutes. So study hard, Privates! At 0330 we will be leaving for a thirty mile hike, so have all your things ready to go and be dressed in your full military gear for an overnight trip. Do you understand?" yelled the Sergeant again.

"Sir! Yes sir!" said all ten conscripts. Then Sergeant Berg left the barracks.

"Just another day in paradise," said Mohammed to Yeshua as he smirked.

"Yeah. It's been one wild and crazy day!" replied Yeshua as he looked down at his gun.

"Wow. Look at this thing. It's the most beautiful and at the same time the most horrible object I've ever held in my hands. I hope I never have to kill anyone with it," said Yeshua.

"I hope not either. Yet, at the same time... you may have to pull that trigger and take someone's life in an act of self defense," said Mohammed.

"I know. Being a soldier is a great responsibility. I pray when the time comes I will do what is best," said Yeshua.

Most of the other soldiers were now sitting on their cots looking at their instruction manuals and learning how to disassemble and reassemble their guns. Yeshua looked over to the clock on the wall and it showed 23:11 on its LED display.

"11:11 wishes!" said Yeshua to Mohammed. Their cots were next to each other in the small barracks room.

"All I know is that I wish I could sleep for a few hours," said Mohammed. They both took out their instruction manuals and started to learn how to master their guns. After about an hour of tinkering, they both seemed to get the hang of taking apart and putting back together their X95s.

Yeshua looked on the floor under his cot. There was his duffle bag he had packed earlier that morning in

Beersheba. Or was it yesterday? He seemed to have lost complete sense of time. He pulled his duffle bag out and opened it. The only thing he really cared about was his Shofar. It was there in the bag! He was so relieved.

"Let's prepare our backpacks and get ready for the long hike. We only have a few hours before we have to leave," said Mohammed.

"I agree. I'd love to get just even one hour of sleep before we go," said Yeshua.

Yeshua opened the large green duffle bag that was next to his cot. He took inventory. There was:

- a first aid kit
- a container of hand sanitizer and sunscreen
- two white towels
- three pair of green army pants
- three pair of long sleeve green army shirts
- three green tee shirts
- six pair of black boxer underwear
- two pair of black combat boots exactly his size
- two brown belts
- a brownish-green beret
- a hard military helmet with attached night vision goggles and telecom system
- a multipurpose army knife with a Star of David on it
- ten 30-round clips for his gun
- a green camouflage sleeping bag and small pillow
- a small camouflage tent pack

He opened his backpack and looked inside. There was food! He counted six containers of military rations. He was so hungry. He opened one and started eating. It tasted so good. He thanked God in his thoughts and prayers for the food.

In the side pocket of the backpack was a small blue case. Yeshua opened the box and there was a stunning black analog watch inside. He read the instructional insert and it said that the watch could send out a distress signal anywhere in the world via GPS activation. It was fully waterproof as well. Yeshua put on the watch on his left wrist and it clicked into place. However, he found that he could not take the watch off. It was locked into place around his wrist.

"I'm going to take a shower," said Mohammed. He was already naked except for the towel around his waist. He walked towards the latrine area and found the shower room. There was already someone in the shower. It was a woman! He saw her bare backside and then he turned away.

"Ahhh hummmmm," he voiced loudly as he tried to make a sound like he was clearing his throat.

The woman, who was stunningly beautiful turned off the shower and grabbed her towel and wrapped it around her.

"I guess our showers are co-ed?" asked Mohammed.

"I guess they are," said the woman soldier. She walked back to the barracks area.

Mohammed took a quick shower. As he finished, Yeshua arrived to take his shower.

"My friend, be careful. These showers and bathroom are co-ed," said a freaked out Mohammed.

"Big deal," said Yeshua. "I don't know why everyone makes a such a fuss about about stuff like that. I mean, we're all human, right? What's there to be so embarrassed or ashamed about?"

"In my Bedouin culture, women keep covered up. And your Orthodox Jews do something similar. It's just not appropriate to see naked women who aren't your wife," said Mohammed.

"Mohammed. It's 2018. It's not the Middle Ages anymore. It's okay to show some skin. Seeing a naked woman isn't going to make you completely lose control of your mind and your senses or your devotion to God. We can all act appropriately here, it's the army. We are here to be professional soldiers," said Yeshua.

"Well said my friend," said Mohammed. "But that woman in our unit. She's the most beautiful woman I've ever seen!"

"Keep it together buddy. We've got to focus here. Okay?" said Yeshua.

"Sir, yes sir!" said Mohammed as he saluted his friend.

Yeshua took a quick shower and looked at the time after he finished. His brand new watch said 1:03am. There wasn't much time left. He went over to his cot and got dressed in his new uniform. He then filled his backpack with a change of clothes, some food, the first aid kit, the pocketknife and some rounds of ammunition. Then he grabbed his Shofar from his duffle bag and slid in into the backpack. There was just barely enough room left and it just fit like a puzzle piece.

Yeshua looked over to Mohammed's cot and saw he was already there sleeping. He was snoring. Everyone else, all the eight other new soldiers were sleeping too. Yeshua set the alarm on his watch to 3:03AM.

"Ah sleep! How I've missed you," he murmured to himself as he lay down on his cot and shut his eyes.

Yeshua went immediately into REM sleep. His eyes started to flutter back and forth under his closed eyelids. He quickly went into the dream state. He was falling, free falling... just like so many times before in his dreams. He knew at the end of the fall there would be the inevitable impaling on large spike or spear through his chest.

This time however, he turned around to see from where he fell from. He looked up and saw that he had just been pushed off a tall cliff. Standing on the top of the edge of a cliff was a man, a very familiar man. He had a scar on the left side of his face. His eyes were bright red and coming from his back were two folded feathery wings. He was laughing at Yeshua. Quickly Yeshua fell faster and the cliff disappeared from view. He could still hear the laughing; it sounded like Vincent Price's laughter at the end of the Michael Jackson's Thriller video. He turned his body back around to face downwards. He was falling through the clouds. Then the ground appeared below, far below. He fell through some more clouds and then he could see the earth below clearly.

Instead of a big spike or spear, he saw a giant bed of nails directly below him. It was getting closer and closer as he fell. This time, in this dream... Yeshua had no fear. He welcomed the end. He stretched out his arms for impact. He knew that the end only meant a new beginning. He was just about to hit the nails and then…

Beep!
Beep!
Beep!

His watch alarm woke him up. It was 3:03AM. He stirred awake and sat up. Everyone else was still sleeping.

"Mohammed! Mohammed! Wake up!" said Yeshua loudly.

"Two more minutes," said a half asleep Mohammed as he lifted up his right hand and flashed two fingers, like a peace sign.

Yeshua got up and started to pack the rest of his things. He attached the sleeping bag and tent to his backpack. He put on his combat boots. Many of the other new soldiers were now up and packing their things. Mohammed was down on his hands and knees doing his morning prayers.

At 3:30AM sharp Sergeant Berg walked into the barracks. He held his helmet in one hand and his gun in the other. All ten soldiers were already standing in attention in a single file line in front of their cots. Everyone had on their helmets, combat boots and full uniforms. They had their backpacks on their shoulders and they were all holding their Tavor rifles.

"Shalom Soldiers," said Sergeant Berg. He walked by each soldier for closer inspection.

"Impressive. Keep this up and we may shorten your Gibbush by one day. Now, I'm sure you were all expecting when you got here that your first day would be full of running up and down sand dunes, crawling on all fours and doing lots of push ups. However, we are going to be switching gears a bit. We will be embarking on a 30 mile hike. It will take approximately nine hours to get to our location. We will stop twice for short latrine and refueling breaks. Otherwise we will keep hiking and not stop. If anyone can't handle this mission tell me now and we will excuse you."

He paused for a moment.

"Anyone?"

There was total silence in the room.

"Okay. Let's do this. Outside the barracks you will find a full water skin on a table for our trip. Sling it around your back. Also, on your helmet there is a three toggle telecom button. Turn it on now to activate your headphones. There's another switch to activate your microphones so when you talk, the rest of our platoon will hear you. If you have that button on, please be very mindful of what you say."

The Sergeant placed his helmet on his head and turned on his telecom system.

"Can everyone hear me in your helmets? Give me a thumbs up," said the Sergeant.

All the young soldiers gave him a thumbs up.

"Okay. On your helmets are your thermal night vision goggles. Once we get outside, put them on and you can toggle them on and off with the button right here. There's another button on the other side of the goggles that toggles on and off the radar heat sensors. That mode will allow you to see the heat imprint of enemy combatants through walls and hiding in dark places. Do not look directly in bright light with the goggles turned on. Now let's head out!"

Sergeant Berg walked out of the barracks followed by his platoon, like a mother duck followed by her ducklings. His large backpack was on a table just outside the building, along with eleven leather water skins. He placed his gun temporarily on the table while he put on his backpack. Everyone grabbed their water skins and slung them over their backs.

It was very dark outside. Yeshua looked down at his watch. It said 3:57AM. He slid down his night vision goggles and turned them on.

"Wow. I can see everything!" he said to Mohammed who was standing next to him.

"Those are the best night vision goggles money can buy, soldier," said the Sergeant into Yeshua's headphones. "Remember, anything you say with your telecom on active mode the entire platoon will hear. So please keep radio silence unless what you have to say is absolutely necessary."

"Yes Sir," said Yeshua. "I'm sorry I didn't realize I had them in active mode."

"There's no room for mistakes here, Private. You all remember that. One little error can put the whole platoon in jeopardy. Do you understand? Now, let's move out!" said

Sergeant Berg into the telecom to everyone as they all started walking to the east following the Sergeant.

"Yes Sir," Said Yeshua. He toggled his telecom to passive mode.

Mohammed was hiking behind Yeshua in the line and shoved him gently in the back. Yeshua turned around and Mohammed gave him a silly face. Yeshua stuck his tongue at him.

Above, the dark sky was full of stars. Yeshua looked upwards with his night vision goggles. He was completely amazed that he could see at least ten times more stars than normal. There was some kind of massive meteor storm going on above. Yeshua could see dozens of shooting stars per minute flash across the sky. He had never seen anything so beautiful, at least in a non-dream or coma state. He wanted to tell everyone about the shooting stars through his telecom, however decided not too.

The Sergeant picked up the pace. They crossed over a road and started walking in a giant cornfield. Yeshua noticed little floating dots all over the place with his night vision goggles. They looked like tiny glowing orbs. It almost looked like it was snowing, as they were everywhere. Then Yeshua turned on his thermal radar setting on his goggles. The little orbs lit up like fireflies in all different colors. They were flashing luminescent orange, red and yellow. Yeshua turned the goggles off and placed them up on his helmet. He looked all around and couldn't see anything in the dark. There were no floating tiny orbs, only moonlight and lots of corn.

Yeshua turned his head around and whispered to Mohammed "Do you see them, in the goggles… all the fireflies?"

"Yes. What the heck are they?" whispered Mohammed back.

"I have no idea," replied Yeshua.

After about a half an hour more of hiking, the Sergeant turned on his intercom and said, "We have a long way to go soldiers. Let's get to know each other a little better. Starting with the first soldier behind me, introduce yourself to the group. State your name, where you grew up and something unique or interesting about yourself."

The first soldier behind Sergeant Berg was the female whom Mohammed saw naked in the shower.

"My name is Tanya Ivanov. I grew up in Tel Aviv. My parents and grandparents are from Russia. We come from a long line of circus performers and acrobats, and since I was a little girl I did the high wire and the trapeze."

"Thank you Private Ivanov," said Sergeant Berg. "I'm sure your skills will come in handy. Okay, next…"

"My name is Simon Avraham. I'm from Haifa. My family is originally from Ethiopia, and my parents were rescued from starvation during Operation Moses in 1984. I am told that one of my ancestors was once the ruler of the Kingdom of Aksum in Ethiopia. My people are descendants of the biblical King Solomon and the Queen of Sheba"

"So you are a King?" asked Sergeant Berg.

"I am descended from a King, Sir. But I am no King. I'm just a soldier, here to defend my country. Oh, and one more interesting thing. My great Uncle is a guardian monk at the Saint Mary of Zion Church in Aksum, Ethiopia. Within the church is claimed to be the Ark of the Covenant, the Holy of Holies."

"The Ark... it still exists?" asked Sergeant Berg.

"I don't know for sure. No one is allowed in the church, except the guardian monks. I've never been there. Perhaps one day I will find my great Uncle and ask him what is truly inside the Ark."

"That would be very interesting to know. Thank you Private Avraham. Okay, next..." said Sergeant Berg.

"My name is Jakub Nowak. I'm from the Yagur Kibbutz near Mount Carmel. My family is Polish. My great grandmother and grandfather both survived the Auschwitz concentration camps and moved to Israel after the war. There's not too much of anything interesting about me. On the kibbutz my job is, I mean was... being a lumberjack. I would go out into the woods and find the fallen trees and limbs and chop them up and bring them back for firewood."

"Thank you Private Nowak. Now I know who to ask for when we need to build a campfire," joked the Sergeant. There was some chuckling in the intercom as a few of the young soldiers laughed. "Okay, next..." said Sergeant Berg.

"My name is Chaim Cohen. I'm from Safed. My family is Orthodox Haredi and my father wanted me to study to become a Rabbi. Instead, I wanted to do my three years of military service. So here I am."

"Well, I hope you make your father proud, Private Cohen. You can always become a Rabbi later. Thank you for volunteering. I know you Haredi are exempt from joining the IDF. So thank you. Okay, next..." said Sergeant Berg.

"I'm Eitan Yehuda. I'm from Jerusalem. My father was is a commando in Sayeret Matkal. He was one of the paratroopers who rescued the hostages in Operation Thunderbolt in Entebbe, Uganda. My father wanted me to follow in his footsteps."

"Do you know, was he also part of the team that rescued Lieutenant Colonel Yossi Ben Hanan from the Syrians during the Yom Kippur War in 1973?" asked the Sergeant.

"Yes, Yes. I believe so. I remember him telling stories about that. His commander was Yonatan Netanyahu," said Eitan.

"My father was part of tank brigade that fought the Syrians in the Golan Heights during the Yom Kippur War. Lieutenant Colonel Ben Hanan was his commander. It's an honor to serve with you Private Yehuda. Okay, next..." said the Sergeant.

"My name is Eli Shapiro. I live in Jerusalem; however, I grew up in Los Angeles California in the United States. I'm American and an Israeli. My parents moved here when I was fifteen. My dad is a filmmaker and producer, so maybe someday we will all be famous characters in a war movie together."

"Yes, well I hope our movie has a nice Hollywood ending, Private Shapiro. Okay, next..." said Sergeant Berg. There was more chuckling and giggles in the intercom.

It was Yeshua's turn. He still couldn't figure out what to say that was interesting about himself. He was somewhat panicked on the inside.

"My name is Yeshua Rabin. I grew up in Beersheba. I don't really know what to say that is interesting about me."

"Private Rabin, surely you can think of something. Anything," said the Sergeant.

"Ummmm. Yeah. Well, I think I was reincarnated. I've think I've been here before," said Yeshua.

"What? How do you know that Private?" asked Berg.

"I know this sounds crazy, but I keep on having these dreams and visions of being in other times, like during the Nazis and the Romans for example," said Yeshua.

"Are you sure you haven't just watched too much TV?" said Berg.

"I don't know, Sir. You asked me to tell you something interesting about myself, and I am telling you something. You don't have to believe me," said Yeshua.

"I believe you," said Private Cohen in the intercom. "I studied Kabbalah in the Yeshiva in Safed. The Book of Zohar describes the soul as being eternal. There are three basic reasons why we reincarnate. One is that we are here to rectify the sins of our past. Another is that your soul was not able to complete its mission in a previous life and is now here in this lifetime to fulfill your destiny. The third reason is that you are sent back here for the sake of another soul or group of souls, to assist, guide or heal them."

"Wow! Like the movie Groundhog Day?" said Private Shapiro. There were several giggles in the intercom.

"I suppose so, yes. Perhaps we keep on coming back here until we get it right. Or perhaps we are sent back here on a specific mission," said Private Cohen.

"That's very interesting, Rabbi Cohen. I suppose we're all here on a mission from above," said Berg. "Let's definitely have more discussions about this in the near future. Okay, next..."

It was Mohammed's turn. He said, "My name is Mohammed Al Heuwaitat. I'm a Beaudoin from Beersheba. I am here to change the world."

"That's your mission, Private Al Heuwaiat? Or do you mind if I call you Private Mohammed. That rolls of my tongue much easier," said the Sergeant.

"Yes sir. And that's fine... Private Mohammed. Just so you know, Yeshua and I are best friends. We grew up in the orphanage together in Beersheba. Both our families were killed by Palestinian terrorists in the Gaza strip before it was evacuated in 2005. And even though I'm a Muslim, my full allegiance is to Israel. I'm proud to be an Israeli."

"Thank you for volunteering Private Mohammed, and I'm very sorry for your loss. But let me ask you a question... are you here in the IDF to revenge your parents?" asked Berg.

"Oh. No Sir," replied Mohammed. "Although at times I find it a challenge to love all of my neighbors, wouldn't it be a much better world if the Jews, Muslims & Christians forgive each other and found peace?"

"Yes it would Private Mohammed. Until then, we will carry these guns? Okay?" said Sergeant Berg.

"Yes sir!" said Mohammed.

"Ok next…" said the Sergeant.

"My name is Judah Richter. I'm from Nazareth. I won the gold medal in wrestling at the 2014 Summer Youth Olympics in Nanjing, China."

"Impressive, Private Richter. Those skills will come in very handy during Krav Maga training later on. Okay, I think there's one soldier left… for a total of ten in this platoon," said Berg.

"My name is Noah Shimon. I'm from Tel Aviv. I play a lot of shooter video games, like Fortnite, Call of Duty and Doom."

"You know Private Shimon, real life is way different than video games. You don't get extra lives here," said the Sergeant.

"I know, Sir. And by they way, I noticed that the bullets in our clips aren't real. Is there a reason why?" asked Noah.

"You are very observant Private Shimon. Do you really think we would give live ammo rounds to a bunch of totally green conscripts on their second day in the army?"

Then, there was radio silence. Yeshua looked down at his gun and was actually somewhat glad and relieved that the bullets inside weren't real. He wasn't ready to kill someone. He had never even shot a gun.

In the east, the sky started to brighten. Sunrise was coming. Yeshua looked at his watch; it read 6:03AM. They had been hiking over two hours already. He was very tired, and not tired at the same time. He took a sip of water from his water skin. The platoon crossed over a road and then walked next to a large industrial site for about a mile.

The soldiers then navigated over a four-lane highway and descended into a dry, winding riverbed. Suddenly there was the loud sound of chirping crickets, and then seemingly a large group of frogs chimed in from a surrounding marshland. Some nearby birds started to sing as the sun came up over the rolling hills to the east. It was a veritable symphony chorus of nature, thought Yeshua. All the beautiful sounds seemed to energize him. He turned off his night vision goggles and placed them up on his helmet.

The sunrise was beautiful. Golden rays of light shone from the sun up into the clouds in a fan-like pattern. There was a misty fog cover hovering just over the green fields around the riverbed, and as the sun rose higher the mist started to rise slowly and evaporate from the heat. It almost looked like spirits or ghosts rising up into the sky. The riverbed widened and exposed several large flat stones.

"Okay, Platoon. It's time for a break," said Berg. "Find someplace to do your business. Eat a food ration. Pray. Meditate. Take a short nap if you need too. Whatever. We roll out of here in exactly 20 minutes."

Just about everyone took off their helmets, backpacks and set their guns down on the flat rocks and then walked into the surrounding bushes to find somewhere private to heed the call of Mother Nature. Afterwards, Mohammed walked back to the flat stones and got on his hands and knees and did his second prayer to Allah of the day.

Yeshua walked over to Sergeant Berg who sat against a tree overlooking the riverbed.

"Sir, I have a question for you," said Yeshua.

"Shoot," said Berg.

"When I turned on my night vision goggles earlier, there were dozens of these firefly like orbs all over the place floating in the dark. What are they?" asked Yeshua.

"Oh. Those," said Berg. "I call them dust Angels. There're little pieces of dust in the air that your highly sensitive goggle are picking up. Don't mind them, I just ignore them and my brain fades them out into the background."

"Ok Sir, thank you. But when I turned on my infrared sensors they all lit up different colors. And they seemed to be flying around almost intelligently, rather than inanimate objects going with the flow of the wind," said Yeshua.

"Well damn. Maybe they are space aliens. Or little tinker bells. Listen Private Rabin, I'm gonna close my eyes for a few minutes and rest. We got a long hike ahead of us. I suggest you get a few moments of rest too, okay? That's an order!" said Sergeant Berg in a raised voice.

"Yes Sir!" said Yeshua loudly and he saluted Berg. As he turned around and walked away, he softly muttered, "Asshole."

Yeshua walked over to Mohammed who had just finished his prayers. He was sitting on the rock Indian style.

"We've come so far, yet have so far to go," said Mohammed. "Come, sit down my friend. Rest."

Yeshua walked over to Mohammed and sat next to him. Yeshua's right ear suddenly started to buzz at a high pitch. He grabbed his ear.

"Uh oh," said Mohammed, looking at Yeshua. "That means trouble. Your right ear is buzzing."

From the west they heard the rumble of thunder in the distance. Almost immediately the wind started to kick up. There were some dark clouds moving towards them from the west.

Sergeant Berg woke up from his catnap from the sound of the thunder. He grabbed his cell phone and checked the weather radar map. His eyes got really big and he stood up.

"Okay, Platoon. Pack up!" he yelled from under the tree. "We got an incoming hostile thunderstorms moving fast right towards us. There's a tornado alert too. Let's move it! Now!"

A huge flash of lightning illuminated the western sky. A few seconds later thunder rolled through the valley.

The entire platoon ran over to their gear and hurriedly put on their backpacks, helmets and grabbed their guns. The sky was getting darker and darker as the storm clouds approached.

Yeshua couldn't remember the last time he saw weather like this. He lived in the dry, arid desert. Even the air felt different. It felt electric.

"Here's the plan," said Sergeant Berg. The whole platoon gathered around him along the flat rocks of the dry riverbed. "About a mile east of here is an old slaughterhouse. We're going to run there to take cover. This storm is going to be right on our butts. Do not stop running. Everyone keep up and stay together. And don't get hit by lightning!"

Just as he said that, the entire sky lit up with massive steaks of white lightning.

BOOMMMMMM reverberated through the entire valley. Yeshua could feel the rock underneath him shake.

"Let's go!" yelled Berg, and he turned and started running east down the riverbed with everyone following him. The wind increased fast and strong. Leaves and debris flew all around the soldiers as they ran full speed carrying their guns and their forty pounds of gear. It was not a pretty sight.

The heavy rain poured into the valley. The storm clouds were upon then. A small twister formed and descended quickly from the black clouds into the riverbed just to the west of the platoon's location. It moved along slowly tearing up the rocks, and then it snapped the tree in half that Sergeant Berg has just been sleeping under moments before.

As he was running full speed, Yeshua's right ear buzzed louder and he turned his head around and saw the half of tree fly up into the air within the violent black tornado. The tree spun within the vortex of the whirlwind and then shot out super fast in the direction of the running soldiers.

Yeshua stopped running and turned around. It was raining really hard. He saw a huge wave of water rushing and streaming towards him from the west. A flash flood! Simultaneously, the huge tree was flying directly towards them with the tornado close behind. Yeshua thought he could see another one of those demonic figures dancing in the vortex of the twister.

Yeshua turned on his helmet intercom. "Run out of the riverbed right now! Take cover in the bushes. Now! Incoming!" he yelled. The giant half of a tree flew over him aimed right at his platoon. Yeshua ducked down to avoid being impaled by the branches. Just in the nick of time, everyone dove out of the way of the tree and into the bushes on both sides of the riverbed. The tree landed and smashed into thousands of pieces.

Yeshua was down on the ground stunned in the middle of the riverbed. He started to get up slowly even though it was difficult with all his gear and his gun. As he got on his knees, a large wave of water from the flash flood overtook him, and he was swept quickly down the river. A tree branch in the water hit him squarely in the forehead. Everything went black.

CHAPTER 12

THE VALLEY OF ELAH

He heard the sound of rushing water. Yeshua opened his eyes. He was lying partially in the water along the black muddy riverbank. The murky water flowed next to him fiercely in the once dry riverbed. Broken branches and debris floated rapidly by his body. The thunderstorm and rain had passed, although the sky was still dark, angry and grey.

Yeshua checked himself. He was still wearing his backpack and his helmet. Somehow, his gun was still next to him. He turned on his intercom and said, "Hello. Is anyone there? Mayday. Mayday. This is Private Rubin." He waited for a response. There was none.

He got up slowly. His entire uniform was soaking wet. His water skin was gone. He took his water bottle from his backpack and drank some water, and then he walked up the muddy riverbank and through the bushes to dryer land.

Up the hill from him was a giant aluminum warehouse structure. Many of the metal beams and supports were rusty, and the whole area looked quite dilapidated. Stacked around the outer walls were many old round metal barrels.

He walked up the incline towards the building. Maybe he could find someone to help him or a phone. He clicked back on his intercom. "Mohammed. Sergeant Berg. Are you there? Is there anybody out there?"

Moments went by... still no response. He arrived at the building. It was massive and shaped like a long rectangle. Yeshua saw a door in the far corner of the building and walked towards it. He arrived at the metal door and turned the handle. It was open! "Thank God," he said. He walked inside.

The first thing he noticed was the smell. It smelled horrible, like death. He almost vomited from the stench and pulled his shirt over his nose.

"Hello!" he yelled. "Hello! Anyone here?" His voice echoed in the vastly large building.

Then he heard some noises coming from within the depths of the building. It was dark inside, and he couldn't see much. There was an electrical switch along the wall which he turned to the on position. Nothing happened. No lights went on.

Yeshua put on his night vision goggles and turned them on. There was a narrow hallway ahead of him leading to a larger room inside. He could hear strange grunting noises coming from the room down the hall. He grabbed his gun and slowly moved forward. Then he remembered that he didn't have live ammo in the clips.

"Damit," he muttered softly. He swung his gun around his back on its sling and grabbed his Israeli pocketknife out of his backpack. He found the largest blade it in and opened it. He held it outwards with his right hand and moved forward in the darkness. As he got closer to the opening of the hallway and closer to the large room, he turned on the infrared thermal filter on his night vision goggles. To his surprise, almost the entire room in front of him lit up with large red, yellow and orange figures. They looked like monsters in his goggles.

"What the heck..." he said out loud as he walked inside the huge room. As soon as he entered, the grunting noises in the room crescendoed and exploded. All the figures with the large heat images moved and shifted from their positions. It was like a panic of energy took over the entire space. There were crashing sounds like metal hitting metal.

Yeshua completely freaked out and switched his goggles' thermal sensor back to normal night vision. Then he could see clearly what was in the room. There were hundreds of cattle in large pens in the massive room. Most of them were young calves. They looked just as scared as Yeshua. They were all now "mooing" loudly.

Yeshua walked deeper into the room, into the many rows of cow pens. Hanging nearby from the ceiling, on hooks and chains, were seven skinned cow carcasses. They smelled horrible and some large horseflies flew around the dead meat. There was blood on the floor. Yeshua had walked into the slaughterhouse.

Yeshua looked around as he walked through and searched the room. There were no people anywhere to be found. .

"Hello. Hello! Anyone here?" He screamed again.

As he called for help, all the cows started to moo louder. However, what Yeshua heard was "Help me. Help me…" coming from the young cows. Their moos were cries for help.

Yeshua walked to the opposite side of the room. There was a door to the outside, and he could see rays of light peeking through its seams. He opened the door and light poured into the dark room. He turned off his night vision glasses and looked outside. There was a huge green pasture, as far as his eye could see. He could see well in the distance that there were two wide mountain ranges with a lush valley in between. There was a massive barbed wire chain link fence surrounding the perimeter of the building with dirt covering the ground. Beyond the fence were the vast green pasturelands.

The cows trapped within the slaughterhouse started to moo even louder. They were banging up against their pens. They were crying for help.

Yeshua had an idea. He walked back into the building. He cut the ropes with his knife that kept each cow pen door closed. There were ten to twenty cows in each stall, and when Yeshua cut them loose the cattle quickly ran outside through the open door to the large fenced area outside the building. He went to each stall one by one and freed every living creature until the giant room was empty.

Once all the cows were outside, Yeshua went through the metal door and closed it behind him. There must have been at least three hundred cows in the large fenced in dirt field next to slaughterhouse. They continued to moo, "Help me. Help me!"

"And now for my next magic trick," Yeshua said to the cows. He walked towards the far side of the fence, in the direction of the green pasture. The cows followed him slowly. He thought of the story of the pied piper. All the cows massed together and walked towards the fence behind him.

He finally reached the locked gate of the fence. It was a large chain linked barbed wire gate with a huge bolt and lock secured around it.

"Hmmmm," said Yeshua to himself as he looked at the big metal lock. He turned around and the huge group cows were about halfway from the building to the fence gate. They continue to walk slowly in his direction in almost a "V" pattern.

Then, Yeshua saw the building door open and some men wearing uniforms came out. They were holding guns. His heart started racing. He looked at them more closely. He had seen those uniforms before. They were Nazi uniforms! One of the men had a scar on his left face.

"Halt! Halt!" screamed scar faced man. The cows heard his yells and went into a panic. They started to stampede towards Yeshua in fear.

One of the Nazis held up his gun and shot a few warning rounds up into the air. The cows started mooing louder and ran faster. "Halt, Halt," they yelled as they started to run in Yeshua's direction.

Yeshua looked at the lock and chain on the fence. He only had a few more moments before the stampeding cows arrived. He took the butt of his gun and started to smash it against the metal lock. He prayed for strength. He hit the lock as hard as he could, once, twice. On the third time the lock broke open and the chain slid off the gate. He opened the gate and held it wide open as the frightened cows ran towards him just a few dozen yards away.

He said, "Come on. Come on. You're free!" As they arrived at the gate, they stampeded through into the wide green pasture. He held the door open until they had all passed, then he let go and the door slammed closed.

The Nazis were still running at him, and as soon as the door slammed closed Yeshua looked closely at the one with the scarred face. It was the same man that had been haunting him in all his other dreams. Yeshua turned around and ran into the pasture, following the freed cows towards the valley beyond.

"Yeshua, Yeshua! Are you okay?" yelled Mohammed. Yeshua opened his eyes. He was lying on the wet riverbank. His entire platoon stood above him.

"Ummmmm. Yeah," said Yeshua as he looked upwards surrounded by ten Israeli soldiers. "Is everyone okay? The storm... the tree! Did anyone get hurt?" he asked.

"Well, there you go again my friend, saving the world. We are all fine, thanks to you. When you warned us on the intercom, we all jumped out of the way of the tree as it crashed in the riverbank. Then I saw you get swept away by the flash flood. We searched all over for you. We thought you were dead! And here you are alive, by the grace of God. You floated down the river over a mile. You must have a really good Guardian Angel," said Mohammed as he winked his right eye at Yeshua.

Yeshua sat up. He looked around to get his bearings. Up the hill from the riverbank was the massive aluminum building. It was the same exact one he had been in just rescuing the cattle from within his dream. Or did he just wake up from another coma?

"What's that building?" he asked as he pointed to the building.

"That's an old abandoned slaughterhouse," said Sergeant Berg.

"Abandoned? There's no one in there?" asked Yeshua.

"It been empty for decades. We are going to go through there to get to get back on our trail," said Berg.

The soldiers helped Yeshua get up on his feet, and they started walking up towards the slaughterhouse. Yeshua tried to turn on his intercom to tell everyone about the cows, but it was broken. It must have malfunctioned from getting wet in the river. He decided not to say anything.

Everything looked the same. The rusty girders, the old barrels and even the location of the door was identical. The platoon walked over to the entrance and Sergeant Berg opened the door. It was dark inside. Berg grabbed his flashlight from his backpack and turned it on.

"Follow me," said Berg. "And don't touch anything." He walked into the building and the platoon followed him in single file.

Once inside, the dark room looked the same to Yeshua. Thankfully, however, it didn't smell like death. Even the same light switch was on the wall and in the "off" position. Ahead Sergeant Berg shined his flashlight as he led the platoon into the large open room inside. Yeshua turned on his night vision goggles to see better. The room was the exact same with all the cow pens. However, it was completely empty except there were a lot of cobwebs everywhere. There were no cattle. He looked in the corner of the room where the seven carcasses had been hanging. The seven hooks and chains were there, just no dead cows. Yeshua was having the biggest déjà vu of his life.

The Sergeant led the platoon over to the far door and opened it. Light poured into the huge room from the sun outside. Yeshua turned off his night vision goggles, just like he had earlier at this same door. Outside was the huge dirt holding pen surrounded by a barbed wire fence, and beyond was the vast green pastures with the two mountain ranges and valley far in the distance.

They all walked outside into the light. Berg led them along the dirt to the closed gate at the far side of the fence. The Sergeant pushed the gate and held it open for the soldiers to walk through. As Yeshua passed through, he looked down on the ground. He was stunned. In the dirt was the same broken lock and chain, exactly as he had left it when he set the cows free.

Although Yeshua's intercom didn't work, he said with a raised voice so everyone could hear him, "Does anyone ever have a sense of déjà vu?"

They started to walk along the rolling green pastures, towards the mountains far off in the eastern horizon.

"What's a déjà vu?" asked Private Avraham.

"It's a feeling like you been somewhere before," said Mohammed. "It's an eerie sense that what is happening has happened before."

"Oh," said Private Avraham. "That happens to me all the time. Like I'm reading a book or watching a movie and it seems so familiar and I feel like I already know what it going to happen next; then I read or watch more and what I thought is going to happen next is exactly what happens."

"Well yes, something like that. It's the familiar feeling you get when you have already lived through something and the same thing or a similar event happens again," said Mohammed.

"Yeah, that happens to me too," said Private Ivanov. A few of the other soldiers said, "me too."

"That's very interesting," said Private Cohen. "King Solomon once said 'That which was, will be again, and what was done will be done again. There is nothing new under the sun.' Perhaps he was alluding that the déjà vu experience is derived from reincarnation and past lives. Maybe the strange feeling you get is that you have experienced the same thing before in a previous lifetime."

"Yeah, wow! Like when I meet someone for the first time and they seem so familiar. Like I feel an instant connection. Is it that I recognize them from a previous lifetime?" asked Private Richter.

Sergeant Berg interrupted on the intercom, "I hate to cut short this deep, metaphysical discussion; however, let's please keep to intercom discourse to only absolutely necessary communications."

"Yes Sir," said Private Cohen.

There was silence amongst the platoon. As they walked along the countryside, Yeshua had the distinct feeling that he had been there before. Everything looked and felt so familiar.

The platoon walked for several hours through green pastures, barren dry open fields, grassy hills and many groves of trees. For a few miles, they walked along a double lane road that said Highway 353. A few cars drove by, and Yeshua wondered what the people in their cars were thinking when they saw eleven fully armed soldiers walking along the road.

The terrain became more hilly and the wide valley with the two mountain ranges became much closer in the distance. The platoon left the road and walked down a dirt path. It was a gentle slope eastward into the valley. They walked through several recently harvested crop fields and then they crossed a road and continued through some more fields.

"Welcome to the Valley of Elah. This is our destination. We have an important mission a couple miles to the east of here, but first we'll take a break just up ahead," said Sergeant Berg.

The platoon left the fields and started walking along a dry riverbed in a middle of the valley. Yeshua looked around to make sure no rain clouds were nearby. There were many large terebinth trees in several groves among the winding riverbed. Yeshua looked up the mountains to his left towards the north. He thought he could see some old ruins of a stone fortress along the highest ridge. Then, he suddenly got that intense déjà vu feeling again. He felt like he had been here in this place before. Sergeant Berg stopped walking and the platoon came to a sudden halt.

"Ok, we are here," said Berg. "This is a special place. It's called the HaElah stream. Nearby is the location where David fought Goliath and the Philistines. We will take a thirty minute rest break. If you need to relieve yourself there's a bunch of trees over there. Girl's trees that way, boy's trees over there." Berg pointed to the south.

All the soldiers took off their backpacks, helmets and placed their guns in a big pile on a large flat rock in the middle of the riverbed. Almost everyone except Sergeant Berg gingerly walked to the south and found a private area to empty their bladders.

"Do you think that it's true about David and Goliath?" asked Private Shapiro. "That it happened right here in this valley?"

Private Cohen replied, "The story of David and Goliath is written in the Book of Samuel. King Saul and thousands of Israelites positioned themselves on the north side of this valley along the mountains, and thousands of invading Philistines with their champion Goliath held the southern part of the valley along the other mountain. It was a forty-day standoff. Each day, the giant Goliath would walk over to the Israelites and taunt them and challenge them to send their champion to fight to death in single combat. No one was courageous enough to fight the giant. Eventually, a young boy named David accepted the challenge. He duels Goliath and kills him with a stone from his slingshot and the Philistines retreated. The Israelites were victorious and eventually David would become King."

"Wow. That would make a great movie!" said Private Shapiro. "How tall was Goliath?"

"No one knows for sure," said Cohen. "Some estimates were that he was nine or ten feet tall."

Mohammed and Yeshua started walking back to the gathering point after relieving themselves and Private Cohen quickly rushed over to talk to them.

"Yeshua. I have a question for you. You said you think you've been here before, that you've been reincarnated. I'm just curious... what's the most the most esoteric or mystical thing that's ever happened to you?" asked Cohen.

"What's esoteric mean?" asked Mohammed.

"The word esoteric comes from ancient Greek. It means 'belonging to an inner circle' and in modern times it usually means a spiritual or religious experience that evolves one's consciousness through revelation or a deeper understanding of the inner workings of the Universe," replied Cohen.

"Wow. Yes. I've had many of those experiences," said Yeshua.

"Really? Please enlighten me. What happened?" said Cohen.

"Well, one time I talked to God," responded Yeshua.

"You talked to God? Really? What did He say?" asked Cohen.

"Honestly, first of all... I don't think God is a he. I don't think God has a sex like male or female. We may be created in God's image; however, it's more like we've been formed from the divine pattern or sacred design the Universe, which all comes from God... the Creator of everything. So when we say God is a "He," like God the Father... we are just placing our own humanness on something that isn't even a physical being," said Yeshua.

"Very interesting Yeshua, it appears you've done some really profound thinking about this. Now what was it that God told you?" asked Cohen.

"Well, let me ask you a question first... if you met God, and you could ask one question about anything, what you ask?" replied Yeshua.

"I don't think I would ask a question. I would just thank him, ahmmmm.... I mean I would thank God for everything. Actually, I think you are right, I don't think of God as a 'he' either," said Cohen.

"Ok, well let's say after thanking God.... God asked you to ask one question, what would you ask?"

"That's a very interesting scenario. What would I ask God?" said Cohen. He paused for a moment and looked in deep thought.

"Okay, I got it!" exclaimed Cohen. "Why is there so much suffering in the world?"

"Ohhhhh. I know how Allah would answer that," said Mohammed.

"Allah?" said Cohen.

"Yes, Allah. Allah is the same Being as your Hebrew God that created the Universe." said Mohammed. "Allah is the same as Elohim in your Torah," said Mohammed.

"Ah I see, we worship and pray to the same God! I never knew that. Thank you for explaining that to me. That means a lot, really. Now, how do you think Allah would answer my question?" asked Cohen.

"If you were to ask Allah, or God... why there is so much suffering in the World, God would likely reply... 'I wanted to ask you that very same question too.'"

There was silence as Private Cohen processed the answer. He reflected for a moment and said, "You are right Mohammed. We are responsible for almost all of the suffering here on Earth. We need to do something about it, and God has given us an opportunity in this lifetime to make the world a better place. Thank you again for your insights Mohammed."

Mohammed smiled and gave Cohen a pat on the back.

"It is my honor, my friend," said Mohammed.

"Ok, back to your story Yeshua. What did God tell you?" asked Cohen.

"Ah, yes. Well... I don't tell many people this because I don't want everyone to think I'm crazy. God came to me in a vision. I asked God 'What is the meaning of life?' the response from God was... the meaning of life is the difference between One and Zero," responded Yeshua.

"What? Say that again..." asked Cohen.

"The meaning of life is the difference between One and Zero," replied Yeshua again.

"Whoa! That answer can have so many different interpretations. That's totally mind blowing! Mathematically, the difference between one and zero is one. Everything is One! That's in the Shema... one of our most important Hebrew prayers. **Hear O'Israel, the Lord is our God, the Lord is One!**" exclaimed Cohen.

The three soldiers returned back to the big pile of backpacks and guns. Sergeant Berg sat nearby under a terebinth tree eating a ration. He nodded at three young men. The rest of the platoon returned to the tree grove and everyone ate some food and drank water. They all geared back up and continued south along the dry Nahal HaEla riverbank for about a half a mile until the reached a two lane road. They left the riverbank and travelled due east along the road for a few miles.

It was very hot in the late afternoon sun. The southern mountain range was just adjacent to the road, and another ruins of an ancient fortress appeared on a nearby hilltop. The platoon passed by a small town in the middle of the valley. Yeshua looked to the left and saw a monument close in the distance by the town. There were two large stone statues of the Hebrew letters "Lamed" and "He" surrounded by many stone columns.

"What's that?" asked Yeshua loudly. His helmet intercom was still broken.

"That's a war memorial," said Sergeant Berg. "The Lamed and He letters means the number thirty five. It's a memorial to thirty-five Israeli soldiers who died here in this Valley during the bloody 1948 conflicts with the Arabs. They were sent to help people in a nearby Kibbutz that were trapped, but they were ambushed here and all killed. According to one account, the last three Jewish soldiers blew themselves up with a grenade rather than being taken prisoners."

"Gosh, that's horrible," said Mohammed. "Why can't we all just get along? We are all just brothers and sisters of the same family."

"I agree," said Berg. "Yet, most of our Arab neighbors absolutely hate us. They want us to die and don't even recognize our right to exist. Maybe someday we will find some way to have peace and reconciliation. In the meantime, we will defend ourselves at all costs. I don't want any of us here to be memorialized in a monument like the one here in this valley."

They passed the town and the Valley of Elah opened up wider along the road. The surrounding grassy fields glowed intense green from the recent rainfall. On both sides of the valley there was a beautiful array of yellow, white and red wildflowers bloomed in a massive display of color. Up ahead, along the road appeared some giant satellite dishes. It was a surreal sight here in this ancient valley to see so many futuristic space-aged structures. There were two giant white dishes pointing upwards into the sky surrounded by dozens of smaller dishes.

"We have arrived at our destination, platoon," said Berg. "This is the Ha'Ela Valley Satellite Station. A couple days ago there was an incredibly violent lightning storm, just like the one earlier today. All of the electrical transformers blew up which rendered this entire station inactive. We are here help remove the old transformers and replace them with new ones. They delivered the new ones today on trucks and we will be unloading them and helping to install them. Do you understand?"

"Yes, sir!" responded the entire platoon in unison.

Chapter 13

The Philistines

Each transformer weighed approximately five hundred pounds. There were ten of them in large wooden crates inside the back of a huge trailer of an eighteen-wheeler truck parked inside the satellite complex. From the truck was a long ramp from the floor of the trailer to the ground.

It took every ounce of effort from all ten of the young soldiers and Sergeant Berg to lift each crate from the back of the truck and slowly walk it down the ramp to the satellite relay center. With the help of an electrician, the old blown out transformers were removed and the new ones were carefully placed into position.

All the soldiers had taken off their heavy gear and just wore their tee shirts and work gloves while moving the heavy equipment. It took about four hours to complete the tasks. Everyone was exhausted as the sun disappeared in the western sky and nighttime fell. Once done, Sergeant Berg told the platoon to pitch their tents just outside the satellite station and get some rest. He told them at exactly 0800 the next day they would be placing the old transformers into the wood crates and putting them back in the truck's trailer for reprocessing.

The young soldiers made their tents, ate some food, and drank some water. Mohammed did his evening prayer to Allah. Everyone was exhausted and welcomed sleep.

Before retiring to their tents, Yeshua and Mohammed looked up at the night sky and the stars from beneath the enormous satellite dishes.

"Mohammed, I wonder something," said Yeshua.

"Tell me what it is, my friend," responded Mohammed.

"I wonder, do you think somewhere up there is intelligent life?" asked Yeshua.

"I bet you.... on some planet far, far away there are two space alien best friends sitting under a bunch of satellite dishes looking up at the stars and our sun and having this very same conversation," said Mohammed with a big smile.

"Ha-Ha. Very funny," said Yeshua.

"Or maybe they are already here, watching us and being very entertained like one of those crazy reality TV shows," joked Mohammed.

"I suppose we would be entertaining to space aliens. We act like idiots and fools most of the time," responded Yeshua.

Suddenly, Sergeant Berg walked out from the satellite relay station building. He looked very tired and a bit worried.

"Ladies and Gentlemen," he said loudly, addressing the platoon. Most of the soldiers were already in their tents. He looked directly at Yeshua and Mohammed.

"I'll be working in the control center for the next few hours trying to get the station back online. Afterwards I'll be getting some R&R inside, so if anyone needs me... you know where to find me. See you all right here at 0800 sharp!" said Berg.

"Yes Sir!" said the soldiers who were still awake. Berg walked back into the building and the door shut behind him.

Yeshua and Mohammed said goodnight and crawled into their tents, zipped them closed and got into their sleeping bags.

Yeshua fell asleep very quickly. His body, mind and soul were drained beyond measure from the outlandish events of the last few days. After a few hours of deep sleep, in the middle of the night... his left ear started to high pitch buzz. He woke up in his tent and it took him a couple of moments to realize where he was.

Through his the tent he thought he could see some lights moving in the dark just outside. He slowly unzipped his tent and peaked outside. To his utter surprise, all around his tent were the thousands of little firefly orbs he had seen in his night vision goggles the night before.

They floated and scintillated in the darkness.

Yeshua walked outside of his tent. Many of the little orbs gathered and flew around him in dozens. Some were yellow, some orange and others white. They glowed and sparkled and frequently lit up brighter like real fireflies. He lifted up his arms above his head and many of the little orbs spiraled and flew around his hands and past his fingertips.

"Am I dreaming?" thought Yeshua. "Is this a dream?"

Suddenly the orbs seemed to speak back to him, almost telepathically.

"We've been waiting for you to join us." The orbs seemed to all speak together in high pitch voices similar to the frequency of the buzzing in his ears.

"Are you... are you the ones that warn me by the noise in my ears?" asked Yeshua.

"We've been waiting for you to join us," they said again. "Follow us. Follow us this way."

The thousands of little orbs started moving towards the north. Yeshua followed them, almost in a trance. It was very dark outside and the orbs illuminated the way as Yeshua walked through several hills and valleys. Above, the black sky was full of millions of stars.

After a while, the orbs floated up a large hill just above a rocky dirt path. Near the top of the hill was an entrance to a cave. The glowing orbs hovered all around Yeshua and guided him into the opening of the dark cave. Like little candles, their lights filled the cave with luminescence.

The first part of the cave was a narrow long tunnel, which opened into a huge chamber. There were thousands of crystalline stalactites and stalagmites that looked like steaming rivers of melted wax from the ceiling to the floor. The light of the flying orbs reflected in the chamber and the shadows seemed to dance among the glittered rock formations.

There was a sandy trail through the large stalagmites on the floor of the cave. The orbs slowly hovered along the path and Yeshua continued to follow. After a short while, a small stream of water appeared running through the middle of the cave. There was a small wooden bridge that arched over the stream. On the other side of the stream, across the bridge was a sandy beach in the middle of the giant cavern.

To Yeshua's surprise, sitting on the beach in a cross-legged lotus position was man wearing a robe. His garments were dark brown and a hood covered most of his face. He reminded Yeshua of the Obi wan Kenobi character from Star Wars. Many of the orbs flew over the bridge and hovered around the man who was facing Yeshua from across the bridge.

Yeshua slowly and quietly walked over the bridge and stood in front of the man sitting Indian-style, who was about ten feet away. The sounds of the trickling stream under the bridge became much louder and filled the large room with its gentle echoes. The robed man's energy seemed so relaxing and peaceful, despite being in this very creepy and dark cave. Many of the orbs descended down to the floor of sandy beach and made a circular pattern directly in front of the sitting man. Yeshua walked over to the circle and sat down in the center of the lighted pattern made of glowing orbs.

The man calmly pulled the hood off from his head with his right hand. He revealed his face yet still had his eyes closed. He had light olive colored skin and dark, short curly hair and a long dark beard. Hundreds of orbs floating around him and his entire body seemed to glow with light from the reflections. He seemed to be in deep meditation.

After a few more moments of silence, he opened his eyes and looked directly at Yeshua. His eyes were blue, like the sky. He raised his hands slightly and held them out towards Yeshua and opened his mouth to speak.

"The Kingdom of God is within you."

The man smiled, then the tiny floating orbs all around both men swirled and contracted into a small area just above the robed man's hands. They organized even more and formed a small shining rotating ball of light. Within the orb were images of many faces… the faces of the prophets, spinning in the globe. Tiny bolts of electricity shot out from the Orb. Yeshua had seen this Orb before… it came to him in a vision a few months earlier when he blew his Shofar in Tel Be'er Sheba and he then travelled back in time through some kind of Biblical wormhole.

The man then looked at the globe just hovering above his hands. It was almost as he was holding it like a ball.

"All is One," he said. "All is One…"

"Yeshua, you gotta see this," whispered Mohammed. Yeshua suddenly woke up and he could hear Mohammed talking to him just outside of his tent. He looked down at his watch and it said 5:03AM.

"Yeshua. You in there? Wake up… you gotta see this. It's incredible!" said Mohammed in a slightly louder voice.

"Ok, OK… I'm getting up," said a tired and grumpy Yeshua. He got out of his warm cozy sleeping bag and unzipped the tent. Mohammed was standing outside looking straight up into the sky. Yeshua crawled out of the tent and looked up into the night. Above them was a brilliant display of shooting stars. Two, three and sometimes four long trails of light streaked across the black sky simultaneously.

"Wow. That's amazing," said Yeshua. "I saw some shooting stars last night, but it was nothing like this."

Just then, a large blue fireball flew overhead rapidly from the east to the west lighting up the entire sky white for a few seconds.

"Whoa. I've never seen one like that before," said Mohammed. "The Earth must be flying through a big comet's dust trail or something like that."

"Mohammed, I have an idea. Will you do something kinda adventurous with me?" asked Yeshua.

"Will we end up in jail?" asked Mohammed.

"No, I don't think so," replied Yeshua.

"Is your right ear buzzing?" asked Mohammed.

"No, it is not. Actually, my left ear was just buzzing not too long ago," said Yeshua.

"Oh, that's a good sign? Right? Count me in. What are we going to do? We have about three hours before roll call," said Mohammed.

Yeshua crawled back into his tent. He opened his backpack and found his Shofar. He removed it and slung it around his back and came out of the tent.

"Ok, follow me," he said. "We are going on a little journey."

Yeshua led Mohammed a short distance from the satellite station to the main road, and then they turned left and walked a couple miles back to the HaElah riverbed. In the east, the sky was getting much lighter as the sunrise was approaching. The two young men left the road and walked along the riverbed until they came to the exact place where they had taken their break the day before with the platoon.

Yeshua stopped in the middle of the riverbed on a large rock.

"Here, here is the spot," said Yeshua.

"Why did you take us back to this place?" asked Mohammed.

"A little bird told me to come back here. Now sit down, right here on this rock," said Yeshua.

Mohammed sat down and Yeshua sat down next to him. Yeshua slung his Shofar from his back into both his hands and he held the mouthpiece of the spiraling rams horn very close to his face.

"Okay, now I want you to hold the Shofar with me as I blow into it. Don't let go, okay? Trust me," said Yeshua.

"Okay. I trust you," said Mohammed.

Mohammed grabbed the Shofar with both his hands as well. Yeshua put the mouthpiece up to his lips and blasted with all his might as loud as he could. Exactly at the same time, the sun rose over the eastern horizon and rays of light flooded into the valley.

Ba-ba-baaaaaaaaaaaaaaaa...

Ba-ba-baaaaaaaaaaaaaaaa...

Ba-ba-baaaaaaaaaaaaaaaa...

At the end of the third Shofar blast the two best friends lost consciousness and passed out. Everything went black for both of them. There was nothing... no light, no sound, no smell, no sensation.

"Mohammed, are you there?" asked Yeshua.

"Yes I'm here. Where are you? I can hear you, but I can't see you. I can't see anything!" exclaimed Mohammed.

"Stay calm. Everything is going to be okay. The Shofar is some kind of time machine. We are both in the portal right now," said Yeshua.

"I can't feel my body. Where are you? What is happening?" asked Mohammed.

Then, all of the sudden they could see something up ahead. Out of the darkness came an array of lights. First it was dim, and then a tunnel of repeating concentric circles formed in front of them. The lights got brighter, and they seemed to be flying through the multicolored patterns of rotating circles.

"This is what happened when I sounded the Shofar at Tel Be'er Sheba," said Yeshua. "I left my body and flew through this magical tunnel. It took me back in time. I think we are just in spirit form now. I can't feel my body either."

"Wow. This is what it must feel like to do drugs, eh?" asked Mohammed.

"I don't know, maybe. I've never done drugs," responded Yeshua.

From the end of the tunnel they could see a bright light approaching rapidly. They were both flying super fast and literally they came out through the light at the end of the tunnel.

Immediately they were right back at the HaElah creek, exactly at the same location as they were a few moments ago before blowing the Shofar. Although now instead of being completely dry, a stream of fast moving water ran through riverbed. It was sunrise and the new day's light shone brightly into the valley.

"Yeshua, are you there?" said Mohammed.

"Yes, I'm here," said Yeshua.

"I can't see you. Where are you?" said Mohammed.

"Like I said, I think we are actually out of our physical bodies. We are in some kind of spirit form. Also, I don't think we are really talking with our voices since we don't have mouths. I think we are communicating telepathically," explained Yeshua.

"Whoa! So I came here with you since I was holding the Shofar when you blew it? Oh wait a sec, I think I can kinda see you. You look like a faint white aura," said Mohammed.

"Yes, we portalled here together. And I think I can see you too. You look like a faint yellow aura. I'm pretty sure if you want to move around, all you have to do is concentrate hard and uses your thoughts to navigate," said Yeshua.

"Ummm. Yeshua, look up there. Look at top of the mountain ranges," said Mohammed.

Just to the north, along the mountain ridge stood thousands of soldiers holding spears, swords and shields. Instead of ancient ruins, the colossal Elah Fortress was completely intact. There were hundreds of soldiers looking out from the massive stone complex into the valley. The soldiers' uniforms were mostly blue and white cloth with leather belts, boots and helmets.

Along the southern mountain range were several thousand troops as well. Many of them wore metallic bronze armor. There were several large fires burning in the hills and smoke billowed up into the sky. To the southeast there was an extensive fortress on a hill, close to where the satellite station would be located in the future.

"Yeshua, I think we did go back in time. On the north hill is the Israelite army, and on the south hill I think is the Philistine army. Look, the Philistines are marching down the valley towards us," said Mohammed.

Unexpectedly, there were some rustling noises coming from around the curve of the river.

"Do you hear that?" asked Mohammed.

"Yes, let's go check it out. Just think hard and you will start moving, okay?" said Yeshua.

They hovered above the river and moved in the direction of the sounds just to the east. Then, they saw a young boy with red wavy hair walking in the river. He was holding a tall wooden staff.

"Yeshua. That boy looks just like you, when you were younger. Whoa! Is that you? How is that even possible?" asked Mohammed.

"I don't know. But he does look just like me! When I was thirteen, exactly! Oh my Gosh!" said Yeshua telepathically.

The young boy reached down into the flowing waters and grabbed a smooth hand-sized stone. He put it in his satchel. Then he grabbed another, then another and yet another for a total of five stones. He then walked up the riverbed to the west, in the direction of Yeshua and Mohammed. He walked right between their two spirits.

"He can't see us. But we can see him. Let's follow him," said Yeshua.

They followed the young boy as he climbed up the sloped riverbed to the south. As Yeshua and Mohammed reached the top of the ravine they saw an incredible sight. Thousands of Philistine soldiers stood in formation about one hundred yards away at the other side of a barren, dry field. The young boy walked in their direction to the south by himself. There was a huge man, nine or ten feet tall standing in front of all the troops wearing an ornate bronze helmet, a magnificent coat of scale armor and bronze greaves on his legs. He held a massive bronze javelin, and he wore a sword in a sheath on his waist. Next to him was a much smaller man holding a giant bronze shield. There was a beautifully designed eagle pattern in the center of the shield.

The young boy and the giant man walked towards each other on the field. They were still quite far from each other and they yelled at each other and exchanged some words in a language Yeshua and Mohammed did not understand.

"I think I know how this ends," said Mohammed. "That little boy is going to kill the big man with a stone from his slingshot."

The giant man continued walking towards the boy into the middle of the field. The boy pulled a stone out from his satchel and placed it into his sling. He wound up the sling and fired the stone at the giant and the stone flew well over his head and missed him.

"Huhhhh? He missed," said Yeshua. "He missed?"

The giant started to laugh and continue to walk towards the boy. He was getting closer to him. The huge crowd of Philistines behind him cheered when they saw the rock miss its target. The boy threw another stone at him, this time it hit his chest plate and bounced off. The giant laughed again and yelled at the boy, taunting him. The soldiers cheered again.

"How many stones did he take from the stream?" asked Mohammed.

"Five, I counted five stones," said Yeshua as the boy slung another stone at the giant. It just barely missed him as the giant man ducked and it landed behind him on the field. The giant started to run towards the boy and scream in anger. He grabbed his javelin from his back and pointed it at the boy.

The young boy calmly grabbed another stone and placed it into his sling. He launched it, and just as the stone was about to hit the giant in the head, Goliath stopped running and took a swing with his javelin and smashed the rock into pieces in mid-air. He held up the javelin in both his hands and let out a huge roar that echoed in the entire valley. He turned towards his army and yelled some words as he brandished his javelin above his head. All the thousands of Philistines followed suit and started to holler and scream at the other end of the field. Then, they all started to run full speed towards the boy and the Israelites along their positions just to the north.

"Dear God. He's only got one stone left. I have an idea," said Mohammed.

"What? What are you going to do?" said Yeshua as he saw Mohammed's yellow aura move quickly into the field towards the boy. Behind them to the north, the Israelites were in full charge coming down the mountain. The sounds of dozens of shofars trumpeted into the valley as waves of soldiers stormed towards the Philistines. Many had already reached the riverbed and were coming up the ravine just behind the wide-open field.

The young boy grabbed his last stone and placed it in his sling. He spun around in a few circles and yelled out a shrilling scream at the top of his voice as he released the stone. The giant was almost upon him; the sharp tip of his javelin just yards away. His massive Philistine horde was close behind him in a full speed onslaught.

The stone flew through the air at near lightning speed and landed squarely in the giant's face along a crack in his gilded bronze helmet. He immediately slumped down and fell to his knees. Then he completely fell to the ground face forward with a loud resounding thump just a few feet away from the boy.

The bulk of the entire Israeli army then reached the battlefield as they navigated through the riverbed and started running full speed towards the oncoming Philistine army. The boy walked over to the giant and removed his dented bronze helmet. Yeshua could see the young boy say something to the giant. He wasn't dead, just stunned from being hit by the stone. There was blood streaming from his face. The giant rolled over onto his side and looked like he was trying to get up. The boy leaned down to the giant's writhing body and pulled the sword from the sheath on his waist. He then raised it up above high above his head with both hands.

Time seemed to shift and slow down. Everything was moving in slow motion. The two massive armies were in full attack speed charging towards each other just a few dozen yards apart. The boy swung the sword downwards and let out a shrilling scream as he sliced through the giant's neck and decapitated him with one blow. Blood gushed from his lacerated neck vessels and pooled onto the dusty, dry ground.

The boy then dropped the sword and lifted the giant's head from the ground and held it straight up facing the Philistine army, like Perseus holding the Medusa. This caused a ripple effect among the Philistines as they broke their charge and many stopped running. Although they didn't turn into stone like the victims of Medusa's snaky head, the sight of their dead champion and the entire Israeli army rushing towards them struck fear and dread in the Philistines. Many of them turned and ran away from the battlefield.

The boy turned around to face his army coming from the north. He was still holding the giant's head. Just a few yards away, Yeshua looked at the giant's face, now without his helmet. There was a large, freshly bleeding cut running down the entire left side of his face from the impact of the stone. Yeshua had seen this kind of scar before, many times.

The oncoming charging Israelites reached the boy and dozens of them surrounded and congratulated him. In the center of the battlefield, the charging Israelite army smashed into the fleeing and disorganized ranks of the Philistines.

The Philistines' front lines crumbled easily and then they went into full retreat. Thousands of Israelite soldiers chased the Philistines towards the west. After a few minutes, hundreds of dead and dying soldiers littered the valley. Dozens of vultures circled high in the sky waiting for the dust to clear.

Yeshua saw Mohammed's yellow aura nearby.

"Mohammed, is that you? Are you there?" said Yeshua.

"Yes. It's me. Did you see what happened?" asked Mohammed.

"I did, yes. What time do you think it is? I'm sure we have to get back to the satellite station now," said Yeshua.

The young boy, still holding the giant's head, was being escorted by ten Israeli soldiers back towards the riverbank. One of the men wore silver armor and looked like a general or a commander of the army. They descended from the dusty field down to the riverbed as Yeshua and Mohammed followed them. Standing around the large flat rock where Yeshua had earlier blown the Shofar, were about a dozen Israeli men in decorative uniforms and regal looking attire. On the rock next to the flowing stream stood a man wearing a gold crown and gold armor, and next to him was a very old man wearing fine robes made from blue, purple and red cloth laced with golden embroidery. He had a long white beard and appeared to be a priest or holy man and he looked just like Rabbi Yohanan from Masada who had given Yeshua the Shofar when he was thirteen.

The young boy placed the giant's head on the stone in front of the old man wearing the crown. He bowed in front of him. He was the King Saul of the Israelites. Yeshua and Mohammed came right up to the flat stone next to the boy.

The King spoke. Somehow Yeshua and Mohammed could now understand what they were saying even though it was a strange language.

"Whose son are you, young man?" asked the King.

"I am David," said the boy. "I am the son of your servant Jesse of Bethlehem."

The holy man in robes standing next to the King now held a long spiraled Shofar. It looked exactly the same as Yeshua's Shofar. He placed it to his lips and blew with all his might.

Ba-ba-baaaaaaaaaaaaaa…

Ba-ba-baaaaaaaaaaaaaaaa…

Ba-ba-baaaaaaaaaaaaaaa…

Everything went black.

Chapter 14

The Virus

"Mohammed, Mohammed... wake up!" yelled Yeshua as he shook his friend's limp body laying on the wide, flat stone in the middle of the dry riverbed.

"Ugggghhhhhh... what happened?" asked Mohammed softly as he slowly came back to consciousness.

"There's no time to talk now!" screamed Yeshua. "It's 7:33AM. We've got to get back to the satellite station, STAT!!!"

"I feel like a brick just hit my head," said Mohammed as he sat up, holding his hand over his forehead.

"We need to leave now," said Yeshua. "If we're not at roll call at 8AM Sergeant Berg will beat us, or worse!" Yeshua helped Mohammed up to his feet. "Let's go, now. Run!"

The two young men ran south through the riverbed quickly and jumped onto the main road. They ran as fast as they could east along the road, although Mohammed was much faster and reached the satellite station first. Yeshua arrived at the tents under the satellites a few minutes later, his Shofar slung across his back. He looked down at his watch and it said 7:58AM. All the soldiers stood there in attention in a single file row and Yeshua joined them. He was completely out of breath.

Sergeant Berg walked out of the satellite relay station building at exactly 8AM sharp. His eyes were bloodshot and he looked exhausted.

"Platoon, we still have a lot of work to do here," he said. "Does anyone speak and read Arabic, and does anyone know how to code computers?"

"Sir, I am fluent in Arabic," replied Mohammed.

"I know SQL, Java, Javascript, C, C++, Python, HTML, iOS, PHP, Ruby, DOS and Fortran, Sir!" said Private Shimon, the gamer expert.

"You two come with me," said Berg. "The rest of you pack up those old transformers in those wood crates and stack them in the back of the trailer!"

"Yes, Sir!" they all yelled.

Mohammed and Private Shimon followed Berg into the building where they walked down a hallway into the control center room. There were dozens of screens and monitors that were turned off all along the walls and several computers and keyboards sitting on multiple rows of tables facing a large black screen along the far side of the room.

There was one man sitting in the center of the room looking at the only computer screen that was turned on. Mohammed recognized him as the electrician who helped them install the transformers the day before. He looked like Newman from the Seinfeld TV show and he was typing furiously on the keyboard in front of his computer.

"We can't seem to get the satellite station turned back on. The main computers and generators won't even activate. It appears that some kind of software virus or trojan horse has sabotaged the entire operation here. We need your help," Berg said to Mohammed and Private Shimon. "Please, sit next to Albert."

The soldiers sat in chairs on either side of Albert, and Berg stood behind them.

"Someone hacked the entire system here," said Albert. "They put up an arcane firewall on all the main servers and routers. I was able to sneak in through a backdoor with this terminal, although I'm blocked by some kind of sneaky AI bot that is coded in Arabic."

"Wow, so you can't even access the mainframe?" asked Shimon.

"No. It took us all night just to get this computer functional and navigate through multiple hoops and curve balls to the primary firewall. I'm even having to use my phone as hotspot for our Wi-Fi connection," responded Albert.

"So this is your only terminal? Are you able to mirror another CPU while you stay parked on the firewall entrance?" asked Shimon.

"Ummmm. Yeah. I think so, I can open another window and portal an offsite server through a remote desktop," said Albert.

"Great. Do that. We don't want the bot to know we are connected to the outside. I think I know how to get through this thing," said Shimon.

"I found some code on the backside of the firewall that I can access, however the entire program is in Arabic. I don't know what it says... I can't read it," said Albert.

"Show me the code!" said Mohammed loudly. He did his best Cuba Gooding, Jr. impression.

"This isn't funny," said Sergeant Berg. "Seriously, this is no laughing matter."

"Yes Sir," said Mohammed softly.

"Albert, let me look at your cellphone for a second. I need to look at your web browser. And what's the IP address of this station?" asked Shimon.

"Its 5.29.181.818," said Albert as he handed the phone to Shimon. "Ok, I got the mirrored desktop up on the split screen."

Private Shimon reached over and punched in a website on Google with the terminal keyboard. His eyes got big and he said, "It looks like our IP address is now 5.134.199.245"

"Okay. What does that mean?" asked Berg. "I don't understand what you are doing?"

"Albert, do you mind? Can I sit there please and use the computer?" asked Shimon.

Albert and Shimon both stood up and exchanged seats. Shimon opened another Google window on the computer screen and typed 5.134.199.245 in quotes.

The first result on Google said:

5.134.198.160 - Iran - IP Address Details - IP lookup - proxio.io
https://www.proxydocker.com/en/proxy/5.134.198.160
5.134.199.228 · 5.134.199.229 · 5.134.199.230 · 5.134.199.231 · 5.134.199.232 · 5.134.199.233 · 5.134.199.234 · 5.134.199.235 · 5.134.199.236 · 5.134.199.237 · 5.134.199.238 · 5.134.199.239 · 5.134.199.240 · 5.134.199.241 · 5.134.199.242 · 5.134.199.243 · 5.134.199.244 · **5.134.199.245** · 5.134.199.246 · 5.134.

"What? The IP address is from Iran?" asked Berg.

"Yeah, they were sloppy. The hackers are from Iran and they didn't cover their tracks very well. Look, this code in Arabic isn't really a bot program. It looks like it's a prompt to a password access with some kind of hint. Mohammed... what does it say?" asked Shimon.

"Okay, I'll read it," said Mohammed as he scooted up closer to the screen with his chair.

"Ah. It's a riddle. It says... Pointed is his spearhead, sharp are his teeth. His progeny are his helpers, dissolving union is his business. He assails his master, clinging to his moustache, inserting his fangs into old and young. Agreeable, of goodly shape, slim, abstemious. A shooter, with shafts abundant, around the beard and the moustache."

"What could the answer be?" asked Berg.

"Hmmmm. I think I remember hearing this when I was a young boy. I think it's an old Persian riddle," said Mohammed.

"I know, it's a scissors!" said Shimon. He started typing on the keyboard however the letters appearing on the screen were in Arabic.

"Oh snap! This whole data link interface in is Arabic. We must be inside the server in Iran, behind their firewall. However, I have no idea how to type in Arabic on an English keyboard," said a frustrated Shimon.

"Ok, let me sit there," requested Mohammed. "I think can figure out how to write in Arabic using the QWERTY keyboard. You just need to tell me what to type."

The two young soldiers switched seats. In the back of the room, Berg was quietly talking to someone on his cell phone.

"Okay, type in scissors," said Shimon. Mohammed found the correct letters on the keyboard and slowly typed in the word 'scissors' in Arabic and hit return.

The response on the screen was "غير المرور كلمة صحيحة" in Arabic.

"Mohammed. What does that mean?" asked Shimon.

"It means... the password is incorrect. That was the wrong password," responded Mohammed.

"Now I remember the riddle," said Mohammed. "I think the answer is A Comb."

"Ahhhhhh. A Comb. That makes much more sense," said Shimon. Mohammed typed in the answer. A bunch of more Arabic writing appeared on the screen. "We're in!" yelled Shimon.

"Now, all we have to do is flip the IP addresses and we are back in business," said Shimon.

"Wait a sec," said Mohammed as he looked at the screen and the Arabic writing. "What is this satellite station actually for?" he asked. "I thought it was just for picking up cable TV and Internet signals and maybe part of the SETI search for extraterrestrial intelligence project?"

"That's actually classified information," said Berg, now off the phone.

"Well, there's something really freaking serious going on. It says here that the virus is deactivating the entire Israeli satellite radar missile detection system. It's put a lock on the whole station," said Mohammed.

"Wow!" said Shimon. "Before we switch the IP addresses, let's see if we can hack into their system or learn more about this virus program. Hopefully, they don't know that we've snuck in through their backdoor."

"Ok, type this command in Arabic. Write Main Menu," said Shimon.

Mohammed wrote in the words and hit return. The screen filled with more Arabic words.

"Wow! It's another riddle," said Mohammed. "These Iranian programmers must be some real jokers."

"What does it say?" asked Albert.

"What is it that tears into small pieces whatever falls in its toothless mouth? If you put your fingers in its eyes it will instantly prick its ears," said Mohammed.

"I know!" yelled Albert. "It's scissors this time, for real."

"I think you are right Albert," said Mohammed as he typed in the answer in Arabic.

The screen filled with more Arabic words. It looked like a list of numbers with options.

"Boom! We're in!" said Mohammed. "Ok, it's the main menu. The options say... number one Site Map, number two Admin, number three Targets, number four

Code Editor, number five Security, number six Accounts and number seven Tic-Tac-Toe"

"Seriously, Tic-Tac-Toe?" asked Shimon. "Shall we play a game?" he said jokingly.

Albert said, "Let's look at Targets. I wonder what other locations they are trying to sabotage."

Mohammed typed in number three and hit return. A digital map of Israel came up with several different colored dots on multiple locations. One was red, the majority yellow and some green.

"There we are... that red dot," said Albert. "They have us deactivated so we are red. Those other sites are all the other satellite relay stations that control the missile detection systems in the entire country. Holy Moly! They are trying to prevent our ability to track and stop incoming missiles with our Iron Dome and Patriot systems. It looks like all the yellow dots are locations they are actively trying to deactivate, and the green sites are locations they haven't hit yet."

Berg walked over. His face was pale white. He had just gotten off his phone again.

"We need to get this station back online right now. Intelligence is reporting activity in multiple hostile locations about a massive impending missile launch," he said.

"Wait. How much time do we have?" asked Shimon.

"I don't know exactly," said Berg. "Based on that map, it looks like they are still trying to sabotage a bunch of other satellite relays and haven't succeeded yet. However, this one is down and is responsible for defending a large portion of Tel Aviv. We've got to get online ASAP as millions of people are vulnerable right now if they launch immediately."

"I think I can jam their entire network and maybe take their whole thing down," said Shimon. "I can do it in less than five minutes, God willing."

"Really? That fast?" said Sergeant Berg. "Yeah, go for it!"

"Ok, Mohammed. Go back to the main menu and select Code Editor," said Shimon.

"Yes, Sir!" said Mohammed. He typed on the keyboard and hit return. More Arabic words filled the screen.

"Oh gosh. Another riddle. What is it with these all these riddles?" said Mohammed.

"Well, at least we are getting hints to the passwords. It would be way worse if it were just a single password prompt. We'd certainly run out of time downloading and installing password generators programs. That could take forever," said Shimon.

"Good point, my friend." said Mohammed. "Okay, here's the riddle… I never was, am always to be. No one ever saw me, nor ever will. And yet I am the confidence of all, to live and breathe on this terrestrial ball."

"Sheesh, what were these programmers smoking? Afghani opium?" said Sergeant Berg.

"What could be the answer?" said Shimon. Everyone looked at each other in confusion.

Mohammed closed his eyes. He went into a deep meditation. A few moments went by. He opened his eyes.

"I got it!" he said. "The answer is tomorrow. I never was, am always to be… that's tomorrow! You can't see tomorrow till it happens, then its today."

"That sounds like the right answer, Mohammed. Type it in," said Berg.

He typed in it in Arabic and hit return. Several pages of Arabic text scrolled onto the screen.

"Viola!" said Shimon. "That's the entire code for the active virus. Wow, these guys are such amateurs. We got them by the balls now. Mohammed, can you find the 'Select All' option on the drop down menu?"

"Sure thing. It's right here," he said. He clicked on the button and the all the words highlighted blue.

"Now, hit the delete button," said Shimon.

Mohammed hit the delete button. Some words appeared on the center of the screen in Arabic.

"What does it say?" asked Berg.

"It says, Are you sure you want to delete? This operation will be irreversible," said Mohammed.

"Yes! Yes! Click Yes!" said Shimon. He seemed super excited.

Mohammed went to push the return button and Shimon yelled, "Wait… NOOOOO!!!!"

"What the heck?" said Mohammed.

"Hold on. I have a really good idea. Click 'no.' and go back and reselect all the text," said Shimon.

"Okay," said Mohammed. He followed Shimon's request and reselected all of the code to the virus. The entire screen turned blue.

"Now, select 'copy' then click on the other open window's google browser. Type in this website… https://translate.google.com and paste the text in there," said Shimon.

Albert said "Ahhhh…. Brilliant."

Mohammed again followed Shimon's instructions and copied and pasted the text into the translator website.

"Now, click translate into English and hit print. There's a printer in here, Albert?" asked Shimon.

"Yes, there is. Over there. It works too, I just printed something out not long ago," said Albert.

Mohammed translated the text and hit print. The printer started shooting out the papers. Albert walked over and he said, "We got it!"

"Ok, now go back to the other window and let's delete the virus," said Shimon.

Mohammed selected the other window and hit the delete button. He then confirmed the delete and typed in yes and hit return. After a moment, the entire screen went black.

"What the heck just happened?" asked Albert.

"Wait for it… wait for it…" said Shimon repeatedly.

The computer in front of them started to reboot. Then all the screen terminals in the entire room turned back on one by one. A digital large map of Israel appeared in the giant screen in the center of the room and there was a green dot over the satellite station location on the map.

"We did it!" yelled Mohammed as he stood up and all the men exchanged high fives. Everyone was smiling.

Suddenly, Yeshua swung the door open to the control center and stumbled inside the room. He was holding his right ear and wincing in pain and there was blood coming from his head, dripping between his fingers.

"Something horrible is about to happen," said Yeshua as he fell to the floor on his knees.

Mohammed and Shimon ran over to Yeshua and lifted him back on is feet. Berg was back on the phone.

"But Yeshua, we just reactivated the entire station and stopped the Iranian virus from disabling the missile defense grid. And your right ear is still buzzing?" asked Mohammed.

"Yes. It's buzzing louder than it ever has. And look, I'm bleeding. It hurts so badly. We've got to do something!" cried Yeshua.

"Buzzing, what does that mean?" asked Shimon.

"There's no time to explain right now," said Mohammed.

Berg and Albert walked over to the three young soldiers. "Our intelligence just reported that the imminent missile launch activity we detected earlier has stopped for now, so well done soldiers. However, since they are aborting their launches... that means they must know we deactivated the virus and that our missile detection system is fully functional. Ehhh... what the heck is going on with Private Rabin?" asked Berg.

"Sir, I can't explain it all right now, however... we need to search the entire station ASAP. There's something very dangerous about to happen. Maybe we're going to be under attack. Maybe the Iranians had a back up plan to take out this station, I don't know..." said Mohammed.

"Okay, let's get everyone outside on this right now!" yelled Berg. He grabbed his Tavor machine gun and backpack from the corner of the room.

"Private Shimon, Albert... search all the rooms in here for suspicious activity," ordered Berg. He handed Shimon his semi-automatic Glock pistol. "Do you know how to use this, Soldier?"

"Yes, Sir!" responded Shimon.

Sergeant Berg, Yeshua and Mohammed walked outside from the control station. The platoon had just finished placing the final tenth wooden crate with the old transformers into the back of the trailer.

"Platoon, gather up!" screamed Berg. Everyone quickly left the back of the trailer and stood in front of Berg in attention.

"We have a situation here. There may be enemy combatants in or around this station complex right now. I want you gear up ASAP and search every inch of this station and set up a defensive perimeter surrounding the entire complex. No one gets in or out, and if you detect any suspicious activity shoot first and ask questions later," said Berg. He reached into his backpack and pulled out several black 30 round NATO magazine clips and tossed one to each soldier.

"These are real bullets," said Berg. "Lock and load them up in your X95s right now. Put your telecom on active mode in your helmets and call out anything that looks out of the ordinary. Now go!" he yelled. "You two, come with me," he said to Yeshua and Mohammed.

The soldiers rapidly scrambled to their tents and grabbed their guns and helmets. Meanwhile Berg, Yeshua and Mohammed started to walk around the outside of the control building. Berg held his X95 in front of him and stepped slowly around the corners of the station as Yeshua and Mohammed followed closely behind.

"Ok. Tell me what's really going on here boys. What the freak is happening?" said Berg softly as he cautiously searched the outside of the station. Behind them, the rest of the platoon scouted and patrolled around the huge satellite dishes and along the outer fence.

"So, it's a long story… I get a warning signal in my right ear when something bad is about to happen. Remember the missile that was going to hit the helicopter the other day? Same thing, I hear a high pitch buzzing noise right before something horrible is inevitable," said Yeshua.

"What? Are you serious? That sounds crazy. How is that even possible?" asked Berg.

"I'm not exactly sure. I'm trying to figure it out myself. I think maybe it's my guardian Angels, or maybe just my own intuition. Or perhaps it's my future self warning my present self about danger. I just don't know. It's been like this since I was a young kid. Although it's real... I know it sounds wacka-doodle," said Yeshua.

"He's telling the truth," said Mohammed. "It's one of his super-powers."

"So you're some kind of psychic superhero?" asked Berg.

"Huh? No, I'm not a superhero. I'm just a Israeli soldier," said Yeshua.

"And you Mohammed. How can you swim and run so fast? I saw you on the beach. What are you two? The dynamic duo?" asked Berg.

"Sergeant. I found something," said Private Ivanov on the intercom. "By the main satellite dish number one."

"Copy. Be right there," said Berg. "Hold your ground. Any other suspicious activity, platoon?" Several "No, Sir." responses immediately came through the intercom.

Berg, Yeshua and Mohammed walked over to one of the huge main satellite dishes. Its massive round dish pointed upwards towards the southwest. Private Ivanov stood waving at them on the upper platform several flights up the white metal stairs that led to rear of the main dish. They walked up the stairs and reached the top of the landing.

"Come inside the control room," said Ivanov. She motioned them with her hand as she opened the door. Computer terminals filled the inside the tiny room. The small glass windows within had stunningly beautiful views of the surrounding valley and the wildflower-filled green grassy fields.

"Is this supposed to be here?" she asked. She pointed to a large metal box bolted to the floor semi-hidden under the main control desk. There were multiple wires coming out from the back of the box and connected up into the control panel. "That looks suspicious, doesn't it?" she said.

As soon as they entered the room, Yeshua's right ear started buzzing louder. He held his ear and winced in pain. Berg looked at him and said, "Your ear is buzzing?" and Yeshua nodded.

Shimon suddenly came on the helmet intercom. "Sergeant Berg, you there?" he asked.

"Copy. Here," said Berg.

"I just read through the print out of the virus program," said Shimon. "It appears that somewhere on the base is a stealth radar jamming system. It's covertly hijacked the satellite dishes to send jamming signals to all our planes, helicopters and tanks. Our military is sitting ducks right now from incoming rocket fire."

"Well that would explain the helicopter incident two days ago. The radar detection systems failed. I think we found the device here wired into the main satellite number one control panel. I'll deactivate it right now," said Berg. He walked over and got out his Israeli pocketknife to cut the wires from behind the box.

Yeshua's right ear started buzzing even louder as Berg went to cut the wires. He screamed "Noooooooo!" however it was too late, Berg had cut the wires. Berg looked at Yeshua with big eyes.

"I think it's a bomb too," said Yeshua. "I'm pretty sure it's going to blow up now since you cut the wires."

Berg yelled some explicatives and looked back at the box.

"Quick, let's open the box and try stop the bomb! Maybe we'll have enough time," said Mohammed holding a screwdriver he had just found in the room.

Berg grabbed the screwdriver from Mohammed and got on his knees in front of the box. He unscrewed the outer panel and pulled it off. Inside was a very complex looking control CPU motherboard, hard drive, battery pack and three bricks of what looked like C4 explosives. There were lots of colored wires connecting almost everything and some Arabic writing on the multiple places inside the box.

"It's a bomb. What does it say in the box, Mohammed?" asked Berg.

"It says Made in China. Ha-Ha. Just kidding," joked Mohammed. "It just says 'Fragile, handle with care.' "

"Quit it with the jokes, okay?" said Berg.

Yeshua leaned down and looked carefully at the electronics. He saw an LED timer next to the CPU. "Look, there's a timer here. It's counting down five minutes. We have five minutes before it blows up," said Yeshua. "I think I can figure this out. Listen, everyone get out of here, now."

"What?" said Berg.

"There's no time to argue. Get out of here now! All of you. I got this!" yelled Yeshua.

"Okay, are you absolutely sure?" asked Berg. Yeshua nodded and turned to look back at the bomb.

"Let's roll. Good luck and Godspeed Private Rabin. Guardian Angels, huh?" said Berg. He opened the door and he, Mohammed and Ivanov quickly ran down the steps back to the ground level.

Yeshua went to grab the wires and pull them from bricks of the C4 explosives. As his hands got closer, his right ear buzzed. "Wrong wires," he said to himself softly. The timer said 3 minutes and 57 seconds and continued to count down. There was a blinking light next to the timer. He took his hands and placed them over the wires by the timer... still, right ear buzzing. Then, he moved his hands by the battery pack; still his ears buzzed. He opened the black plastic cover connecting the CPU and the hard drive, and on the inside were about ten rows of multi colored wires. Yeshua held each one in his fingers for a moment, and still his right ear buzzed, so he moved to the next wire carefully and methodically. The timer was under one minute. He grabbed the red wire and his left ear buzzed loudly. "Finally, got you!"

Yeshua pulled the red wire and the timer stopped. He placed his hand over the hard drive, and his left ear buzzed more loudly. He pulled the hard drive out of the unit and stood up. He did it! He defused the bomb!

Yeshua walked out of the control room and stood on the outside platform. He could see the whole platoon waiting for him outside the fence by the main road. He gave them a thumbs up, and everyone started yelling and cheering. Just down the main highway, an armored Israeli transport vehicle approached. "Ah, thank God," said Yeshua to himself. "I hope that transport is coming for us. I'd love not to have to hike all the way back to the base."

CHAPTER 15

THE EGYPTIANS

Four weeks later
Nitzanim Army Base, Israel

"Ok platoon, you have done very well so far," said Sergeant Berg. The entire group stood in attention inside their barracks. "Everyone here has scored in the top five percent in rifle training and small arms proficiency. Also, you are all excelling in your infantry basic training skills. And Mohammed, you just beat the base record in the military obstacle course... well done soldier!"

"Thank you Sir," said Mohammed.

"Tomorrow morning at 0630 we will be starting our three week parachuting and paratrooper course, and at 1600 sharp we will begin Krav Maga training. So get a good night's sleep soldiers. Strong work so far!" said Sergeant Berg. He saluted his platoon, and everyone saluted back.

"At ease," said Berg as he left the barracks.

"What's Krav Maga?" asked Yeshua to Mohammed.

"It's like a combination of Bruce Lee style ninja martial arts and advanced street fighting on steroids. It's a special method of self defense invented by the IDF. I've been waiting patiently for this part of the training. Woo Hoo!" said Mohammed excitedly.

"Tomorrow will be a very exciting day. Do you think we will get to jump out of an airplane or helicopter or just sit in a boring class and learn about how to operate a parachute?" asked Yeshua.

"I hope we get to jump with parachutes. I've never done that before. As a matter of fact, I've never even been in an airplane," said Mohammed.

"Me neither!" Yeshua paused for a moment. "I've been meaning to ask you something Mohammed. It's about what happened in the Valley of Elah. It's been so crazy busy we've never really had a chance to talk about it."

"Yeah, that was pretty epic… being in that huge battle between the Israelites and the Philistines," said Mohammed. "What's up? What's your question?"

"Well, I remember right before David threw his last stone at Goliath… I saw your aura actually go into David. Then he made that shrilling yell like you made on the beach while we were running to the flagpole. What did you do?" asked Yeshua.

"Let's just say I helped him," replied Mohammed.

"What do you mean? How did you help him? I don't understand," questioned Yeshua.

"Okay, we both saw him miss with the first four stones. If he missed with the last stone, he's dead. Goliath puts his javelin through David's chest. So I went into him and gave him a little extra strength," said Mohammed.

"You went into him? Like inside his body?" asked a confused looking Yeshua.

"Yes. That's what I did. Yes. I put my aura, my spirit, into him. It was so cool! I could see through his eyes, and I supercharged him with all my might. In my mind, I made the shrilling yell, and it came out of his mouth," said Mohammed.

"So, you took over his body? You controlled him?" asked Yeshua.

"Hmmm. I didn't see it that way; it was more like I boosted his energy. But yeah, maybe I did control him in a way, although it was more like I assisted him. However, there was something more too. When he released the rock... my spirit travelled into the stone. It's like I helped smash the stone right into Goliath's ugly face," said Mohammed.

"Whoa. So you powered up David and then you telekinetically guided the stone into Goliath? That's incredibly fantastical!" exclaimed Yeshua.

"I know, right? That Shofar of yours is astonishingly miraculous. We should definitely travel back in time again soon. And by the way... David looked just like you as a boy, red hair and all. What do you think of that?" asked Mohammed.

"Yeah. It's beyond belief. Do you remember when I disappeared in Masada? I went back in time to the days of the Roman siege. I saw another boy who looked just like me," said Yeshua.

"So, this wasn't the first time you saw a boy who looked like you?" said Mohammed.

"No. There's other times too. Like my dream about the Nazis. They come to get me and I'm me as a thirteen year old boy," replied Yeshua.

"Wait a sec. What if it's not actually a dream? What if it's a real memory? Could it be that it was actually you in each time period? What if you are seeing yourself as you reincarnate through different eras of history?" asked Mohammed.

"Oh my God. I think you could be right. That makes so much sense. You think I actually was David, King of the Israelites in a previous lifetime?" said Yeshua.

"It is a honor to know you, my friend," said Mohammed.

"Likewise, Mohammed. But what about you?" asked Yeshua. "Do you remember any of your past lives or reincarnations? You looked just like that young boy I helped get water from the well after I blew the Shofar in Tel Be'er Sheba."

"Sadly, I do not," replied Mohammed. "I hardly remember any of my dreams like you do. Everything just kinda goes black, and then I wake up."

"I wonder if we have been reincarnating together... like perhaps we've been friends forever, always reincarnating and helping each other in every lifetime? Hmmm. I have a little experiment I'd like to try," said Yeshua.

"Are you sure? Last idea you had we battled against the giant Goliath and almost missed roll call," joked Mohammed.

Yeshua handed Mohammed his Shofar.

"Tonight, when you go to bed hold the Shofar in your hands. As you fall asleep, try to enter into my dream. Let's try to dream together, like that quantum entanglement you talk about. What happens to me happens to you. Let's see we if can trace our past lives together in a dream," suggested Yeshua.

"Wow. This sure would make a really cool sci-fi movie, wouldn't it?" said Mohammed as he took the Shofar into his hands.

Everyone in the platoon prepared for sleep after the long day of training. Each soldier got into his cot and said goodnight to the others. Mohammed turned off the lights as he was the last one to get in his bed. He held the Shofar. The clock on the wall said 23:11.

It became very dark. There was the sound of rushing waters, and then the rhythmic whooshing of paddles or oars. Above, the night sky was vast. The bright constellation Orion was directly above. In the east, a large object in the sky shone brightly. It was Halley's comet, with its bright center and long tail. In the west, the full moon was close to the horizon. A few shooting stars whisked across the Universe overhead.

"Yeshua, are you there?" asked Mohammed.

"What, Mohammed? Are you in my dream?" asked Yeshua in his mind, telepathically.

"Yes, I'm here. We are in some kind of boat," responded Mohammed.

Yeshua looked down. He saw his muscular body below, only wearing a white loincloth. He was lying on some kind of ornate bed with a tall wooden canopy on a long wooden boat. There were comfy cloth pillows behind him.

Around him were about twenty young men with bald heads and dark skin also wearing white loincloths. They were on either side of the boat and rowing long paddles in a very wide river surrounded by huge dark silhouettes of palm trees along the edges of the water.

"Where are you? Mohammed... I don't see you," thought Yeshua.

"I think I'm with you... in your mind," replied Mohammed. "I'm seeing what you are seeing."

"Whoa. You are in my mind talking to me in my dream? That's crazy!" thought Yeshua.

"Well, I guess this is the new normal now. I seem to be able to walk into people's minds lately," said Mohammed. "I wonder where this boat is going? Wait a sec, look up ahead to the left."

The boat was traveling downstream with the flow of the river towards the north. Far in the distance, the moonlight illuminated three large massive triangular structures. Each one had a glowing beam of light like a laser reflected upwards into the heavens from the tip of each apex.

"Oh my... that's the Pyramids," said Yeshua. "We're in Egypt!"

"Incredible. They appear as brand new," said Mohammed. "Look at the smooth limestone walls and smaller golden pyramids at the top."

"Wow. Yes," thought Yeshua. "We've travelled over four thousand years in time! We're on a boat in the Nile River. Look, I'm an Egyptian."

Yeshua looked down again at his body and held up his hands to his face. Although it was night, he could see that his skin was dark. He wore sandals on his feet. On his head, he wore a blue headdress similar to the one he had seen on the Internet from the golden mask of the King Tut mummy.

"It looks like I'm some kind of royalty," thought Yeshua.

"This is truly amazing. I've always been fascinated with Egyptian archeology and history. My Bedouin ancestors are from Egypt," said Mohammed. "Okay, I'm thinking hard about this. I recall that the first Great Pyramid was made by the Pharaoh Khufu. He reigned for many years during the Fourth Dynasty. Surprisingly, only one little statue of him was ever found, and they never found his mummy."

"So, do you think I'm Khufu, the Pharaoh?" asked Yeshua.

"I don't think so," responded Mohammed. "You look like you're a young Egyptian man. Khufu would have been an old man around the time his Pyramid was completed. It reportedly took over twenty years to finish."

"Okay. Could this dream be something to do with my being Jewish? Did the Jews build the pyramids as slaves? Or maybe could I be Moses from the Torah coming to tell the Pharaoh to let my people go?" asked Yeshua.

"That's a lot of questions," replied Mohammed. "It looks like we are getting closer to the Great Pyramid. Look at it! It's incredible! I've only seen photos of it from our modern times with the huge bricks on the outside. I've never been here in person… I mean never been there. Apparently all the smooth limestone was looted to build other buildings after the fall of the ancient Egyptian culture around the time of the Romans."

Ahead, along the west bank of the river a large stone dock appeared far off in the distance. There were some burning torches on poles that made it visible in the dark. The oarsman rowed in the direction of the dock.

"Ok, let's think about this," said Mohammed in Yeshua's mind. "In your Torah Holy Book, the actual names of the specific Pharaohs are never mentioned. It's like their names were purposefully omitted. He is always referred to as the 'Pharaoh' so we don't know the exact period when Hebrews might have been here as slaves. Furthermore, there's not much archeological evidence or even hieroglyphics proving the story of the Israelite Exodus. However, history was erased many times by some Pharaohs, and I'm sure they didn't want to have any evidence in writing of a huge embarrassing slave revolt. So, anyhow... I think most Biblical historians guestimate that the Hebrews were slaves in Egypt around the time of Pharaoh Akhenaten or Ramses. That was a very long time after the Great Pyramid was supposedly built."

"Ok," said Yeshua. "So, what does that all mean?"

"It means the Great Pyramids were built long before the Hebrews would have come here to Egypt," explained Mohammed. "So based on that timeline, you are definitely not Moses. At least not in this dream."

The boat approached the dock and turned to the left. There was another narrow waterway that went inland towards the Giza Plateau. The canal was lined by huge Egyptian columns. There were statues of Sphinxes lining the walkways in between the columns. Directly ahead was the massive Pyramid of Khufu. It glowed in the dark night, brightly illuminated from the stars and the moonlight.

"Look, there's someone up ahead at the end of the canal," said Mohammed.

Standing alone along the walkway was a beautiful Egyptian woman. She looked like Elizabeth Taylor from old the Cleopatra movie. She had stunning eyes surrounded by the traditional black makeup and had long black hair woven in tight braids. She wore an ornate gold headdress and a long, flowing white dress. She smiled as the boat docked next to her.

Yeshua got out of the boat and approached the women. She greeted him with a kiss on each cheek. He looked down at her almost bare chest and saw her exquisite gold Ankh necklace.

"Wow. She's so stunningly gorgeous," said Mohammed telepathically to Yeshua.

She spoke ancient Egyptian; however, her words translated and were understandable in the dream.

"I assume your time in Abydos went well. Our father Khufu is on his deathbed. He has summoned you to see him in the morning. The Pyramid tomb is complete and ready for his journey into the afterlife. Are you ready to ascend to the throne?" she asked.

"Oh wow!" said Mohammed in Yeshua's mind. "You're the first son of Khufu! You're going to be the Pharaoh!"

"What?" thought Yeshua. "I'm going to be the Pharaoh of Egypt?"

"Tell her yes… and tell her that you are going to inspect the Pyramid. I want to check it out before your dream ends," requested Mohammed.

"Ok sure," replied Yeshua.

"I am ready," said Yeshua to the woman. "But first, I will inspect this glorious Pyramid. Thank you. I will be on my way. I will see you in the morning."

He reached down and grabbed her hand and kissed it. She gave him a strange look and then turned around and walked away.

"Let's go, it's going to be morning soon!" said Mohammed. The eastern sky was starting to get lighter. Halley's comet and Orion were directly over the Pyramid from their perspective on the dock.

"You sure do have some extraordinary dreams my friend. Let's walk to the Pyramid and explore a bit, okay?" said Mohammed.

"Yes, Sir!" said Yeshua in his mind. He walked down the long stone causeway towards the Great Pyramid to the west. As he got closer, three much smaller pyramids appeared on the left.

"Those are called the Queen's Pyramids," stated Mohammed. "I guess Khufu had multiple wives. I forget which one was your mother. And up directly ahead is the Mortuary Temple. I think the main entrance is on the north side of the Pyramid, so let's see if we can find our way there through the Temple."

As they approached the Mortuary Temple, a man stepped out from behind the shadows and into the causeway. Yeshua was shocked... the man looked just like Mohammed in real life.

"What the... ???" thought Yeshua.

"Brother Kawab! How are you? I did not expect to see you here," the man said. He came up and hugged Yeshua.

"Ya Lahwy!" yelled Mohammed inside Yeshua's head. "That's me! I'm your brother!"

"We talked about this since we were young boys... the day you would become Pharaoh. Now the time is upon us. Father will pass any moment now. Are you ready?" the Egyptian asked.

"Yes, I am ready. Yes," responded Yeshua.

"I am so very happy for you!" said the man as he hugged Yeshua again. Then he stepped apart from him, staring at him with a very strange expression.

Yeshua looked down and saw blood. A knife was deep in his left chest, just under his left nipple. Blood was pouring out from around the blade. He fell to the floor and everything went black.

"You killed me!" screamed Yeshua as he woke up in the barracks. The clock on the wall said 5:55AM. He got up from his bed and walked over to the sleeping Mohammed in the next cot.

"What the freak! You killed me!" yelled Yeshua as he grabbed and shook Mohammed's body in anger.

"I'm so sorry!" mumbled Mohammed as he woke up. "I'm sorry." He started crying tears. "I'm sorry…"

"Break it up!" yelled Private Cohen as he pulled Yeshua away from Mohammed. "What's going on here? He killed you? You must of had some kind of nightmare… settle down Soldier!"

Yeshua grabbed his Shofar back from Mohammed and sat down on his bed. He put his hand over his forehead. "I guess it was just a dream. I dreamed he stabbed me. Right here." He pointed to the birthmark on his chest.

Chapter 16

Krav Maga

Nitzanim Army Base, Israel
1600

The platoon stood in attention in a single line inside their barracks. There was a large foam mat covering most of the floor in front of their cots. They had just come back from hours of paratrooper instructional courses and learning the ins and outs of their military grade parachutes. Yeshua and Mohammed had not spoken to each other the entire day since their confrontational episode earlier that morning.

The door opened to the barracks and in walked Sergeant Berg followed by a very pretty tall blond woman wearing the standard olive colored green tee shirt and camouflage pants with black combat boots. She looked very familiar to Yeshua and Mohammed. It was Miriam! She was the nurse who took care of Yeshua while he was in a coma back when he was thirteen.

"Soldiers, this is Corporal Taylor," said Sergeant Berg. "She volunteered to temporarily come out of civilian duty to teach you Krav Maga. She's the best instructor I've ever known, and I personally invited her here, so please treat her with the same respect you would treat me as your troop leader. I know she looks like a movie star; however, she will put you on your butts quicker than you can say Marilyn Monroe."

There were some laughs and chuckles from the platoon. Sergeant Berg left and Corporal Taylor walked over to the center of the mat in front of the soldiers.

"Shalom platoon!" she said. I'm here for next four weeks to teach you the Sayeret Matkal introduction course on Krav Maga. Sergeant Berg has very high expectations for all of you and he says you are some of the finest young soldiers he's ever seen. So, let's not disappoint him!"

"Before we start, I want two volunteers," she requested.

Everyone raised their hands. She pointed to Yeshua and Mohammed. "You two. Come here; stand in front of me and face each other."

Yeshua muttered under his breath "It's payback time," as they walked onto the mat.

"You both look somewhat familiar. Do I know you?" asked Taylor.

"Yes Corporal," said Mohammed. "You were Private Rabin's nurse five years ago at Soroka Medical Center in Beersheba."

"Yes! You were his friend who sat by his side? And you were the boy who was in a coma after the bus explosion?" she asked them.

"Yes ma'am," responded Yeshua.

"What a small world. I suppose everything does happens for a reason," she said and smiled.

"Okay, we're going to start with a little demonstration for the class. When I say go, I want you... Private Rabin to attack and take down Private..."

"Mohammed. Private Mohammed," said Yeshua.

"Yes, this is a nice soft floor mat," said Taylor. "So no worries about getting hurt too badly. You are all grown up now, no longer boys. Okay, Private Rabin... get him, now... GO!"

Normally calm and easy-going, Yeshua still harbored quite a bit of anger towards Mohammed from the murder dream and desired some retribution. Both friends put up their fists and started circling each other. Yeshua faked a few jabs, and Mohammed pulled back each time. Some of the platoon cheered them on. "Get'em Yeshua, hit him!"

Yeshua saw that Mohammed let his left fist down a few inches, exposing his face. He jabbed him with his left fist a few more times, trying to get him distracted and then wound up a punch with his right fist. Instead of landing the blow, Mohammed quickly blocked with his left hand. Yeshua then directly lunged at him in a tackle move, but Mohammed quickly sidestepped him and lifted his knee up into Yeshua's abdomen as he charged forward. Yeshua fell to the ground wincing and holding his stomach in pain.

"Well done, Private Mohammed," said Corporal Taylor. "Do you already know Krav Maga?"

"Well, not really. I've watched a lot of YouTube videos," said Mohammed.

"Get up soldier," she said to Yeshua. She lent down slightly and offered her right hand. Yeshua grabbed her hand, and she helped pull him up to a standing position.

"Are you okay?" she asked.

"Yes ma'am," Yeshua said and then he slowly walked back to the line of soldiers standing in attention.

"One of the most important principles of Krav Maga, more than anything… is to avoid confrontation," she said. "You should do everything you can to prevent a situation from escalating. Once, however, when you determine that violence is inevitable… you need to master the quickest possible way to disable your opponent."

"When Private Rabin tried to tackle Private Mohammed, he handled the situation perfectly. He blocked his punch and then quickly countered with a knee to the stomach. He delivered a strike that incapacitated his attacker. In Krav Maga, your body becomes a lethal weapon. You will learn how to outsmart your enemies and simultaneously attack and defend yourselves during a conflict. This is not martial arts training. There are no scored contests here. This is real world fighting, sometimes to the death. Do you understand, platoon?"

"Yes, Corporal!" said everyone in unison.

"Does anyone know who the founder of Krav Maga is?" asked Taylor.

Private Richter raised his hand. Taylor nodded at him.

"Imi Lichtenfeld, Ma'am," said Richter.

"That's right," said Taylor. "His name was Imi Lichtenfeld. He grew up in Slovakia in the early 1900's and was a highly accomplished and skilled boxer and wrestler. His father was the chief police inspector there and owned the gym where Imi trained. During that time fascism and anti-Semitism worsened and Imi and his Jewish boxer friends teamed up to defend their neighborhoods against violent gangs and mobs. They developed a special method of street fighting based on self-defense in life threatening situations.

Fortunately, Imi escaped the Nazis and got on the last immigrant boat out of central Europe. Through a series of incredible misadventures, he eventually reached British Occupied Palestine in 1942, where he was recruited by the Haganah and Palmach to train Jewish fighters. In 1948 Israel and the IDF were formed and Imi was promoted to be the Chief Instructor for Physical Fitness and Krav Maga. Since then, hundreds of thousands of Israeli soldiers and police have been instructed in defending themselves during hand to hand combat. My teacher was taught by personally by Imi... and now, I have the honor of teaching you. Any questions so far?"

There was silence.

"Over the next few weeks, we will focus on advanced skills such as strikes, takedowns and groundwork," continued Taylor. "You will all become specialists in defense against attackers holding knives, sticks, and guns. Also, we will work on your strength, endurance and conditioning. Today, we are going to start with a warm up run around the base. So let's go!"

Corporal Taylor opened the door to the barracks and quickly ran outside. The platoon followed her as she ran to the south perimeter fence and she then turned and headed west. The platoon followed her single file. After a half a mile of running, Yeshua's right ear started to high-pitch buzz and he grabbed his ear in pain. Mohammed was running behind him and stopped immediately. A few of the other soldiers slowed down and stopped running too. They were on the western perimeter of the base along the fence. On the other side of the fence was a vast field of sand dunes and just beyond the dunes was the Mediterranean Ocean.

"Oh no!" said Mohammed. "What's going on?" He looked scared.

Corporal Taylor stopped running and turned around when she heard Mohammed's voice.

"Excuse me soldiers. Did I say to stop running?" she said in a very irritated way.

"I'm sorry," said Mohammed. "Something very bad is about to happen."

At that exact moment, the base's emergency warning system turned on and activated. Loud sirens blasted and red lights started flashing all over the place.

"What the…" said Corporal Taylor.

Just then, streams of incoming missiles flew overhead from the west and into the base. A few landed around the main barracks and huge explosions rattled nearby. Smoke billowed up into the sky. More missiles flew towards the base, their contrails streaking behind them.

"Take cover! There!" yelled the Corporal. There was an old underground bunker entrance connected to a network of defensive trenches about forty yards away from the fence. Above the platoon, two AH-64 Apache helicopters flew towards the west in the direction of the incoming missile fire.

"Go! GO!" screamed Taylor as the entire platoon ran in the direction of the trenches. Another missile landed just on the other side of the fence in the sand dunes, and a huge explosion shook the ground. Sand and rocks flew everywhere and pelted the soldiers as they ran.

As they reached the trenches, another barrage of missiles reached the base. Scattered explosions rocked the entire area. Huge fires rose from several of the larger buildings. Yeshua looked towards the barracks and saw someone running out from a door on fire. There were some soldiers on the ground, and he wasn't sure if they were dead or unconscious.

The entire platoon jumped in the trenches.

"What the freak is going on?" said Private Cohen. "Who is shooting at us?"

"It must be a gun boat off the shore," said Mohammed. "There's no way they could be launching this many missiles from the ground."

"Why isn't our Iron Dome shooting them down?" asked Corporal Taylor.

"Well, apparently the Iranians have some advanced radar jamming technology," said Private Shimon. "We've been playing cat and mouse with them."

Private Nowak started screaming in pain with his back against the wall of the trench and was holding his right leg. "My leg... I think it's broken!" he yelled.

"Ummmm. Corporal Taylor," said Private Ivanov. "We have a problem."

A few more missiles flew over the platoon and exploded in the middle of the base.

"We sure do have some big problems. What's up?" asked Taylor.

"Look right there," said Ivanov. She pointed over the trench just to the west.

"Oh my God," said Private Cohen as he looked at what Ivanov was pointing too.

Everyone peeked their heads over the edge of the trench, except for Nowak. Right in front of them was an unexploded missile that had landed just a few feet away. It was broken in half with its sharp point partially burrowed in the ground. Some of its electronics were exposed, and there were small bolts of electricity sparking from the crack in the bomb.

"Gosh, I really dislike bombs," said Yeshua.

"What is it with you and all these bombs?" asked Corporal Taylor. "They told me you diffused a bomb at the satellite station. Is that true? That you have some kind of gift?"

"Yes. I guess I do," answered Yeshua.

"Then get up there and see if you can deactivate that bomb. Or we might all die here today," said Taylor.

Overhead, two more missiles flew nearby and exploded in huge fireballs as they landed, rocking the entire trench. Dirt crumbled from the sides of the tunnel. Yeshua looked at one of the massive explosions and thought he could see a giant demonic figure unravel its contorted body into the blue sky as fire and smoke.

"Okay. I'll do my best," said Yeshua as he pulled his body up and over the trench into the dirt. The missile was just a few yards away.

Yeshua heard a loud noise overhead and looked up. He saw two Israeli F-15 fighter jets approaching the base from the east and flying quickly towards the west. They both launched missiles in the direction of the Mediterranean.

Yeshua then diverted his attention downward as he got close as he could to the malfunctioning missile on the ground. He could see the open electronic case on the side of the bomb. There were many wires sticking out from the circuit boards.

He went to place his hand closer to bomb and then he heard a huge explosion above. Yeshua looked up in disbelief. One of the fighter jets had just been hit by an incoming missile. The pilot had ejected and was far up in the air in his open parachute. The fiery debris from the plane started to shower down towards the base, directly above Yeshua and his platoon.

"Ok. Not much time left. We got this," said Yeshua to himself softly. He stepped closer to the unexploded bomb and kneeled down. Sparks shot out from the electronics. He placed his left hand next to the wires coming from the complex looking circuit boards. His right ear buzzed loudly. He then placed his hand inside the cracked missile. His left ear started buzzing. He looked inside the bomb and saw a large battery pack connected to the circuitry. He placed his hand over the battery pack and his left ear buzzed even more loudly.

"I got you," said Yeshua. He unplugged the battery back. As he pulled the wires, electricity shot through his body. Bolts of white lightning streaked up his left arm and went into his chest. He fell backwards and lost consciousness.

"Did you see that?" screamed Mohammed from inside the nearby trench. "He just got electrocuted!"

Some of the debris from the exploded plane started to come crashing down around the platoon. Mohammed looked up and saw one of the plane's engines heading directly towards Yeshua's flaccid body.

"Oh Jesus!" said Mohammed. He jumped out of the trench and quickly ran over to Yeshua. As he grabbed him by the arms, he felt strong electrical shocks jump into his own body. He almost passed out, but he fought through the intense energy and pulled Yeshua's body back towards the trench with all his might. The huge engine crashed exactly on the spot where Yeshua had been lying.

Within the trench, the soldiers in the platoon grabbed Yeshua's motionless body from Mohammed with their outstretched hands and brought him down carefully to the bottom of the floor. Mohammed jumped back down into the trench as more pieces of the destroyed plane landed all around them.

Private Ivanov knelt down to Yeshua's body and felt his neck.

"He's got no pulse!" she yelled. "We need to do CPR."

Mohammed started doing chest compressions, and Ivanov did the rescue breaths.

Above, a huge part of the blown up airplane's wing was falling directly towards the platoon. It was moments from hitting all the soldiers in the trench.

Mohammed looked up in the sky while he was pounding on his best friend's chest. The broken wing was about to directly land on them and likely kill them all. In the chaos, in between compressions... Mohammed saw Corporal Taylor put her hands up into the air and make a triangle with her two thumbs and index fingers. She closed her eyes.

The wing shattered in a million pieces directly above the platoon. Yeshua suddenly sat up and took a huge, deep breath.

"Private Ivanov... ummm...were you just kissing me?" asked Yeshua.

"You just died, my friend," said Mohammed. "You got electrocuted; we did CPR and brought you back. Are you okay?"

"I'm fine. Never been better," Yeshua said calmly.. "Did the bomb go off? I can't seem to remember everything," he asked. The entire platoon stared at Yeshua in amazement.

"Yes! You disarmed the bomb Private Rabin!" said a grinning Corporal Taylor. "You saved us all! Thank God."

Yeshua turned to Mohammed. "Thank you for saving my life, again."

"I haven't heard any explosions for a while," said Private Cohen. "Maybe it's safe to come out from the trench."

"I believe it is," stated Yeshua. The entire platoon climbed out from the ground. All around them looked like a scene from an armageddon movie. The shattered remains of the exploded airplane littered the surrounding area. To the east, the base had been badly decimated by the missile attacks. Several of the buildings were either completely destroyed or on fire. All the base's sirens and alarms turned off as the platoon walked back towards their barracks. Privates Avraham and Richter helped Nowak walk due to his broken leg.

There were firefighters throughout the base holding long hoses attempting to put out the multiple fires. Standing in front of the soldiers' destroyed barracks stood Sergeant Berg and Lieutenant Colonel Eliora. They looked very sad, as the entire barracked had collapsed.

Mohammed silently walked up behind the Sergeant and the Lieutenant Colonel.

"Private Mohammed here reporting for duty!" he said loudly.

Berg and Eliora turned around and immediately smiled. "You are all alive! We thought your entire platoon perished in the barracks when the missiles hit. "Thank God!" said the Lieutenant Colonel.

Corporal Taylor walked up to Berg and Eliora. "What happened? Why didn't the Iron Dome stop this?" she asked.

"There was a hijacked Turkish registered boat off the coast that was disguised as a fishing vessel," replied Eliora. "Apparently it was armed to the teeth with Iranian guided missiles, and somehow they jammed our defensive systems, again. We're not sure if they were Hamas, Hezbollah, Syrians or Iranians."

"How many casualties? There must have been at least twenty direct missiles hits," asked Mohammed.

"Luckily none," said Berg. "Miraculously no one was killed. Just heavy damage to the base and one lost fighter jet. There's about 30 wounded, maybe more. Speaking of wounded, get Private Nowak to the infirmary over there." He pointed to the hospital building to the north of the barracks. "Is there anyone else in the platoon injured?"

"Well, Private Rabin got electrocuted disarming an unexploded missile. We had to do CPR," said Mohammed.

"What? Really?" said Berg. He looked at Yeshua.

"Are you okay? Do you need the see the medic?" asked Berg.

"I'm fine," said Yeshua. "I actually feel better than ever, Sir."

"Well, you sure do have some amazing bomb karma, soldier," joked Berg.

"Corporal Taylor, please stay here for a full debriefing," said Eliora. "The rest of you report to the mess hall until further notice."

"Yes, Lieutenant Colonel!" said the rest of the platoon. They all walked over to the cafeteria building.

The mess hall was full of soldiers. The platoon walked over to the cafeteria line and got some unappetizing looking food. Yeshua and Mohammed sat down next to each other.

"I guess your secret is out," said Mohammed. "Everyone knows about your special powers now."

"I guess so. I wonder why I was given these gifts in this lifetime. Why couldn't I just had an easier life and reincarnated as a plastic surgeon or a movie star," joked Yeshua.

"In each lifetime, you have a purpose and a destiny to fulfill," replied Mohammed. "Your fate is predetermined."

"So what about free-will?" asked Yeshua. "If everything happens for a reason, do we actually get to make choices or are they already made for us? Do we get to choose what we do or is it just an illusion of choice?"

"It may seem like free-will, however... every decision you make is already determined by all the events and experiences of your past," replied Mohammed.

"That's very deep," said Yeshua. "I always enjoy our conversations. So... what do you think your purpose is in this lifetime?"

"Well, for one... I'm trying to make up for murdering you in Egypt over 4,000 years ago. What was the name I called you when we met by Great Pyramid, again?" asked Mohammed.

"Kawab. You said my name was Kawab," responded Yeshua.

"Oh... and I forgot to ask you," said Mohammed. "When you got electrocuted and passed out, did you remember anything?"

"Yes! Now that you ask I do remember," said Yeshua. "I remember all of it. When I removed the battery pack, electricity surged through my whole body. I passed out and everything went black. Next thing I knew, I was on a huge military airplane high up in the sky. I was alone. There was a door open and I looked down. Everyone in the platoon had already jumped out of the airplane with their parachutes. I was wearing full gear except my parachute was next to me on the ground. I went to put my parachute on, and suddenly I was pushed out of the airplane. I started free falling and looked down. Far below I could see the fortress of Masada and to the south the Negev desert. I thought to myself I must be dreaming, as I've had so many other dreams where I'm falling to my inevitable death. As I got closer to the ground, I decided I would try to fly. I figured since I was in a dream, why not fly? I put my thumbs and index fingers together and concentrated... then I started to fly!"

"Wait a sec!" said Mohammed. "You put your hands together and made a triangle, like this?"

Mohammed simulated with his hands the position Yeshua described.

"Yes, just like that. Like the Illuminati symbol," said Yeshua.

"Oh my gosh. While we were doing CPR on you, Corporal Taylor made that same symbol with her hands, then mysteriously a bunch of airplane debris that was just about to hit us disintegrated into thin air," said Mohammed.

"Whoa, do you think she has superhero powers too?" asked Yeshua.

"Maybe. Or just another of many synchronicities," said Mohammed. "Okay, so what happened after you started flying in your dream?"

"Oh yeah. So I stayed flying south, towards the town of Eilat, on the Red Sea. It was an incredible feeling, to be flying! As I got closer to Eilat I saw something far in the distance. There was a great plume of smoke, like you would see from a volcano," said Yeshua.

"Really?" said a surprised Mohammed. "There's no active volcanoes in the Middle East. Where was it coming from?"

"I saw it far to the south, on the east side of Red Sea. Then I woke up. Private Ivanov was kissing me!" said Yeshua.

"She wasn't kissing you silly! She was doing CPR. Are you sure you saw the volcano on the east side of the Red Sea?" asked Mohammed.

"Yes. Why?" asked Yeshua.

"Because that's Saudi Arabia," said Mohammed.

The two soldiers finished their food and walked over to throw out their trash and put up their trays.

"I have an idea," said Mohammed. "Follow me."

They left the cafeteria building and walked over to the adjacent recreation hall. There were several Internet kiosks along the back wall. One was empty and the two best friends pulled up chairs in front of the unoccupied terminal.

"Okay, type into Google Pharaoh Khufu," said Mohammed. Yeshua typed in the words and hit return.

"Great! Now click on that first Wikipedia entry on Khufu. Let's read that," requested Mohammed.

"Khufu... known to the Greeks as Cheops, was an ancient Egyptian monarch, who ruled during the Fourth Dynasty in the first half of the Old Kingdom period (26th century BCE). Khufu was the second ruler of the fourth dynasty; he followed his possible father, King Sneferu, on the throne. He is generally accepted as having commissioned the Great Pyramid of Giza, one of the Seven Wonders of the Ancient World, but many other aspects of his reign are rather poorly documented," read Yeshua.

"Hmm. Well, that doesn't make any sense. If Cheops or Khufu built the Great Pyramid, why were all three Pyramids already there in my dream?" asked Yeshua.

"Well perhaps Khufu didn't build it. Maybe it was already there and they renovated it for his tomb," replied Mohammed.

"Oh my. So could all the Egyptologists be wrong? Perhaps the Pyramids are way older than they are saying. Maybe even the Sphinx. And if so... who built them?" said a very perplexed looking Yeshua.

"I don't know, although maybe we can find out somehow," said Mohammed as he winked and gestured towards Yeshua's Shofar.

"So, your name was Kawab in your dream. Let's look more in the Wikipedia entry for Khufu's descendants. Scroll down a bit," said Mohammed. "Okay, there… oh my gosh, it says Kawab! Click on that link and let's read it."

Yeshua read aloud "Kawab was the eldest son of Pharaoh Khufu and Meritites and half-brother of Pharaohs Djedefre and Khafre. He was possibly born during the reign of his grandfather Sneferu. Kawab died during the reign of his father, so the next ruler was Djedefre, who married his widow Hetepheres II. It used to be believed that Djedefre had Kawab murdered, since Djedefre was buried in Abu Rawash, instead of Giza, which was the custom."

"Murdered? That's what happened in your dream!" said Mohammed. "So, I apparently was Djedefre, your younger half brother. You were going to become Pharaoh and I killed you to take the over throne. Sheesh. I'm really sorry about that. Ok, click on the Djedefre link now."

Yeshua had an expression of disbelief after he clicked the button. On the screen was an image of a statue of the head of Pharaoh Djedefre from the Louvre Museum in Paris.

"Oh my God," said Yeshua. "That's you. You look exactly like him, Mohammed. How is this even possible? Ok, let me read what it says… Djedefre was an ancient Egyptian king of the 4th dynasty during the Old Kingdom. He is well known under his Hellenized name form Ratoises. Djedefre was the son and immediate throne successor of Khufu, the builder of the Great Pyramid of Giza; his mother is not known for sure. He was the king who introduced the royal title Sa-Rê (meaning "Son of Ra") and the first to connect his cartouche name with the sun god Ra."

"Whoaaa," said Mohammed. "This goes way down the rabbit hole. It says here that he was the first Pharaoh to connect with the sun god Ra."

"Okay, why is that important?" asked Yeshua. "What does that have to do with anything? And it seems we've perhaps solved a 4,000 thousand year old murder mystery."

"Okay, this is incredible," said Mohammed. "So for thousands of years, the Egyptians worshiped many gods. They had a pantheon of holy deities, like the Greeks and the Romans later. Ra was the God that signifies the Sun. It says Djedefre declared himself the son of Ra. Now, hundreds of years later after his death, another Pharaoh named Akhenaten changed the entire country's religion to believe in only one God. That God was Ra, also called Aten. And around this time the Jews were slaves in Egypt. They believed in one supreme Creator God as well."

"So, you are saying this is all connected?" asked Yeshua. "Khufu, Kawab, Djedefre, Akhenaten, God and the Jews are all connected?"

"Yes. It is all connected. It must be. Everything happens for a reason," said Mohammed. "Otherwise, it wouldn't have been in your dream. Yeshua, I think you may be some kind of Prophet."

Yeshua just stared at Mohammed in silence for a few moments.

Mohammed typed something on the keyboard, and a map came up. It was a map of the Middle East.

"Yeshua, here's a map of the Red Sea. Can you point to me where you think you saw that volcano?" asked Mohammed.

"Sure. I think it was right about there," said Yeshua. He pointed to a place just inland about halfway down the Red Sea in Saudi Arabia.

"That's the mountain called Jabal al-Lawz," said Mohammed. "That's also the area called the land of Midian from your Torah Holy Book."

"Wait a sec, isn't that where Moses saw God come to him as the burning bush?" asked Yeshua.

"Same exact place," said Mohammed. "I'd like to go there and check out that mountain."

"But it's in Saudi Arabia," said Yeshua. "It's not like we can just fly there."

"Hmmm. Maybe we can. Not right now, but maybe later when the time is right," said Mohammed.

"Ok, now I need to do something really important," said Yeshua. "Will you come with me?"

"Will we end up in jail?" asked Mohammed.

"No. I really doubt it. Let's go," said Yeshua.

They left the recreational building and walked back to what used to be their barracks. The entire structure was burned and collapsed. Some of the fallen walls still smoldered from the recent fires.

Yeshua stepped over the perimeter into the charred remains of what was left of the barracks. He put his hands into a heap of debris and pulled out his Shofar. He held it up in the air. "Got it!"

"What are you two doing here?" yelled Lieutenant Colonel Eliora. "This area is restricted. Now report to the transportation center immediately. Your entire platoon has been reassigned to another base to complete your training."

CHAPTER 17

HABAHADIM

IDF training center, Negev Desert
Four weeks later

"Okay, platoon... we have a special mission today," said Sergeant Berg. "Our intelligence reports some newly built tunnels that go from Gaza under the fence into Israel near Kerem Shalom. Under cover from the border rioting, Hamas has almost completed the tunnel, and they are about to use it for a massive suicide attack on the surrounding villages."

Berg showed a high-resolution satellite map on the large AV screen to the fully geared troops in the main helicopter hanger. He pointed to the most southern part of Gaza, near the Egyptian border.

"We are going to stealth parachute at night and dig down into the entrance here," said Berg, pointing with his laser pointer to spot in an open field just by the 1950 Armistice line.

"We need to avoid detection by the Hamas scouts and spies, so silence is key," continued Berg. "Avoid live fire at all costs and focus on the prime directive, which is to blow up this tunnel. You've all had two days to study the protocols and contingency plans, so I want no mistakes. And today, we have a special helper that will assist us."

A door opened to the hanger and Corporal Taylor appeared. She started to walk towards the platoon and another figure appeared behind her. It was a robot. It looked very much like the male cyborg from the Terminator movie, except it was all black instead of silver metallic. Its face had a skeletal appearance and its eyes looked like real human eyes. It wore an elaborate large black metal backpack. He walked with normal strides over to the platoon and then stopped next to Sergeant Berg.

"Whoa! Full metal jacket. It's hammer time!" said Private Richter.

"This is Gurion," said Sergeant Berg. "He's a prototype class one robot soldier, top secret. We are still working on his neural network, and we have a whole team of programmers and scientists controlling his actions. His AI isn't perfected yet, so for now he's just a puppet controlled via Wi-Fi by headquarters. He's designed to help us dig into the ground down to the Hamas tunnel, and then he will follow us and carry the explosives in his pack. He is not programmed for active combat yet."

"Any questions?" said Berg.

There was silence.

"Ok, let's roll. The helicopter is outside waiting for us. Keep your telecoms on active mode and communicate only when absolutely necessary," said Berg.

Everyone in the platoon put on their combat helmets and then they left the huge hanger and walked outside to the helipad. It was nighttime, and sky was full of low-lying clouds. The helicopter was a brand new Boeing CH-47 Chinook tandem-rotor beauty. Both rotors were spinning, and Yeshua was impressed at how quiet it was. Everyone boarded through the front door by the main cockpit. Yeshua looked into the cockpit and saw a complex array of digital controls. Behind him, Gurion walked up the portable steps and into the helicopter effortlessly. Berg sat down in the pilot's seat and Taylor sat in the co-pilot's seat.

Inside, the platoon sat down in their seats and strapped in. Next to each seat was a standard military parachute and a black X95 machine gun.

"Chinook Eighteen ready for take off," said Sergeant Berg in the telecom. He was talking to air traffic control. "Awaiting clearance, check."

"Clearance granted," responded a woman's voice. "Good luck, Sergeant."

The helicopter pulled up and lifted off the ground. It did a one eighty turn and flew towards the northwest. Yeshua looked down at the massive military base in the desert from above; then they broke through the clouds. The sky was full of millions of stars, and the outline of the Milky Way galaxy was fully visible. It was new moon, and the shadow of the giant ball was visible as dark round space obscuring the stars behind it.

After approximately twenty minutes Sergeant Berg spoke through the telecom. "We're almost at our drop point. Get your parachutes on and get ready!" Everyone stood up and followed his orders.

The helicopter stopped moving westward and hovered. Sergeant Berg came out from the cockpit and put on his parachute. Taylor took over the main controls. Berg opened the main door, and strong winds blew into the cabin. He gave the troops a thumbs up and everyone thumb upped him back and got in a single file line holding their Tavor X95 machine guns. They all had silencers on the muzzles of their guns. Gurion was the last in line, and he held a large metal shovel.

"Okay. Let's do this!" said Berg. He pointed out the door. "Put on your night vision goggles before you jump." Private Ivanov jumped first, then Shimon. The rest of the platoon followed. Gurion walked up to the open door, then jumped out without hesitation, and Berg followed him.

Each soldier's parachute opened and they all glided downwards, through the dark clouds. Once past the clouds, Berg directed everyone to the target landing point using a laser pointer. As Yeshua parachuted down, he saw thousands of the tiny glowing orbs flying around him through his night vision goggles. One by one, all the troops landed very close to each other in a barren field just an arrow shot from the security fence.

Everyone gathered their parachutes and repackaged them, including Gurion. Berg pointed down to a spot in the ground, and then Gurion walked over with his shovel. At seemingly lightning speed, the cyborg robot shoveled the sand and dirt. After a few minutes, he was down about four feet. The rest of the platoon pushed the huge amount of loose dirt away from the enlarging hole in the ground. Gurion then jumped into the deep hole and continued digging.

After a few more minutes, the dirt collapsed under Gurion as he shoveled, and he fell into the tunnel below.

"We're in!" said Berg quietly on his telecom. "Now follow me! Be ready to disable any hostiles." Berg climbed down the hole and waited for the rest of the nine soldiers to follow him. The tunnel was dark and narrow. Along the floor were two small bands of metal that looked like mini railroad tracks. Just to the east was the end of the tunnel, and there was a small cart on the tracks full of dirt and stones.

Berg pointed to the west and gave a thumbs up. He starting walking slowly with his gun pointed forward and the platoon followed him. After approximately fifty feet, the tunnel opened up into a larger space and two other tunnels appeared to the north and the south.

"I don't remember there being four crossing tunnels on the map," said Private Shimon quietly on the telecom.

"Okay. We have a change in plan. Turn on your heat sensors on your goggles. Shoot anything that moves down here," said Berg. He walked over to Gurion and opened the bottom of his large black backpack. He grabbed some small rectangular objects with timers on them and started handing them out to the platoon. They were the bombs that were going to be detonated to blow up the tunnel.

"Avraham, Yehuda, Shimon... you go that way forty yards and place the charges then come back and get out," said Berg as he pointed to the north.

"Mohammed, Rabin, Cohen... you go that way and do the same," said Berg. He pointed to the south.

"Ivanov, Richter, Shapiro... you come with me, we are going that way westward down the main passage," commanded Berg.

"Gurion, you stay here and guard the tunnel," Berg said to the robot. Gurion nodded his head and held his shovel up in the air in response.

The three groups went their separate ways. Yeshua led the way down the south tunnel, gun pointed forward. In his goggles, a few of the tiny glowing orbs floated around him.

"Yeshua, is your right ear buzzing?" asked Cohen.

"No, it's not. I think we are safe," replied Yeshua.

After a minute of slowly walking down the dark tunnel, they came to a closed door.

"Sergeant Berg. Copy. We've come to a closed door. What are we supposed to do now?" said Mohammed quietly in the telecom. "Do we open the door?"

There was no response. Silence.

"Sergeant Berg. Copy. Are you there?" said Cohen.

Still, no response.

"We haven't gone forty yards yet," said Yeshua. "That was the order, go forty yards and place the bombs. So that means we have to go on the other side of this door."

"Okay," said Mohammed. "Okay," said Cohen.

"Mohammed, grab the door handle and slowly open the door," commanded Yeshua. "I'll look inside as you open it."

Mohammed followed his order and grabbed and turned the door handle silently. He pulled the door open a crack while Yeshua peered inside.

The room was dark. Yeshua could see several bunk beds lining walls inside with his night vision goggles. Sleeping in the beds were about a dozen young children.

"There's a bunch of kids inside, sleeping," said Yeshua. "Oy Vey! What should we do?"

"The orders were to place the bombs and leave," said Cohen. "It's a tough call, but I think we should just place our bombs here and go back. I don't think we should go through that room."

"But there's kids in there!" said Yeshua. "I'm not killing children."

Just after Yeshua said that, a door in the back of the room with the beds burst open and the overhead lights turned on. The light blinded Yeshua's vision. Two masked militants with guns came into the room and starting shooting at Yeshua, Mohammed and Cohen through the slightly open door. They all took multiple bullets to the head, chest and abdomen.

"Dammit!" said Cohen as he took off his virtual reality headgear. "Yeshua, you just got us killed!" he yelled.

Yeshua took off his headgear as well in the large, high-tech simulation room. The rest of the platoon was there. Each soldier stood on their own virtual treadmill and wore advanced haptic sensory gloves and space age looking VR headsets.

"I'm not killing children with bombs," said Yeshua.

The rest of the soldiers removed their headgear and looked at Yeshua.

Sergeant Berg walked into the simulation room from the control station. "Okay, platoon, the mission is over," he said. "Yeshua, you put your men in jeopardy when you hesitated in the tunnel. In real life, you would all be dead."

"I'm sorry Sir," said Yeshua. "I'm not going to murder kids."

"Okay, platoon. Let's wrap it up," said Berg. "You all have Krav Maga training in the gymnasium in thirty minutes."

Everyone de-geared and left the huge newly built technology center and walked towards the massive athletic center next door.

"I would not have killed those kids either," said Mohammed to Yeshua as they walked outside. "We could have just closed the door and turned around."

"It's such a catch twenty-two, Mohammed. "The Palestinians hate us, and then when we kill them when we are attacked or pre-emptively in defense… they hate us even more. There's no solution. What ever happened to the Golden Rule? That which is hateful to you do not do to others?" said Yeshua.

"For every problem there is a solution," said Mohammed.

"What solution? They are all caged in there like the Jews were in the Warsaw Ghetto. Like animals. Are we no better than the Nazis?" said a very upset Yeshua.

"We are not the Nazis. Not even close," said Mohammed. "We are not trying to exterminate the

Palestinians. Actually, it's them that want to exterminate us. They don't even recognize our right to exist. We are just defending ourselves. It's their fault they are in this situation, they voted in terrorists as their leaders and use innocent women and children as shields."

"Yes, but in their eyes... we stole their land," said Yeshua. "Just like the United States settlers did to the native Americans. It's almost the same thing... we forcibly kicked them out of their land and put them in reservations, just like the Americans did."

"Wow, I never thought of it like that before," said Mohammed. "I think we need to find some way to have peace. One day. There must be a way."

"I hope so," said Yeshua. "Without having to blow up children. I'm so tired of hate, death and wars."

The platoon reached the athletic center and entered through the reinforced glass doors. They walked up the spiral stairs in the large modern lobby and arrived at the new Krav Maga center.

Inside their assigned room Corporal Taylor was waiting for them. Standing next to her was... Gurion.

"He's actually real!" said Shimon. "Wow, I thought he was just a VR simulation."

Gurion looked exactly as he did during the training simulation, except he did not have the backpack. He turned his head to look at the platoon as they walked through the door. The expression on Mohammed's face was priceless as he walked into the room and looked at the robot.

"Yes, he's real. Very real," said Taylor. "This model is a sparring bot with full neural network artificial intelligence. He's basically a black belt in Krav Maga. However, he's purposefully designed not to be lethal in training mode."

"So he is lethal in not training mode?" asked Yeshua.

"We haven't put the bots in real combat situations yet," said Taylor. "We're still programming their skillset. They all seem to learn from each other's experiences and better themselves."

"Bots? There's more than just one?" asked Shimon.

"We've made ten. A full minion. Each one has a special purpose," said Taylor. "This one, Gurion... is a Krav Expert. You all have excelled in your Krav training, so you all are going to help us today by sparring with him and make him better. There's only so much it can learn from programming. We need more real world situations now."

Taylor walked over to the table behind her and grabbed some boxing gloves and pads. She walked over to Gurion and placed them carefully on his hands, arms and knees. She then grabbed some soft shoe pads from the table and stood in front of Gurion. The robot lifted his leg up and Taylor slipped the pad onto his foot, then the other foot.

"Ok, great. Now I need a volunteer," said Taylor.

Richter was the only one to raise his hand.

"Ah Private Richter, you are very brave. Are you feeling lucky today?" said Taylor with devious smile.

"Yes, Ma'am. I'm feeling very lucky," said Richter.

"Ok, your job is to put Gurion on the ground and disable him," said Taylor. "Do you accept the challenge?"

"Yes," said Richter.

"Okay. Now, go!" said Taylor.

Richter quickly moved towards Gurion and the robot immediately went into a defensive position with its padded fists up. Richter did a leg sweep and tried to trip up the cyborg. Gurion leaped up into the air, completely avoiding the attack. Richter then spun three sixty and did a leaping kick into the robot's chest and scored a direct hit. Gurion stumbled backwards and hit its back against the padded wall behind him. Some of the platoon started to cheer.

Richter then did a few jab punch combinations and the robot blocked all them with lightning speed. Then, Richter knee'd him hard in between the legs, and there was a loud metallic clunk sound. Richter backed off and held his knee in pain.

"Uggghhhhh. That hurt bad." said Richter.

"Ahh, I guess we should have put some pads on that area too," said Taylor. "Okay, Mohammed. You are next."

"What. Me?" said Mohammed.

"Yes, you soldier. Take this robot down, now!" yelled Taylor.

Mohammed approached Gurion. The robot walked out from the wall towards Mohammed and put its fists up into the defensive position. Mohammed started to circle the robot and jab with his left hand. The robot turned with

Mohammed and blocked each jab, and then Mohammed laid in some hard punches. Each time, the robot blocked with his padded fists.

"He's very good, Corporal Taylor. Very fast," said Mohammed. "Your programmers should be proud of themselves."

Mohammed then circled faster around Gurion and quickly got behind him. He placed him in a headlock, then swept his right leg under the robot and tripped him. They both fell down to the ground, Mohammed's body on top of Gurion.

"Well done, Private Mohammed!" said Taylor.

Mohammed got off the floor and helped the robot up back into the standing position.

"Yes, well done," said Lieutenant Colonel Eliora from the open door in the back of the room.

All the soldiers stood in full attention when they saw Eliora.

"At ease soldiers," said the Lieutenant Colonel. "I see you all have got to meet Gurion. Someday, we will have an army of these robot soldiers. Men and women will no longer die in wars."

She paused and stared into space, almost seemingly looking into the future with her mind.

"Privates Rabin and Mohammed, come with me please," said Eliora.

Yeshua looked at Mohammed who looked back at him. They then left the room with Eliora in silence.

So many thoughts went through Yeshua's consciousness as they followed Eliora out of the athletic building and towards the main command and control center. He decided to say nothing. Mohammed looked very concerned, as if they had done something wrong.

The new command center had been recently finished. It was a massive brick building with many rows of small glass windows.

They entered the main lobby and passed through security. There were three elevators behind the front desk. Yeshua and Mohammed followed Eliora over to the elevators where she pushed the button on the wall. The door of the middle elevator opened, and the three entered. Once, inside she pressed the third floor button. The elevator went down instead of up. It went down three floors, and the door opened. There was a long hallway ahead with marble floors and white walls.

Eliora led the Yeshua and Mohammed down the hallway to the metallic door at the end. She opened the door and they entered the room inside. Sitting behind a ancient looking wooden desk sat General Geller. He motioned Yeshua and Mohammed to sit down in the two chairs on the other side of his desk. Lieutenant Colonel Eliora stood by the door.

"Soldiers, it's been quite some time since we first met on the beach of Ashkelon. I've been following you two very carefully. What do you think of our new training facilities here at Ir Habahadim?" asked the General.

"They are first class Sir," said Mohammed.

"So, I'm just going to get to the point here," said Geller. "We just don't think you two are cut out for Sayeret Matkal Special Forces."

Mohammed and Yeshua exchanged surprised glances.

"We understand both of you have some special skills, and those skills can be applied in a more utilitarian way. I've recommended that you be transferred to the Institute."

"The Institute?" asked Yeshua.

"Yes. The Institute for Intelligence and Special Operations. Also known as Mossad. Effective immediately," said the General.

"But, what about finishing our military training…" said Mohammed.

"Consider your training completed," said the General. "You both have scored off the charts in just about everything. We are very impressed. Son, you even took down the Krav Maga robot… no one has been able to do that. And Yeshua… you have some kind of special intuitive gift we've never seen before. So, don't consider this a demotion from Sayeret, it's actually a promotion. Do you accept?"

"Yes, Sir!" responded Yeshua and Mohammed.

"We've taken care of all the security clearances," said Geller. "And we already have your first mission planned. In three days time, you will escort an Israeli diplomatic contingent with the Americans to Saudi Arabia. Yeshua, you will be on assignment with the security team. If there is any danger present, we understand you will be help mitigate the situation. And Mohammed, you will be undercover as a translator and interpreter. You will help communicate between our diplomats and the Saudi Arabian delegation."

"So, we are going to Riyadh, Sir?" asked Mohammed.

"Yes," said the General. "You will now be transported to the new American Embassy in Jerusalem for a full debriefing with our American colleagues. I'm sorry but there's no time to say goodbye to your friends in your platoon. The Lieutenant Colonel will be going with you as all. You are dismissed."

The General stood up and Yeshua and Mohammed immediately stood up and saluted him. He saluted back. Lieutenant Colonel Eliora opened the door, and the two best friends starting walking out of the room.

"Oh. Just one question," said General Geller, still standing. "Son, why do you carry around that Shofar so much? It's not Yom Kippur or Rosh Hashanah."

"Ahhh," said Yeshua as he turned around to face the General. "It's a very special Shofar. It's my only possession."

Chapter 18

Jerusalem

King David Hotel, Jerusalem
Two days later

"I'm getting really tired of all these endless meetings and debriefings," said Yeshua, sitting in a comfy lounge chair wearing a beige button down short sleeve shirt and brown khaki pants in the opulent green and teal decorated lobby of the King David Hotel.

"Me too," said Mohammed, sitting next to him wearing similar earth-toned attire. "I'd love to explore the city before we go. I've never been here before, and all we've seen is this fancy hotel and the American Embassy."

Lieutenant Colonel Eliora walked up to them wearing some casual civilian clothes. "We are all set to meet back here in the lobby for a shuttle bus departing to the airport at 0800 tomorrow morning. You both have free time the rest of the afternoon and evening, so enjoy some well-deserved time off. And don't get in trouble, okay?" she said.

"Yes, ma'am! I mean yes, Eliora," said Yeshua.

Eliora smiled, left the lobby and walked outside through the main entrance.

"So, how much time do we have?" asked Mohammed.

Yeshua looked down at his watch.

"It's 1530. So we have about five hours till sunset. Where do you want to go?" asked Yeshua.

"Let's go to the Old City. I want to go pray at the Dome of the Rock," said Mohammed.

"Okay, great! I'll go to the Western Wall. I've never been there," said Yeshua as he pulled out a map from his pants pocket of the city and placed it on the table in front of them.

"Here's where we are," said Yeshua and he pointed to the location of the hotel on the map. "And here's the Temple Mount. It will take less than thirty minutes to walk there."

"Fantastic, this is like a dream come true. Let's go!" said Mohammed.

"Wait a sec. I need to go grab something from my room. I'll be back in two minutes," said Yeshua.

"No problem," said Mohammed. "I'll just wait here in this swanky lobby and people watch."

Yeshua came back to the lobby after a few minutes with his Shofar slung around his back. "Let's roll," he said to Mohammed. They both walked out the lobby and turned north on the very busy King David Boulevard. They made a right on Yitzhak Kariv Street that led them through the ancient white stonewalls of the Jaffa Gate and into the Old City.

"Is your ear buzzing?" asked Mohammed. "Is anyone following us?"

"No. Negatory on the buzzing," said Yeshua as they snaked their way through the narrow cobblestone streets filled with street vendors along David Street. After several minutes, they entered the large open Western Wall Plaza after walking through Sha'ar ha-Shalshelet Street along the Jewish Quarter.

"Wow, there it is," said Yeshua. He was in a state of wonderment as he looked at the massive ancient structure in front of him. There were dozens of people along the base of the wall praying. They looked so tiny compared to the two thousand year old sixty-two foot wall made from huge sand-colored ashlar stones.

"This is one of the most holy places in the entire world. I will be walking up the Mughrabi Gate to the Al-Aqsa Mosque and then to the Dome of the Rock," said Mohammed as he pointed the covered wooden raised walkway on the south side of the plaza. "I assume you will be going over to pray by the Wall?"

"Yes. Then I'm thinking about taking a tour of the tunnel that goes along the Wall. I'm so excited!" exclaimed Yeshua.

"Okay. How about this... why don't we meet in an hour and half at the Lion's Gate, on the edge of the Old City just to the north of the Temple Mount?" suggested Mohammed.

"Perfect! Can't wait to hear all about your experience up there." said Yeshua.

"Likewise, my friend," said Mohammed. The two young men fist pumped each other then parted ways. Mohammed walked south towards the entrance to the Mughrabi walkway, and Yeshua walked through security to get to the base of the Western Wall.

"You're not allowed to sound that here," said the security guard to Yeshua as he walked up to the huge wall.

"Huh?" responded Yeshua.

"Your Shofar. Please do not sound that here," declared the young man in uniform.

"Yes Sir," said Yeshua as he kept walking closer towards the base of the Western Wall. Yeshua saw an open spot along the crowd of men standing and praying and walked up to the Wall and stood right next to the huge vertical stones. A man right next to him was wearing all black placed a small white piece of paper into a crack of the stone in front of him and then starting praying.

Yeshua closed his eyes and prayed for a few moments. He prayed for peace. Then, Yeshua put both his hands on the Wall. He felt warmth and energy flow into his body.

Something happened and Yeshua's perspective seemed to dramatically change, eyes still closed. He saw himself from just above his body touching the Wall, and then he quickly flew up into the sky while looking down at himself. He continued to fly upwards away from Jerusalem and soon he was looking at the big blue ball of earth spinning, and then continued to zoom through space and saw the sun and surrounding planets of the solar system. Then he went even faster and was looking at the entire spiral vortex of the Milky Way galaxy. Time and space shifted again and Yeshua was then looking at many galaxies spread in intersecting linked patterns throughout the Universe. Then, massive waves of energy blazed through the interlinked channels of celestial matter. Yeshua thought it looked like groups of neuron cells firing signals within a giant brain.

"Excuse me son, where did you get that Shofar?" said a voice from behind Yeshua.

Yeshua opened his eyes, and in that precise moment of coming back into his body, he completely forgot where he was. He forgot what time it was and what day it was. He even forgot who he was. His consciousness then returned back to normal and he remembered everything up to that moment, his hands still touching the ancient stonewall.

Yeshua turned around and looked at an old man wearing all black except for his large white Tallit prayer shawl standing behind him. He looked very familiar. He had a very long white beard.

"You gave it to me," said Yeshua.

"I did?" he said.

"Yes. Aren't you Rabbi Yohanan? You Bar Mitzvahed me on Masada five years ago," said Yeshua.

"Yes. I am," the old man said. "That's a very special Shofar, young man. Have you sounded the Shofar here in Jerusalem?" he asked.

"No, no yet," responded Yeshua. "I had this dream that I'm supposed to go to one of the gates here and blow it."

"Ah. Yes," said Yohanan. "The Golden Gate. It's on the other side of the Temple Mount."

"Wait a sec," said Yeshua. "How did you know that?"

The Rabbi suddenly stepped away from Yeshua into the now very large crowd of tourists and religious Jews surrounding the Wall. Yeshua walked quickly into the sea of people trying to find the Rabbi to ask him more questions; however, he had completely disappeared.

Yeshua stopped walking and stood there in silence looking at the Israeli Flag flying in the center of plaza for a few moments. Time seemed to be moving in slow motion. Then, he turned his head to the right and saw the gate to the Western Wall Tunnels along the stone-faced buildings just to the north. He walked over to the entrance and bought a ticket to go inside.

Instead of taking the hour and a half guided tour, he decided to just walk inside along the tunnels himself. He made his way through the narrow arched tunnels until he reached a small room. There was a scale model of the how the Great Temple looked before the Romans destroyed it in the year 70 CE. He turned left and walked along the small excavated tunnel supported by iron beams next the colossal Herodian stones that formed the outer base of the Western Wall.

Yeshua came to a larger open area along the tunnel where there was one massive stone at least 45 feet long. There were a few tourists gathered around and he overhead someone say, "This stone weighs almost six hundred tons. Archaeologists say this is one of the largest stones ever moved by man in the ancient world." Yeshua paused and stopped to look at the mammoth stone. He placed his hands on the stone and thought to himself, "How could men without technology move a 600 ton stone? How is that possible?" He tried to imagine hundreds of men, pulling the stone into place. It seemed miraculous that they could do that with just their bare hands and no modern tools.

Yeshua continued down the tight tunnel along the wall. It was almost like a dream. He passed over some large panes of glass covering the floor, exposing some excavations below. It appeared that the wall went down dozens of more feet from the level of the tunnel. This structure was much larger that he had imagined.

Next, he came to an area called Warren's Gate. There was a sign near the wall that read...

Entrance Gate to the Temple Mount

Warren's Gate is one of the four Western Wall entrance gates to the Temple Mount from the Second Temple Period. During the Early Muslim Period the internal space of the gate-passage served as the main synagogue of the Jews in Jerusalem. The synagogue was located here because of its proximity to the Holy of Holies. It was named "The Cave" because of its location under the Temple Mount. Today, the whole passage functions as a large cistern serving visitors to the Temple Mount. The Gate is named after Charles Warren who discovered it in 1867.

Yeshua felt a déjà vu feeling. He got goose bumps on his arms, and his brain tingled as it felt like he had been here in this place before. He continued to walk to the north and came upon another sign. His left ear started to high pitch buzz. He felt almost intoxicated. The sign read...

Holy of Holies Room

You are standing at the point closest to the site of the Holy of Holies on the Temple Mount. According to tradition, this is the place from which the world was created; the place where the binding of Isaac took place

and where Abraham was commanded 'Lay not thy hand upon the lad'; the place where the Tablets of the Covenant written by God on Mount Sinai were kept; the place where prayers are gathered and from where they rise to Heaven. The High Priest would enter the Holy of Holies only once a year on Yom Kippur, to plea for the entire Jewish Nation. Jews from all corners of the globe came to this place during the long 2000 years of exile, to share their sorrows with the Divine Presence, to pray for its return to Zion, and for Jerusalem to renew its days of old. As you stand here at this sacred site, your prayers join an eternal chain of faith and prayer.

Hear our voice, O God our God, spare us and have compassion on us, and accept our prayer in compassion and favor, for You, O God, hear prayers and supplications, and let us not return empty from Your presence our King, for you hear the prayer of Your people Yisrael in compassion.

There were many people sitting in chairs all along the walls and praying. Yeshua sat down in an empty chair and placed his hands on the walls. He cleared his mind and started praying again for peace.

"Yeshua. Can you hear me?" a voice in his head said.

"What? Who is this? Is it God?" asked Yeshua in his mind.

"No, it's not God. It's Mohammed! Can you hear me? I'm in the cave under the Foundation Stone beneath the Dome of the Rock. I just started praying and I thought I would try to telepathically reach out to you. Where are you?" said Mohammed in Yeshua's mind.

"I'm in the Western Wall Tunnel, at the Holy of Holies room. I think I'm directly across from you along the Wall. How are you talking to me?" asked Yeshua.

"I think that Shofar linked our minds together," said Mohammed, telepathically. "When I go into deep prayer, it's like I can leave my body and go into yours. I think I can even see what you are seeing. Are you sitting in a chair in front of some stones in a tunnel supported by beams?"

"Yes. I am," said Yeshua. "Oh my God, how is this possible?"

"I don't know, although everything does happen for a reason. I'm going to head back up and meet you at the Lion's Gate. I have so much more to tell you, my friend," said Mohammed.

"Yes, me too. See you soon," thought Yeshua in his mind. He opened his eyes and got out of the chair and continued north along the tunnel. He passed through The Quarry, the Hasmonean Channel and through the Outdoor Cistern and finally out the exit tunnel back up to surface in the Old City by the Umariya Elementary School along the Via Dolorosa Street in the Muslim Quarter.

While walking towards the Lion's Gate directly to the east, Yeshua overhead a group of about ten visiting American nuns talking amongst each other in the street.

One said, "Did you know, this is the path that Jesus walked to his crucifixion almost two thousand years ago?"

Another said, "Sister Mary, I just learned today that Jesus wasn't Jesus's real name."

"What? Huh?" responded several of the nuns.

"Sister Teresa... how is that possible? He had a different name? Why don't we know about that?" asked Sister Mary

"Yes, it's true. His real name was Yehoshua in Hebrew. He was a Rabbi. Back in the biblical ages, the letter 'J' didn't even exist at that time," responded Sister Teresa.

"Are you serious. I'm shocked! How can that be true?" asked Sister Mary.

"Well, I learned that his name Yehoshua was translated to the name 'Lesous' in Greek, and than later to 'Issues' in Latin, then finally 'Jesus' in English in the 1500s. It's true! Look it up on Google," said Sister Teresa.

"Yehoshua?" said Sister Mary. "You mean Joshua? That's the English translation of Yehoshua. So, we should be praying to a man named Joshua instead of Jesus?"

"Wait a sec, are you saying we worship the only Son of God's wrong name?" asked another nun.

"Sister Lilah," said Sister Mary. "We've had this conversation before... is it possible that we are all children of God?"

Another nun interrupted. "It doesn't matter what his name is or was. God has many names. It's not the name that's important. It the belief and faith in him that's the most important."

"Yes, but what if faith isn't enough by itself?" said Sister Mary. "What if what you actually do in actions in this world to make it a better place is more important? Jesus... I mean Yehoshua, said 'For I was hungered, and ye gave me meat: I was thirsty, and ye gave me drink: I was a stranger, and ye took me in.' and 'I was naked and you clothed me, I was sick and you visited me, I was in prison and you came to me.' Isn't following the example of Yehoshua and selflessly helping the less fortunate a better pathway to knowing God rather than just belief alone?"

"What are you talking about?" said sister Teresa. "Are you saying we should all attempt to be more like Jesus? That we can each become like Jesus? Like the Buddhists think they can all become enlightened like Buddha?"

"Well, Sister," said Mary. "I do think the world would be a much better place if we all did our best to act more like Jesus..."

"I think she's right," said Sister Lilah. "Yeshua said... If you want to be perfect, go, sell your possessions and give to the poor, and you will have treasure in heaven. Then come, follow me."

Yeshua reached the arched stone Lion's gate inside the Old City. Mohammed was waiting there for him.

"My friend, it feels like forever since we have last seen each other!" said Mohammed while he smiled.

"Yes, it has been an eternity," joked Yeshua.

"So, was it as good for you as it was for me?" asked Mohammed.

"Ha-ha. Very funny," said Yeshua.

"This is cool, while I was waiting for you a tour group walked by and the guide told a little story about this Lion's gate. Come out here, look at the outside on the other side of the gate," said Mohammed.

The two young men walked through the arched gate along the narrow street to the outside of the walled Old City. They turned around to look back at the massive arched gate on other side. It almost looked like a giant cathedral, and there were two large stone lions on either side of the arch entryway.

"So the story goes like this…" said Mohammed. "The Ottoman Sultan was planning on completely destroying the city after they captured it in the 1500s. Apparently, the Sultan had a dream about some lions that were about to eat him. He was spared from death when he promised to protect the city. So, he then build this huge wall around what is the Old City including this gate with the lions you see here that were symbolized from his dream. Little did he know that since Biblical times that the Kingdom of Judah's emblem was a lion. The Ottomans brought an age of hundreds of years of religious peace where Jews, Christians and Muslims enjoyed freedom of religious expression."

"That's a fascinating story Mohammed," said Yeshua. "Especially about the lions. You could be a tour guide! I wish we could have a new age of hundreds of years of peace between the Jews, Christians and Muslims."

Yeshua left ear started buzzing. He felt a wave of bliss roll over him, and he spaced out for a few seconds.

"What, what's going on?" said Mohammed. "Is your ear buzzing? Which one?"

"My left ear," said Yeshua. "It's like an Angel just passed by me and went... that way."

He pointed to the right. There was a gateway next the Lion's Gate surrounded by several large signs written in Arabic.

"That place. That's the entrance to the Bab al-Rahma cemetery," said Mohammed. "Buried there are three of the Prophet Muhammad's companions. May peace and blessings of Allah be upon them."

Yeshua started walking towards the gateway of the graveyard and two Arab men quickly came out holding their hands up and blocking Yeshua from entering.

Mohammed walked over and started a conversation with the two men in Arabic. After a few minutes, they all shook hands and smiled and laughed together.

They let Mohammed and Yeshua pass into the graveyard.

"What did you say to them?" asked Yeshua.

"I told them... those aren't the Mossad agents you are looking for," joked Mohammed.

The two best friends belly laughed as they walked through the ancient graveyard. Almost all the graves had Arabic written on their headstones and plaques. To their right was the massive wall of the Temple Mount. To their left was the Mount of Olives, with the Church of Mary

Magdalene and the Chapel of the Ascension visible in the distance.

"What happened to you at the Dome of the Rock?" asked Yeshua.

"It was incredible!" said Mohammed. "The inside of the Dome was beautiful beyond measure. Inside the center on the floor is the massive Foundation Stone. It is the holiest place in the universe. Sages have said it is from that stone that the Earth was created. And it is said that Adam offered sacrifices to God there. It is the place in the Great Israelite Temple where the Ark of the Covenant containing the two stone tablets of the Ten Commandments given by God to Moses were kept. It's also where the Prophet Muhammad, peace be upon him, ascended to Heaven."

"Amazing," said Yeshua. "All in that one place?"

"Yes. All is one," said Mohammed with a smile. "So, I kneeled down to do my afternoon prayers by the Stone, and something truly miraculous occurred. As I was in deep transcendental prayer, I had an out of body experience. I seemed to float up into the room and then I found myself seeing the room from the perspective of the other people near me."

"Huh?" said Yeshua. "Like you were going into their minds and seeing what they were seeing?"

"Yes!" exclaimed Mohammed. "It's called remote viewing. I was also hearing their thoughts. I could just float from one person to the next, like my spirit was free and I just could move from one person's mind to another."

"Wow! So what happened next?" asked Yeshua.

"So, I was literally floating above the stone and I saw a small hole in rock in the east corner. Did you know there is a cave under the Foundation Stone called The Well of Souls?" asked Mohammed.

"No, I didn't know that," said Yeshua. "What's in there?"

"So, I came back to my body and walked over and asked one of the Dome guards about the cave," said Mohammed. "He directed me to the entrance of the Well of Souls right next to the Foundation Stone. They had just finished some renovations and it was open! I walked down sixteen marble steps through the bedrock into a small chamber. The floor was beautifully decorated and there was a small altar with columns in one corner. The energy was off the charts! So, I kneeled down and prayed some more. That's when I reached out to you telepathically. I went into your mind."

"Whoa. So, while I was praying not far away from the Well of the Souls along the Western Wall... you tapped into my consciousness and saw what I was seeing?" asked Yeshua.

"Yes," said Mohammed. "Exactly. It's a miracle."

Yeshua stopped in front of the Wall and turned and stared towards a huge double arched structure jutting out from the Temple Mount.

"This place was in one of my dreams. I came here and put my hands on this Gate," said Yeshua. "And the Rabbi just told me to come here and blow my Shofar."

"This is called the Golden Gate. It was walled off and blocked hundreds of years ago. Wait, what Rabbi?" asked Mohammed.

"Yohanan. He was the Rabbi who Bar Mitzvahed me on Masada five years ago. He was at the Western Wall and said I should come here," responded Yeshua.

"Whoa. Yes! I remember him. He's also the one who came to the hospital when you were in a coma and gave you that Shofar. You woke up the next day, thank Allah. He was here?" asked Mohammed.

"Yes," said Yeshua as he stepped over the black wrought iron fence directly in front of the Golden Gate.

"Wait... what are you doing? You're not supposed to go in there!" shouted Mohammed.

Yeshua pulled his Shofar from around his back and held it in his hands. It seemed to almost glow.

"Ahhh. Well... I guess here we go again, my friend. To eternity and beyond!" said Mohammed as he stepped over the fence and approached the Gate.

Yeshua placed his left hand on the large stones under the left arch blocking the opening of the Golden Gate and held the long, spiraled Shofar in his right hand. Mohammed placed his right hand on the Gate's right archway stones and his left hand on the Shofar.

Yeshua placed the Shofar up to his lips and blew with all his might.

Ba-ba-baaaaaaaaaaaaaa…

Ba-ba-baaaaaaaaaaaaaaa…

Ba-ba-baaaaaaaaaaaaaaa…

Everything went black.

Out of the darkness came an array of lights. First it was dim, and then a tunnel of repeating concentric circles formed in front of them. The lights got brighter, and they seemed to be flying through the multicolored patterns of rotating circles.

"Mohammed, are you there?" asked Yeshua.

"Yes, Sir!" said Mohammed. "This tunnel never gets old."

From the end of the tunnel they saw a bright light rapidly approaching. Then they came out through the light at the end of the tunnel.

The Temple Mount was gone. The entire city of Jerusalem was gone. Yet, they stood on the same exact spot, on the hill with the Mount of Olives to the east full of trees and all the surrounding graveyards had disappeared. The sun was setting in the west, and it was getting dark outside.

Yeshua could see the faint glow of Mohammed's yellow spirit aura hovering near him.

"I think this is Moriah," said Mohammed, telepathically. "This is definitely Mount Moriah, the same hill that Jerusalem was built on."

"So, we've travelled back in time, again?" said Yeshua. "We are in the exact spot that the Temple Mount and the

Golden Gate will be built thousands of years from now?" asked Yeshua.

"I believe so," Mohammed responded.

There was some noise nearby in the shrubs. Suddenly, and old man holding a burning wooden torch followed by a young boy holding several cut logs of wood appeared. They were walking up the mountain. The young boy had red hair, and looked to be around thirteen years old.

"Yeshua… is that you? Again? That boy looks just like you." said Mohammed.

"Ummm. Yes?" responded Yeshua.

After the old man and boy had disappeared from their view on their way up the hill, Yeshua and Mohammed heard some more noise ruffle nearby. Then, a very large horned male sheep crossed his path in front of them.

"Yeshua, that ram… he looks very familiar," said Mohammed.

"What? You recognize that big sheep, really?" said Yeshua in the best joking telepathic voice he could muster.

"Look at his horns. What do you notice?" said Mohammed.

"Oh my God! That's the same horn from my Shofar. They are identical," responded Yeshua.

"Do you see what is happening here?" asked Mohammed.

"I'm not exactly sure," said Yeshua. "The old man. The boy who looks like me. Am I reliving one of my past lives?"

"Do you remember the story about Abraham and Isaac from the Torah?" asked Mohammed.

"Of course I do. Yes," said Yeshua. "To prove his faith in God, Abraham went to sacrifice his son.... Wait a sec! That was Abraham and Isaac walking up the hill?"

"I think so... Yes," said Mohammed. "And do you know what this ram is for, in the story? Do you know why we were sent back here now?"

"Yes. I know now. We are Angels sent here to bring that ram to Abraham to sacrifice instead of Isaac," said Yeshua. "Just like we were sent to help David defeat Goliath. Just like I was sent to show Hagar and Ishmael the well."

"Yes, my friend," said Mohammed. That Shofar, it's like... we're on a mission from Allah."

The ram that had been grazing nearby immediately raised its head in an alarmed stance and looked at exactly in the direction of Yeshua's and Mohammed's spirit aura. It had a fearful look in its eyes, as somehow his intuition detected danger.

"Did the ram just hear us talking? Can it see us?" asked Yeshua.

"I don't know, but we've gotta get that ram up to the Foundation Stone before it's too late." replied Mohammed.

The ram looked at Mohammed and made a husky grunting noise and looked very angry. He then turned around and started galloping full speed away eastward down the valley towards the Mount of Olives.

"Holy Moly!" said Mohammed. "This is not good. Ummm…"

"Quick, you go get the ram," said Yeshua. "Bring him up to the top of the mountain. I'll go up to the Foundation Stone and delay Abraham until you get there."

"Great plan! I'll see you on the other side!" said Mohammed. Yeshua saw his yellow aura quickly zip down the mountain eastwards following the path of the ram.

Yeshua concentrated and moved his spirit up the mountain, towards the direction of where the Dome of the Rock would stand thousands of years later. As he got closer to the top, he saw the light and smoke trail from Abraham's torch up ahead.

Yeshua came to Abraham and Isaac, on the mountain. They were approaching the large stone on top of the apex. It was dusk and getting darker and darker as the light disappeared in the western horizon.

Isaac was struggling holding the bale firewood in his arms, and looked very tired from the long, arduous trek up Mount Moriah.

He said "My Father!"

Abraham, walking just ahead of Isaac said, "Here I am, my son."

Isaac responded, "Here are the fire and the wood, but where is the lamb for the burnt offering?"

And Abraham said, "God will provide for Himself the lamb for the burnt offering, my son." And they both went together.

And they came to the rock, the Foundation Stone. And Abraham built the altar there and arranged the wood, and he bound Isaac his son and placed him on the altar upon the wood.

And Abraham stretched forth his hand and took the knife, to slaughter his son.

Yeshua looked down the mountain. He did not see Mohammed. He did not see the ram.

He thought with all his might, and said "Abraham! Abraham!"

Abraham looked up at the sky, in response to Yeshua's words. He put down the knife. He was crying as tears streamed down his face. Isaac was crying too, bound in twine on the firewood of the makeshift Foundation Stone altar.

Yeshua felt a huge surge of energy come through him. He then spoke the words "Do not stretch forth your hand to the lad, nor do the slightest thing to him, for now I know that you are a God fearing man, and you did not withhold your son, your only one, from me."

Then, suddenly... the ram appeared. Yeshua could see Mohammed's yellow aura inside the huge male sheep.

The ram walked into a nearby terebinth tree and its horns got tangled in its lower limbs.

Abraham stared at the ram caught in the tree. He walked over to the ram, and then with his perfectly sharp knife made a swift, smooth cut through the ram's neck.

Immediately, Yeshua and Mohammed were back in the mystical tunnel of repeating beautiful colored concentric circles. A light came from the end of the tunnel, and then they were blinded by the light.

It was nighttime. Yeshua heard someone yelling in Arabic. He opened his eyes and saw the two Muslim men who were previously guarding the entrance to the cemetery standing above him. They looked very upset.

Mohammed woke up next to Yeshua at the base of the Golden Gate and responded back to the angry men in Arabic. Mohammed stood up from the stone floor and helped Yeshua to a standing position. He handed Yeshua his Shofar and said, "They said they put the iron fence here to stop the false Messiah from coming here. They want to know if the prophecy is true. Did you resurrect all the dead from their graves here? Are you the Messiah?"

Yeshua looked at Mohammed with a perplexed expression on his face. "Me? I don't know. I don't think so. Are you are the Messiah?"

Mohammed shook his head.

"Yeshua, that boy on the mountain. Abraham's son, Isaac... looked just like you as a child," said Mohammed.

"And you looked just like Ishmael as a boy at the Well near Beersheba," said Yeshua "That means…"

"We were brothers," they both said in unison.

Chapter 19

The Saudis

The next morning, 9am
Ben Gurion International Airport, Tel Aviv

The US Air Force Gulfstream C-37A took off exactly on time with its five crew and twelve passengers.

Yeshua and Mohammed sat next to each other, across from Lieutenant Colonel Eliora and Moshe Katz, the Deputy Minister of Israeli Foreign Affairs.

"Did you know that the engine on this plane was built by Rolls Royce?" said Eliora.

The plane's captain came over the intercom. "We are now at our cruising elevation of 51,000 feet and flying at 650 miles per hour. We will arrive in Riyadh, Saudi Arabia in approximately one hour. The seatbelt signs are now off, so please enjoy the rest of the trip."

After a few minutes, Mohammed looked out the window and his eyes got really big. "Yeshua, look down there. Inland from the Gulf of Aqaba, the Red Sea, at that mountain with the black top. Does that look familiar?"

"Yes!" said Yeshua, looking down. "That's the mountain from my dream. The one that was burning like a volcano."

"That's Jebal al-Lawz, in Saudi Arabia," said Mohammed. "I wonder why it was in your dream? We will have to go there someday and bring your Shofar."

Eliora stood up and excused herself to the restroom. As she walked down the airplane aisle, a young man in a dark expensive suit stood up from the other side of the plane and walked over to Eliora's empty seat and sat down.

"Good morning," the man said in an American accent. He looked very young. "My name is Elijah Spencer. I'm in charge of the United States Peace Delegation on this mission."

He stretched his arm outwards to shake Mohammed's and Yeshua's hands, and they both accepted.

"Yeshua, I understand you have a special gift," said Elijah. "That you know when something bad is about to happen. How does that work?"

"Well, Sir... I'm not exactly sure. I suppose I just have really good intuition," responded Yeshua.

"But, your Israeli colleagues say it's much more than that," replied Elijah. "You have some kind of very impressive psychic powers? That something alerts you when danger is near. How is that possible? I'm quite intrigued. Tell me, please?"

"Well, I honestly don't know for sure one hundred percent. Just perhaps my future self is alerting my present self about a possible threat," said Yeshua.

"Fascinating," said Elijah. "So you think that the 'You' in the future is coming back in time to tell the 'You' in the present time about a potential crisis? Like a warning system?"

"Yes. Exactly, something like that," said Yeshua.

"What a wonderful gift you have," said Elijah. "So it's like a special intuition?"

"I guess so. But isn't that what intuition is anyway?" said Yeshua. "It's a little voice in your head that tells you what the best thing to do in any giving situation. Where does that voice come from? Does it come from the past or does it come from the future?"

"Very interesting," said Elijah. "I've never thought of it that way."

"How does your intuition know what to right thing to do is?" questioned Yeshua. "It's an inner voice that helps you make the best possible choices for your future self. And how many times do you wish you listened your intuition, when you didn't follow it? You see, every choice you make creates a different possible future, so it's your intuition that guides you to chose wisely."

"I really like this kid," said Elijah to Moshe Katz, the Israeli Deputy Minister, sitting next to him.

"So Yeshua, this is a very important mission," said Elijah. "We are on the cusp of peace in the Middle East. However there are many, many forces against us. If your special intuition triggers and tells you about an imminent threat... I want you to make a special signal, so we will know that we need to protect ourselves immediately from harm, okay?"

"Yes Sir," said Yeshua.

"So what do you think should be the signal?" asked Elijah. "How about you scratch your nose with your right index and middle fingers, like this..."

Elijah took his two fingers and placed them on his nose and started rubbing and scratching the tip and bridge of the front of his nose.

"Perfect, Sir. I will do that," said Yeshua.

"And you Mohammed. I hear great things about you," said Elijah. "I understand you will be our Arabic translator and interpreter?"

"Yes Sir," said Mohammed. "I am fluent in Hebrew, English and Arabic."

"Tell me a little about yourself," requested Elijah.

"Well, I'm a Bedouin Israeli Arab," said Mohammed. "I'm an orphan. My parents and family were killed by Palestinian Hamas near the Gaza Strip in 2005 because they were considered traitors. I grew up in the Beersheba Orphanage with Yeshua. We're best friends."

"Oh, I'm so sorry," said Elijah. "And Yeshua… you are an orphan too? What happened?"

"My parents and family were Israeli settlers in a Kibbutz in occupied north Gaza," said Yeshua. "They were killed by a suicide bomber in 2005 just before the Israeli government evacuated the Strip and turned it over to the Palestinians."

"Dear God. I'm so sorry for both of you," said Elijah.

"The Universe works in mysterious ways," said Mohammed. "Everything happens for a reason. It's Allah's plan."

Elijah looked at Mohammed for a few moments in silence with a very contemplative look. "I believe you are right," he said.

"Mohammed, I have a question for you," said Elijah. "Why do you think so many Sunni and Shia Muslims hate each other? I'm trying to understand the conflict better."

"It is very complex," said Mohammed. "My best analogy is the Catholics and the Protestant Christians."

"What?" said a surprised Elijah. "What does that have to do with the Muslims?"

"It's was a similar situation," said Mohammed. "The Roman Catholics and Protestants fought many wars in Europe for hundreds of years during the middle ages. The Catholics saw the Protestants as being not true Christians, as heretics. It is similar in that fundamentalist Sunnis don't see the Shia as real Muslims. There are also many political factors involved."

"So where does the rift come from? Why can't they get along?" asked Elijah.

"Well, there are many religious practices that are divergent... like differential acceptance of Hadith, which are basically books that were written by many authors about the Prophet Muhammad, peace be upon him. The Shia accept some, and the Sunnis others for example. Also, Shia hold great significance to some historical shrines that the Sunnis don't," explained Mohammed.

"That doesn't seem like a reason to kill each other," said Elijah. "There must be a deeper reason."

"Yes. In the year 632, The Great Prophet Muhammed died and there was a rift about who his successor would be," said Mohammed. "One group elected Abu Bakr, a companion of Muhammed. The other group elected Ali ibn Abi Talib, Muhammed's cousin and son-in-law. So that is the root origin of the conflict… the Shias believed that Ali and his bloodline were to become the subsequent leaders of Islam, and the Sunnis did not. Ali became the Caliph leader and was subsequently assassinated, and there has been discord ever since."

"So, it's been over 1300 years since that split… surely you would think the two factions would 'hug it out' and make peace over all that time, just as the Catholics and the Protestants finally did. What is the main current issue that is causing most of the friction?" asked Elijah.

"Well, if you don't mind me saying Sir, in my opinion… it's mostly become a political issue between Iran and Saudi Arabia," said Mohammed.

"Tell me more," said Elijah.

"Have you heard of Wahhabism?" asked Mohammed.

"Yes. But I'm not that familiar with it. It's some kind of fundamentalist form of Islam, correct?" said Elijah.

"The Wahhabist are strict Sunnis who believe that the Shia are not true Muslims," said Mohammed. "The movement started in the 18th century and their leader, Muhammad ibn Abd al-Wahhab, adhered to a strict literal interpretation of Islam and banned the practice of admiration of Islamic Saints and visiting their tombs and shrines as impure. He started a fundamentalist revival movement to purge what they thought was a distortion of

Islam. The most conservative Wahhabis believe that anyone who doesn't practice their form of Islam are their enemies. And, there was a strong alliance between Abd al-Wahhab and Muhammad bin Saud."

"Muhammad bin Saud? The founder of the First Saudi State and the Saud dynasty?" said Elijah.

"Yes. The two worked together to purify Islam. Their children even married and the leaders of modern Saudi Arabia are descended from them," explained Mohammed.

"Okay. Wow. I had no idea. So what is the exact relevance now? You said that all that happened over two hundred years ago," asked Elijah.

"Well, The House of Saud made Wahhabism Saudi Arabia's dominant faith," said Mohammed. "Coming into modern times, the dominance of the Sunni Saudis was challenged by the 1979 Islamic Revolution lead by the Shia Grand Ayatollah Khomeini in Iran. I believe during that time, there was quite a crisis with American hostages."

"Yes. There was," said Elijah. "The Iranians held our people there captives for over a year. It was a disaster."

"So, now… you Americans are aligned with the Sunni Saudis, the mortal enemies of the Shia Iranians," said Mohammed. "So basically the enemy of my enemy is my friend, yes? It's a shame, really. We all worship the same God… Allah, God the Father of the Christians and the Hebrew God of Abraham are all the exact same Creator Being, yet so many are willing to kill the others based on their perception of how to correctly worship Divinity."

"Well said and I completely agree. We all need to accept each other and find peace. What form of Islam do you practice?" asked Elijah.

"I am on the Sufi path," answered Mohammed.

"Sufi... isn't that some kind of Islamic mysticism?" asked Elijah.

"Yes. The practice is a very spiritual form of worship," said Mohammed. "We focus on opening our hearts and souls and connection with Allah through prayer, meditation and chanting."

"I'm very impressed," said Elijah. "You have a fantastic and deep understanding of what is going on here. I'm glad you will be our translator, and I'm extremely happy you're on our team."

"Thank you Sir," said Mohammed.

Elijah stood up and walked back to his chair, and Lieutenant Colonel Eliora sat back down in her seat.

"We will be arriving at the Riyadh airport soon; then we'll be transported to the Grand Sultan Hotel," said Eliora. "Yeshua, you must alert us immediately if you sense any danger, okay?"

"Yes ma'am," said Yeshua.

"Please, call me Eliora for now on," she said and smiled. "We're not in the IDF anymore, technically."

The airplane made a smooth landing at the King Khalid airport, just north of the Saudi Capital city of Riyadh.

Everyone departed the airplane, and the group was greeted by several black luxury limousines on the runway.

Over by one of the limousines, Yeshua saw Elijah and Moshe shaking the hands of three bearded Saudis, each wearing the traditional red and white-checkered ghutra headdress secured by a black rope-like cord on top of their heads. They all wore long, dark robes.

Yeshua, Mohammed and Eliora got into one of the limousines; then Moshe entered a few moments later. All the cars left the airport in a caravan and headed south on King Salman Road.

"Mohammed, you will be our main interpreter here," said Moshe. "Once we get to the hotel, we will check into our rooms and then there will be a diplomatic luncheon meeting at noon. Most of the Saudis diplomats speak at least some English... however they will often converse with us in only Arabic, so we will be depending on you to translate back and forth, okay?"

"Yes Sir," said Mohammed.

"And Yeshua. You are Eliora are in charge of security during the meetings," said Moshe. "You will be introduced as part of our diplomatic staff and sit with us during the lunch. We will have no weapons to defend us of course, so if something dangerous happens it's up to you to take action to protect our people. There will also two American Secret Service there at the table."

"Yes Sir," said Yeshua. "If anything seems off, I will rub my nose... just like I showed Mr. Spencer."

"Perfect. Just remember, only speak when spoken too," said Moshe. "And do not say anything that would offend our hosts, please. This is a very important meeting, and everything we discuss is absolutely top secret. Also, please be very careful about what you say while here, even in private, okay?"

Both Yeshua and Mohammed nodded.

Instead of driving through the center part of the sprawling metropolis with vast city blocks full of massive skyscrapers, the convoy continued west on King Salman Road and then headed south on King Khalid Road closer to the sand dunes of the desert. They past the huge campus of the King Saud University, and then arrived at the massive palatial Grand Sultan Hotel a few minutes later near the foreign embassy district.

Yeshua looked out the window of the limo and was blown away at lavish and colossal building. He jokingly asked, "Is this the hotel or is this the Royal Palace?"

All the limousines stopped at the huge arched entrance lined with giant columns and decorated with elaborate fountains and tropical plants. Several men wearing tuxedos walked up to the cars and opened all the doors, and the entire delegation got out and walked over to the beautifully carved front main doors of the hotel. A doorman greeted them and opened the door and another man escorted them into the main lobby.

The enormous circular room was spectacular, with a huge domed ceiling supported by tall columns and arches. The ceiling had some kind of magnificent digital display, which gave the room the appearance of a real sky and clouds moving overhead. The delegation was led over to the check-in desk where the very friendly receptionist gave each person a key to their room.

Elijah said to the entire group "Okay. Everyone settle into your rooms and freshen up. We will meet in Ballroom One at exactly noon for the lunch session. It's right over there." He pointed to the east side of the main lobby.

"What room are you in?" Yeshua quietly asked Mohammed.

"I'm in 619. How about you?" said Mohammed.

"I'm in 618. Right next to you! Let's go check out or rooms," said Yeshua.

Several members of the diplomatic mission were already walking over to the elevators and Yeshua and Mohammed followed them. Someone hit the elevator button and the door opened. The inside of the elevator was elegantly designed and looked like it was covered in gold. Everyone entered and Mohammed hit the 6th floor button. The elevator stopped on some of the other lower floors and several of the others members of the mission walked towards their rooms. The elevator reached the 6th floor and Yeshua and Mohammed exited.

The hallway was almost as equally stunning as the elevator. All the surfaces… the floors, walls and ceiling were exquisitely decorated to the finest detail. They walked down the hallway and found their adjacent rooms. Yeshua opened his room first and they both looked inside.

"Wow!" said Yeshua. "I never saw such a beautiful place. We've come a long way from the Beersheba Orphanage."

The room was absolutely splendid. There was a sitting area with plush chairs and couches with a large glass window overlooking a beautiful domed mosque in the distance. The space was filled with wonderful carved wood decor and the high ceiling had stunning crown molding surrounding a splendid glass chandelier. The adjoining bedroom was even more pleasing with a large king size canopy bed with spiral wood columns.

Yeshua walked into the bedroom and looked into the bathroom. "Whoa. This bathroom is fit for a King!" There was a marble hot-tub Jacuzzi and a shower with elaborate granite, tile and mirrors covering all the surfaces.

Yeshua sat on the bed for a moment and gazed out the window at the giant white domed mosque surrounded by its tall minarets in the distance. Mohammed left to check out his room and perform his prayers. Yeshua closed his eyes and did some meditation. He reflected on all the extraordinary interconnected events of his past that had brought him to this very moment. Was he predestined to be here at this peace summit in Saudi Arabia, or was it just chance events and luck? Surely, he had been guided here by fate and destiny... like a character in some kind of divine play. He thought about all his recurrent dreams, the Shofar, the Biblical adventures, the Orbs, the reincarnations, talking to God, the Angels... everything went through his mind and consciousness as if he was watching a movie in the theater. Yet, he could not see at all into the future. He could only follow the dots like breadcrumbs from the past into the present.

Mohammed knocked on the door. "Yeshua! It's time to go!" he said. Yeshua came out of his deep trance and walked over the door and opened it. Mohammed looked anxious. "We can't be late. It's time to get to the Ballroom. Are you ready?" he asked.

"Yes. I am ready," said Yeshua. "I've always been ready.

Yeshua and Mohammed walked down the hallway, pressed the down button to the elevators and waited in front of the door. The elevator door opened after a moment and three women were inside, all wearing long black abayas cloaks and black niqabs covering their entire faces except for their eyes. Yeshua and Mohammed stepped aside from in front of the open door and the three women exited elevator quietly. As they walked down the hallway, they started speaking in Arabic. Then, two of them started laughing and giggling.

Yeshua and Mohammed got into the elevator and the door closed. Yeshua hit the L button and they started to go downwards.

"The women walking down the hall, I'm really curious... what were they talking and laughing about?" asked Yeshua.

"Do you really want to know?" asked Mohammed.

"Yes, please. I do. What were they giggling about?" asked Yeshua.

"One of them said that you are really cute," said Mohammed.

"Seriously? I mean really? It's hard to know when you are kidding around because you joke so much," said Yeshua.

"Well, it's true, life isn't always full of rainbows and unicorns, my friend," said Mohammed. "But believe me, it's quite a challenge to keep a positive, fun, optimistic attitude in this very cruel and unforgiving world. I often use humor often as a way to lighten up the mood, because someone certainly needs too."

"Well said, my friend," responded Yeshua. "I really appreciate you… even though you killed me in Egypt."

"See, there you go! Some sarcastic humor finally," said Mohammed. "I love it! Keep it coming."

The elevator door opened and they exited into the gigantic ostentatious lobby. There were a few groups of Muslim men wearing different colored keffiyeh spread throughout the huge room. Mohammed and Yeshua started walking in the direction of the hallway towards Ballroom One.

"Mohammed. I have a question," said Yeshua. "Why do Muslim women wear those cloaks and scarves covering their entire body?"

"I don't think I have enough time to entirely explain that to you right now," said Mohammed. "My best analogy is the kippah or yarmulke that the Jews wear."

"Oh, I see… it's a religious custom that shows devotion to God?" said Yeshua.

"Yes. Exactly like that," said Mohammed. "As Muslims, we are instructed to dress modestly. However it's always been debated as to what the interpretation of dressing modestly means. Here in Saudi Arabia, all women are required by law to cover their hair and wear a full body garment."

"And women are just now being able to drive a car here?" asked Yeshua. "I'm glad they are starting to make some modern reforms. That makes me very happy."

They reached the foyer to Ballroom One. There were two armed Saudi military guards flanking the entrance.

Mohammed walked over to the reception desk. Two young Saudi men sat there with some paperwork in front of him. Mohammed spoke to them in Arabic, and one of the young Saudis motioned the military men to open the door.

Yeshua and Mohammed entered the room. It was just as beautiful and opulent as the hotel's lobby. There was a massive crystal chandelier in the center of a spectacularly designed domed vault ceiling. The tall walls had dozens of grand columns supporting the high ceiling. In the middle of the room was a giant round carved wooden table surrounded by at least forty chairs. Most of the chairs were already occupied, and Moshe waved Mohammed and Yeshua to come over to him. Elijah Spencer, the Head American Diplomat, was sitting next Moshe.

"Mohammed, you will sit here next to me," said Moshe as he pointed to the empty chair next to him. "And Yeshua, you will sit over there by Eliora." He motioned to where Eliora was sitting, about ten seats away. She was the only woman in the entire room.

Sitting in most of the chairs were Muslim men wearing different colored keffiyeh, although the majority of them wore the red and white checkered ones with a black headband and full black robes with gold lining.

Yeshua was the last one to sit down. In front of each delegate around the table was a full set of gold silverware and exquisite China dishes. Suddenly, the room was full of servers wearing tuxedos and glasses of water and Caesar salads were brought to each setting. Yeshua counted one server per person at the table.

One of the Saudi men with a short black beard stood up at the head of the round table and starting talking in Arabic, then he sat back down. Afterwards, Mohammed stood up and addressed the Israeli and American delegation.

"The Prince says... welcome to Saudi Arabia. He hopes your travels went smoothly and he says please enjoy your stay here. They want to discuss making an official peace treaty between their country and the Israeli government. They have some terms to discuss, and their goal here today is to agree at least in principle to the terms that will become the basis of a permanent formal settlement."

Moshe stood up and said, "We are humbled by your invitation to come here and are deeply grateful for the wonderful accommodations and hospitality. We feel blessed to have the opportunity to forge a real, lasting peace between our two nations. As you know, the ancestors of our people and yours were born to the same Father, Abraham... so we are all truly brothers here, family. There is nothing more we wish to do here than to be able to find peace with our brothers."

Mohammed, still standing, translated Moshe's words into Arabic and addressed directly the Prince and the other

Muslims sitting around him. When he was done, several of the Muslim delegates started talking and whisper amongst themselves. An older Saudi man with a white beard sitting directly next to the Prince leaned over and whispered in his ear. They whispered back a forth a few times, then the Prince stood back up and spoke again in Arabic. Mohammed took a moment to work on the translation in his mind and then spoke the words back in English to the other side of the table.

"The Prince says... We are prepared to accept Israel's right to exist as a Jewish State, just as Saudi Arabia is a Muslim State. We are prepared to recognize your people's historical claim to the land of Israel and Jerusalem as your Capital City. We are ready to open direct connections, trade and exchange as well as placing diplomatic embassies in each of our nations."

Just then, the huge entourage of servers came to the table and removed the salad dishes and placed the main Kabsa traditional Saudi Arabian entree... a plate full rice, chicken, nuts and spices.

Moshe stood up again and spoke to the Prince in English. "Your Highness, we are beyond appreciative of your goodwill and kindness. What in return can we do for you?"

Mohammed translated the words of Moshe and spoke to the Prince in Arabic, and then the Prince quickly responded a few phrases back in Arabic to Mohammed.

Mohammed listened to him, looked surprised for a moment, and then quickly regained his composure.

"Sir, the Prince says you must make first make peace with the Palestinians," said Mohammed.

Moshe stood back up. "We are doing the best we can to make peace with the Palestinians. However, they have refused to sit at the table with us since the Americans moved their embassy to Jerusalem. Also, we refuse to negotiate with a Palestinian delegation that also represents Hamas, a internationally condemned terrorist organization."

Mohammed interpreted Moshe's words and communicated them back to the Prince in Arabic, then the Prince whispered back and forth a few times with the older man sitting next to him. He stood back up and spoke in Arabic and then Mohammed translated...

"The Prince has helped solved all of these issues. Sitting here is the Fatah Palestinian representative, Tazik Fatmid. He is authorizing to directly negotiate with you and is not associated with Hamas. Also, Saudi Arabia has agreed to help rebuild the Gaza Strip and heavily invest in the Palestinian infrastructure based on the success of the talks today."

Moshe looked at Tazik, sitting next to the Prince and he smiled. Moshe stood up and said... "We are forever grateful for Saudi Arabia's assistance and generosity in these matters. Mr. Fatmid, we wish to know your specific terms for a final agreement, as well as your plans to address the expected Hamas interference in a mutual peace plan."

Mohammed interpreted the English into Arabic, and then Tazik stood up and spoke in Arabic. Mohammed then interpreted... "Our basic terms are simple. We wish for a two state solution and declare the autonomous and sovereign nation of Palestine to include the current West Bank and the Gaza Strip with our capital in Jerusalem. We demand a cessation of all Israeli construction in the disputed occupied territories which would allow for mutually acceptable land swaps to form the final borders. We are willing to share international border control to help address all obvious safety concerns. We are not demanding the right of return of displaced Palestinians back into their original homes in Israel proper; however, we will need to be able to create safe passageway between our two separated lands. For this we will recognize the right of Israel to exist as our neighbor nation and collaborate on peaceful relations. "

Moshe stood up and smiled. He said, "We would be willing to agree to all of this. However, what is your solution for Hamas?"

Tazik stood up and spoke in English. "Allah willing, I will be endorsed as the new leader of Fatah soon. We will hold a unified Palestinian election within the next year, in both Gaza and the West Bank. If we win the popular vote of all of the people, we will simultaneously sign our two state peace declaration and ban and outlaw the Hamas Organization."

Elijah, the American representative, motioned Moshe to sit down next to him. They whispered in each other's ears a few times back and forth, and then Moshe stood back up.

"You are willing to have a potential civil war with Hamas for Palestinian Statehood and peace with Israel? There will be many casualties and challenging consequences amongst your people," said Moshe.

"We see this as the only logical option moving into a future where our two nations can coexist peacefully. If we continue to take an eye for an eye, eventually we will all go blind. We will no longer accept widespread terror activities and using women and children as shields. We must find a better way to live together," responded Tazik.

"We in principle accept your offer Tazik and look forward to further negotiations with you," said Moshe.

The Prince stood up and spoke in Arabic again. Mohammed interpreted... "The Prince says Saudi Arabia fully endorses this plan. However, for now they wish to be silent partners, as word about this publicly could cause significant unrest and backlash amongst their surrounding Middle Eastern neighbors. This concludes our meeting and your transportation back to the airport will be outside. The Prince thanks you."

The Prince stood up and nodded to the Americans and Israelis. He said something more in Arabic and Mohammed walked over to him and shook his hand. They both smiled and the Prince and Mohammed conversed some more words in Arabic. Then, the Prince and his entire entourage started to leave the room. He walked over and shook everyone's hands in the room on his way to the exit. Mr. Fatmid also came over and shook everyone hands. There were many smiles. Finally, the room cleared out and the entire American and Israeli delegation walked back to the lobby and then outside to the limousines waiting by the main entrance.

Yeshua, Mohammed, Moshe and Eliora all entered one of the limousines and then all the cars departed the Grand Sultan Hotel and headed north.

Eliora said, "I don't think that could have gone much better. Mohammed, what did the Prince say to you at the end of the meeting?"

"He invited me as his personal guest to the next Hajj pilgrimage in Mecca. It is quite an honor. I've never been there," said Mohammed.

"You did very well today translating," said Moshe. "This is a tremendous breakthrough. I hope the Palestinian can make good on his promises. Yeshua, did you have any warnings of danger?"

"I did not Sir," said Yeshua. "Everything went smoothly, thank God."

Just then, his right ear started to high pitch buzz.

Eliora looked out the window and appeared to be surprised. She yelled at the driver in the front cabin. "Where are the other limousines? Why are we going into the city? Driver! You are supposed to take us to the airport."

Mohammed stared at Yeshua with a stunned expression. "Which ear is buzzing?" he asked.

"My right ear," said Yeshua.

"Uhhh-Ohhhhh," responded Mohammed.

The driver hit the button for the black glass window to raise up between the front and back of the limousine. All the doors clicked lock. He started rapidly speeding up the car and raced along the highway towards the downtown district full of skyscrapers.

"The doors are all locked," said Eliora. She hit the black glass window hard in the front of the cabin with her fist and it didn't break. "We are trapped in here," she said.

Moshe got on his cellphone. He called Elijah Spencer, his American counterpart and put him on speakerphone. Elijah answered. "Elijah... this is Moshe. We've been hijacked inside our limo by our driver. He's taking us to the downtown district."

"What? Where are you?" he asked.

Moshe looked outside the window. "I can see the Al Mamlaka Tower Kingdom Centre up ahead."

"Ok, I'm calling security right now. Help will be on the way soon. Hold tight!" said Elijah.

Mohammed started kicking the black window to the driver's compartment without success. After a few moments, Eliora pointed up in the sky and said, "Look, those two helicopters, they are following us."

Then, two police cars with flashing sirens appeared behind the limousine. The driver sped up even faster and was weaving dangerously through traffic. One of the police cars pulled right on next to the limo; then the driver veered hard into police car, which then smashed into the median in the middle of the road and flipped over. This caused a huge pile up of cars behind the limo, blocking the second police car from following them.

The limo made a hard right and took the off ramp to the King Abdullah Financial District. A huge mass of tall skyscrapers was just ahead. One of the helicopters got very close to the limo, and a sharpshooter peered out the window with his gun.

"My gosh!" said Eliora looking out the window. "They are going to shoot us! Who the hell are the good guys and the bad guys here?"

The sharpshooter aimed his high power rifle at the car and pulled the trigger. The right front tire of the limo exploded and the driver started to lose control of the car. He swerved and sideswiped and hit a few other cars driving next to him. Everyone in the back of the limo tossed around violently.

The limo pulled into one of the taller financial district's skyscraper's covered parking garages and abruptly stopped on the second floor. There was smoke coming from the ripped up front tire. The limo driver opened his door and ran away. Then, a black SUV pulled up and four armed men wearing black masks got out and all of them walked over to the back of the limo.

Moshe tried to call Elijah on his cell phone without success. "Damn. There's no cellular signal in here!" he yelled.

The masked men were yelling loudly in Arabic outside the limo.

"They are saying if we don't get out right now and put our hands up, they will kill us all," said Mohammed.

"Are the doors locked?" asked Yeshua. His right ear was high pitch buzzing very loudly.

"No, it looks like the driver unlocked them when he ran away," said Eliora.

"Lock them!" yelled Moshe. Eliora tried to push down the button on the side door. "They won't lock!" she said.

They could hear police sirens in the distance getting closer.

After a moment, the masked men started to shoot rapidly at the back of the car with their handguns. Thankfully, the limo was a bulletproof and the all the bullets glanced off the doors and windows, although the windows heavily cracked in fractal, spider web like patterns. One of the masked men approached the back door and placed his hand on the door handle to open it.

Mohammed jumped out forcefully from the car with a big black seat cushion covering his head and body. The masked man trying to open the car was slammed by the door as Mohammed burst out and fell down on the ground.

Two of the masked men started shooting at Mohammed, and the bullets went into the seat cushion. The other masked man standing there reloaded his gun with a new clip.

Eliora jumped out of the car and drop kicked one of the masked men shooting his gun, his bullets just barely missing her. Mohammed smashed his seat cushion into the other man shooting and knocked him down.

Yeshua followed Eliora out of the car and quickly ran and tackled the last man who was reloading his gun. They both fell to the ground and rolled on the floor away from the limousine. They wrestled intensely to take control of the gun.

Suddenly, another large black SUV pulled up and stopped a few yards away. Three more masked men got out near where Yeshua and the man were wrestling on the ground. One the men had a crowbar and quickly hit Yeshua hard on his head. He lost consciousness and blood started to pour from his scalp. The other men hastily grabbed Yeshua and threw him in the back of truck.

Mohammed saw them put Yeshua's limp body in the vehicle. He screamed "Nooooooooooo!" Both he and Eliora were desperately fighting in hand-to-hand combat with the three masked men by the limousine. The police sirens were getting closer, and then all the masked men stopped fighting and ran away from the limo and jumped into the SUV as it sped away towards the exit of the parking garage. Mohammed and Eliora starting running after the SUV, and as it was leaving the back window opened and one of the masked men starting shooting towards them. Eliora took a bullet in her leg and fell down. Mohammed kneeled beside her on the ground and held pressure on her wound as the SUV left the garage.

CHAPTER 20

THE IRANIANS

Yeshua walked alone in the barren, hot desert. There were no roads or any nearby signs of civilization. It was almost sunset and the bright sun blazed in the western horizon. The arid wind blew strongly and whistled through Yeshua's wavy, long red hair. His skin was quite sunburned and freckled, and he now had a medium length red beard. His lips were dry and cracked, and he stumbled up and down the large sand dunes towards the west. He lost his balance and fell down one of the larger sand dunes and lay at the bottom of the valley for a few moments in exhaustion. Above, a dozen or so vultures circled in the sky.

"Get up," an inner voice said in his mind. "Get up! Fly…"

Yeshua dug deep with all his might, got on his knees, and crawled slowly along the next sand dune to the top of its ridge and stood up. He placed his two index fingers and thumbs together and made a triangular shape with his hands. Then, he held his hands up into sky and centered his hands so the setting sun was in the center of the triangle that his fingers formed. He looked at the glowing sun in the western sky through his hands, and then the glorious beams of light radiating from the sunset transformed into thousands of small multi-colored floating orbs. The tiny balls of light came to Yeshua and seemed to magically swirl all around him. They circled and illuminated his entire body, like an aurora borealis would shimmer as the northern lights in the dark Arctic sky.

Yeshua jumped into the air and leaped off the top of the tall sand dune, just as a diver would in the Olympics surging off the highest platform. His led with his arms forward, his hands still together in the triangular pattern.

Instead of falling into the depths of the valley of the sand dunes in front of him, his body defied gravity and he starting flying forward and upwards, towards the west. He could see mountains and an ocean in the far distance, and then even further away… the black mountain that looked like it was burning like a volcano from his previous visions. He started flying in the direction of the mountain and the huge plume of smoke coming from it.

"Yeshua." said a loud resonant voice in his head.

"Yeshua, where are you?" the voice asked. It was Mohammed's voice.

"I'm flying towards the Mountain, the Mountain of Fire," responded Yeshua in his mind.

"Yeshua, you've been kidnapped. Where are you?" asked Mohammed.

Just then, Yeshua seemed to lose his concentration. He started falling, free falling from the sky back towards the Earth. His arms were flailing, and he started to scream as he fell rapidly back down towards the sandy desert floor.

He hit the ground hard, and his stomach really hurt. It took all the wind out of him.

Then he felt even more pain in his stomach.

"Wake up Jew!" said the masked man in a very bad English accent. He punched him again in the stomach.

Yeshua was tied to a chair, with his hands bound behind him.

The man punched him again hard and Yeshua started spitting up some blood.

"Yeshua, where are you?" asked Mohammed, telepathically. "Do you know where you are? I'm back in Israel at the command and control center and remote viewing through you. I'm trying to help find out where you are. Who is that hitting you? Can you tell me anything?"

"I don't know Mohammed. All I remember is fighting those men in Saudi Arabia in the parking lot and then I blacked out," said Yeshua in his mind.

The masked man pulled off his mask. He had a deep scar on the left side of his face. Yeshua stared at him in horror. He had seen that scar many, many times before. He looked Arabic with olive skin and had a black beard and moustache. The room was very dark and Yeshua could see four or five other masked men standing in the shadows of the room.

Yeshua could feel the floor move somewhat, almost rocking back and forth. It felt like the waves of the ocean.

"Mohammed! Are you there?" asked Yeshua in his mind.

"Yes," said Mohammed.

"I think I'm on a boat, somewhere on an ocean," said Yeshua.

"Okay, great. Do you have any idea where? And who are all these masked men around you?" asked Mohammed.

"I don't know? Wait... you can see what I'm seeing?" asked Yeshua.

"Yes. I can see through your eyes. It's like we a quantumly entangled. What you see, I can see too," responded Mohammed.

The man with the scarred face punched Yeshua again in the stomach. He winced in pain.

"Tell me the name of the Palestinian you met in the meeting in Saudi Arabia. Or we will kill you," the man said.

"Don't tell him!" said Mohammed. "I think these very bad actors are Iranian or Hamas, and they probably want to assassinate the Palestinian politician and stop the peace treaty from happening."

"What Palestinian?" said Yeshua to the scar-faced man.

The man punched Yeshua in the face hard, and blood spurted out from his nostrils.

"We didn't meet any Palestinians. There were only Saudis there. What a nice hotel that Grand Sultan. Have you ever stayed there?" said Yeshua in a mocking tone.

"You are lying," said the man. One of his masked friends brought over a table next to Yeshua's chair with some equipment on it. There was a device that looked like an EKG machine.

"Yeshua. I have an idea," said Mohammed in his mind. "Are you still wearing your watch?"

Yeshua's hands were tied behind his back on the chair with rope. He felt with his right hand that his watch was still there on his left wrist. It had been on there since their first day of IDF training, and he had never been able to remove it. It was locked on there on purpose.

"Yes," thought Yeshua. "It's still on my wrist."

"Great," responded Mohammed. "Can you activate the emergency locator distress beacon on the watch? It will ping your exact location to the Cospas-Sarsat satellite system. We will be able to find you and rescue you."

"Yes. I think I can," said Yeshua in his mind. "I'll work on it, although literally my hands are tied behind my back."

The scar faced man sliced Yeshua's shirt off with his knife. He put the knife up to the side of Yeshua's neck and the sharp tip started to pierce his skin. Blood started to ooze from his neck.

"Tell me his name, Jew!" the man said. "Do you want to die?"

"Even if there was a Palestinian there, why would I tell you?" asked Yeshua. "You are going to kill me either way. So just do it. Kill me…"

"Yeshua, what are you doing?" asked a concerned Mohammed in Yeshua's mind.

"Don't worry," responded Yeshua. "I'm buying some time. He's not going to kill me until he gets what he wants."

Meanwhile, Yeshua had opened the two mini dials on the watch and pulled out the two tiny antenna cords.

"I've activated the watch," said Yeshua in his mind to Mohammed.

"Okay, great," said Mohammed. "We'll wait to get the signal and send some help wherever you are. Do your best to stay alive, my friend. I'm going to go do something to help you as well. I'll be back in a little bit. Don't die, okay?"

"Wait!" said Yeshua. "You are leaving me?" There was only silence, Mohammed had left Yeshua's mind.

The scar-faced man placed two rectangular shaped adhesive pads onto Yeshua's chest and connected them to wires from the machine on the table.

"You are correct, Jew. I need to know who your Palestinian friend is," said the scar-faced man. "You are not going to like this. Feel free to tell me his name at anytime."

The man turned on the machine. It was a cardiac defibrillator. Yeshua was shocked with super high voltage. His whole body shook violently and electrical bolts shot out from his hair. He screamed in pain, and then he passed out.

Yeshua saw the old man, the Rabbi. It was Yohanan. He was wrapped in a tallit, the traditional white Hebrew prayer shawl. He had a long white beard and mustache. Behind him in the distance was the Temple Mount, in Jerusalem. The Rabbi held the Shofar in his hands, the one that he gave him when he was thirteen. He held it up into the sky and blew it as loud as he could.

Ba-ba-baaaaaaaaaaaaaaa…

Ba-ba-baaaaaaaaaaaaaaa…

Ba-ba-baaaaaaaaaaaaaaa…

Yeshua woke back up. He had the taste of blood in his mouth, and there was a burning smell in the room.

The scar-faced man put his ugly face right up to Yeshua's face. He had horrible breath. "I can make the suffering stop. All you have to do it tell me his name."

"Whose name?" said Yeshua. "I don't know who you are talking about."

"Fine," said the scar-face man. He pushed the button again on the machine. Yeshua's body jolted again as his heart was forcefully defibrillated. He screamed in agony as his heart finally stopped, then he lost consciousness and everything went black.

"Yeshua, Yeshua… are you there?" asked Mohammed in Yeshua's mind.

"Yes, I am here. But I don't know where here is," responded Yeshua. "I think I may have died. I'm just floating in nothingness."

"Listen, we know where you are," said Mohammed. "We picked up your watch's distress signal. You are in a boat off the coast of Bahrain in the Persian Gulf and heading rapidly towards Iran. An American Navy Seal team is coming to rescue you right now from Qatar. Don't die! Stay alive! Come back to life, please!"

Yeshua opened his eyes. He was in horrible pain and could barely see. There was no one in the room. He heard the faint sound of helicopters in the distance, and the masked men were all yelling at each other in Arabic outside the room. They had left the door open and he could see the masked men running back and forth along the edge of the boat. It was nighttime outside, and the full moon reflected off the shimmering rolling waves of the Persian Gulf.

The man with the scarred face came back into the room holding a large knife. He had a crazy look in his eyes. He walked up to Yeshua and put his knife up to his chest.

"That birthmark, I recognized that mark," said the man. "I know you. We've met before, haven't we?"

Yeshua was fading in and out of consciousness. He looked at the Iranian, but his vision became very blurry. Then he saw the Nazi officer's face from Amsterdam with the same scar, then he saw the Roman soldier's face from Masada, then he saw the dark Angel's face from Abraham's well, then Goliath's face, then once again the Iranian's face.

"Yes. You know me," said Yeshua. "You've always known me. I am the exact opposite of you."

"This is your last chance," said the scar-faced man. "Tell me the name of the Palestinian."

"This is not the last chance," said Yeshua. "There will be many, many more."

"Then die," said the scar-faced man. He raised his blade and held it with both hands. Just as he was about to plunge it into Yeshua, a masked man from behind him smashed the back of his head with a crowbar. The scar faced man slumped forward and landed at Yeshua's feet.

Heavy gunfire started outside the room on the boat, and Yeshua lost consciousness and passed out. Everything went black.

CHAPTER 21

THE AMERICANS

Al Udeid Air Base, Qatar
Two days later

Mohammed, General Geller and Elijah Spencer landed in their C-27J Spartan transport airplane on the runway of the Abu Nakhlah Airport in Qatar. They deboarded and were taken in a fully armored four-wheeler L-ATV over to the military hospital. They were escorted by security to the Med-Surg Step Down Unit nursing station.

"Can, I help you?" asked the charge nurse.

"Yes, we are here to see Yeshua Rabin," said Mohammed.

"He's in room eighteen. Over there," she said as she pointed down the hallway.

The three men walked down the hall and into room eighteen.

Yeshua's was lying asleep in his hospital bed. He eyes opened and immediately brightened when they all entered the room.

"Mohammed! Mr. Spencer. General Geller, Sir!" said Yeshua as he sat up and saluted the General.

"At ease, son," said Geller.

"My gosh," said Mohammed to Yeshua. "You look like hell."

Yeshua had a left black eye, staples in his scalp, stitches in his neck and lower lip. His nose was swollen and bruised.

"I'm doing great! Almost good as new," said Yeshua. "I feel like a million bucks."

The General closed the room door behind him.

"What's up?" asked Yeshua. "What's going on now? I sense something very serious."

"We are here for a debriefing," said Elijah. "This is all top secret. We are here on a joint collaboration between the CIA, Mossad and the NSA."

"Does it have something with those bad dudes on the boat?" asked Yeshua. "One of them helped me... did we blow his cover?"

"Well actually, that was me," said Mohammed.

"You? You were on the boat? You were one of those masked guys?" asked a surprised Yeshua.

"Well, technically it was a radicalized Iranian terrorist... but I was mind controlling him," said Mohammed.

"So you can mind control people now? Niiice!" said Yeshua.

"I didn't know I could... until that very moment," said Mohammed. "This is all because of that Shofar of yours. First we went back in time and helped King David, then I could go into your dreams, and then in real life I could read your mind and thoughts and see what you are seeing. Now I can go into other people's minds and control them."

"How is that even possible?" asked Yeshua. "What's happening to us? I just had this vision I could fly. Are we turning into some kind of superheroes? I should be dead, right? Those bad guys zapped me and stopped my heart!"

"So, after you pulled the watch tracking system... I left your consciousness and went into one of the masked Iranian's dude's minds," said Mohammed. "By the way, I can only do that when I'm in deep meditation. I saw that the guy with the scarred face was about to kill you, so I made the man I was remote viewing through hit him on the head with a crowbar."

"So, you saved my life again, thank you," said Yeshua.

"Speaking of flying, tell him more," said General Geller.

"Okay. So, while I was in the Iranian guys head, I got more information about their nefarious plans," said Mohammed. "Those guys were pretty high level. They knew all about the Iron Dome and Patriot missile defense systems in Israel. They are the ones responsible for arming Hamas with the missiles that were used to try to destroy the helicopter we were flying on and the gunboat that attacked our IDF training base. They are also the ones responsible for hijacking and booby trapping the satellite station in the Elah Valley."

"Wow. They are really hell-bent on our destruction," said Yeshua. "And they wanted to know who the Palestinian politician was so they could kill him and stop the peace treaty?"

"Yes," said Elijah. "But there's more. Apparently Mohammed found out that there's a master plot. There is a plan in play to nuke Israel. Their final solution is an atomic attack on Tel Aviv and the other major population centers in

Israel. The Iranians have been chanting 'Death to Israel, Death to America' for decades. Now they mean it."

"The Iranians and Hamas have been testing our defense systems for some time now," said General Geller. "We've been playing cat and mouse with them. They have developed jamming technology, hijacking our controls and even now they are trying to disable our entire Global Satellite missile detection system."

"What? How can they do that?" said Yeshua.

"Thanks to you and Mohammed, we now know their plan," said General Geller. "The Iranians have been designing and launching long range ICBM missiles that are capable of suborbital trajectories as well as holding an atomic bomb payload. They also have been secretly launching their own satellites up into space. The Americans have been watching all this very carefully."

"Here's what is happening right now," said Elijah. "The Iranians launched a secret satellite recently, under the guise of a weather satellite. From their satellite, a remote controlled robot bomb is being guided and is about to land on the main Israeli Global Defense Satellite. It is set to explode on Yom Kippur, when all the Jewish Israelis are praying and fasting. Once the satellite goes down, there will be a massive launch of nuclear bombs, as well as diverting conventional attacks from Hamas in Gaza and Hezbollah in Lebanon and Syria. It's going to be a bloodbath."

"We've got to stop that bomb!" said Yeshua.

"Exactly. And we know just the team to do it," said General Geller as he gave Yeshua a thumbs up. Mohammed gave Yeshua a thumbs up too.

"Wait a sec. Us? We're the team? We are going into space?" said a half surprised and shocked Yeshua.

"Well, son. You are the best bomb specialist we have," said Geller.

"Yeshua. They got a rocket ship ready for us... in Florida, United States. We are going into space!" said Mohammed with a big smile.

"Count me in," said Yeshua.

"Sir?" said Mohammed to General Geller.

"Yes, son," said Geller.

"Afterwards, when we stop the bomb... can we go to Disney World?" asked Mohammed. "I've always wanted to go there. Never been."

General Geller gave Mohammed a strange look and paused. "I believe we can arrange that."

One Week Later
Kennedy Space Center
Cape Canaveral, Florida

"This is Captain Alexa Smith," said Elijah Spencer to Yeshua and Mohammed. They shook her hand. They all stood outside in the humid Florida heat next to the huge NASA Vehicle Assembly Building, with the huge American Flag and NASA emblem displayed on the giant outer wall. In the distance, on Space Launch Complex thirty-nine stood a massive Atlas V Rocket.

Captain Smith was a short, middle-aged woman with sandy brown hair and some freckles. "She's the best pilot we have," said Elijah. "She is going to give you a crash course in zero gravity training today."

"We are going to suit up and do an EVA in the NBL today," said Captain Smith.

"Excuse me, ma'am," said Mohammed. "What does that mean?"

"Please, call me Captain Smith," she said. "EVA means a simulated spacewalk and NBL means the Neutral Buoyancy Laboratory. Basically, we are going in a huge pool of water to practice our mission."

"Cool. That's just really cool," said Mohammed.

Elijah and Captain Smith escorted Yeshua and Mohammed to the nearby brand new NBL Training Center.

"Welcome to the NBL," said Captain Smith. They entered a huge room with the largest swimming pool Yeshua and Mohammed had ever seen. There were several men in full scuba gear swimming at the bottom of the pool amidst two large objects.

Elijah's cell phone rang, and he answered the call. He said, "Yes, yes," a few times and then he hung up.

"Please excuse me," said Elijah with a very serious look on his face. "I have to go attend to some important things. I will catch up with you later. Hope you have a productive training today. We will be in touch." Elijah turned and walked out towards the exit of the Laboratory.

"What's at the bottom of the pool?" asked Yeshua. "And what's the ship in there, it looks like a mini space shuttle. I thought they were all retired?"

"So the object in the middle of the pool is a life sized scale replica of the Israeli Defense Satellite," said Captain Smith. "And the ship you are looking at is a modified X37."

"X37?" asked Yeshua.

"Yes. That's the ship we will be commanding," said Captain Smith. "Did you see the Atlas Rocket on the launch pad out there?"

"Yes. I saw it," said Yeshua. "So we are going to fly through outer space in that little shuttle and launch from Earth in that giant rocket out there?"

"That's the plan," said Captain Smith. "My job is to get you to and from that satellite safely."

"Great. We got this," said Yeshua. "What's next?"

"We are going downstairs to spend some time going over the instructional course on the spacesuits you will be wearing; then we will get in the tank and do a simulation mission, okay?" said Captain Smith.

"Yes, Captain!" said Yeshua and Mohammed in unison.

Captain Smith turned and walked down the stairs to the bottom of the training center. Yeshua and Mohammed followed her, and she rolled her eyes and said under her breath, "Gosh, these boys are green."

They entered a large room with about a dozen full spacesuits hanging in glass cabinets on the walls. Mohammed walked over to one and looked at it very closely. "Wow. I feel like I'm in some kind of surreal science fiction movie," he said.

"Guys, listen," said Captain Smith. "We don't have time to joke around here today. We have a lot of work to do and you guys need to focus, okay?"

Mohammed and Yeshua looked at her and nodded.

She walked over to one of the spacesuits on the wall and hit a button. The glass door went up into the ceiling with a whooshing sound.

"This is called an Extravehicular Mobility Unit, or EMU for short," said Captain Smith. "It will keep you alive in the harsh vacuum of outer space. On the chest is the display control module. Now pay careful attention and remember what each thing is as I point to it. There will be a test on this later, okay?"

Mohammed and Yeshua looked at her and nodded.

"Here is the power mode switch; here is the CWS switch, the mode selector switch and the feed water valve switch. This is the purge valve," said Captain smith as she pointed to the top panel of the device. "Here is the fan switch and the suit pressure valve, the cooling control valve, and here is the communication button to talk. Here are the volume controls, the display intensity control and O2 Actuator control. Got all that?"

"Yes, Captain," said Mohammed and Yeshua.

"The suits have enough oxygen for eight hours of primary life support and thirty minutes of backup life support," said Smith. Before we put on the Hard Upper Torso or HUT assembly and the soft Lower Torso or LTA and the Primary Life Support Systems or PLSS we put on the MAG and the LCVG."

"Wow. That's a lot of acronyms," said Mohammed. "What do MAG and LCVG stand for?"

"The MAG is the Maximum Absorbency Garment, and the LCVG is the Liquid Cooling and Ventilation Garment," said the Captain. "Finally, the Snoopy communication cap is placed containing earphones and microphone and lastly the helmet and gloves. I'm going to play this one hour video on how to put on your suits while I go out to the airlock and work on getting the simulation started. When I get back, I want both of you to have your suits on and ready to go."

The Captain pressed the play button on a laptop sitting on one of the nearby desks. She left the room through the door located in the back of the room.

As the video was playing, Yeshua asked "Mohammed, why does Captain Smith seem so nervous. Is it us?"

"I don't think so," replied Mohammed. "Although we are total newbies, I think it's more about that ship, the X37. It's some kind of top-secret military spaceship. I follow this stuff on the Internet. I've never heard of one having passengers, it's supposed to be only remote controlled. They must have made a new prototype to fly passengers. I think she must be super nervous about this mission. I don't think anything like this has ever been attempted since they tried to fix the Hubble telescope. It must be like trying to thread the eye of a needle while walking and chewing gum at the same time flying that ship."

"It's all in God's hands now," said Yeshua.

The two best friends watched the video and started the long process of putting on their suits. A few times, they rewound the instructional video to look at the correct order of the suit placement. They helped each other through each step, and as they placed their glass helmets and got the airtight seal to lock as the final step, Captain Smith entered the room.

"Well done boys!" she said. She walked over and inspected both their suits. "Perfectly done. Now let's go over to the airlock. Remember, if you want to talk to each other, press the talk button on your EMU DCM."

They all walked through the door in the back of the room and entered a long tall hallway. It had huge aquarium windows on the right side with an incredible view of the Neutral Buoyancy Laboratory. Inside the massive pool was the X37 and the model of the Defense Satellite. Scuba divers swam around the two large metal objects and their air bubbles slowly floated to the top of the pool, 40 feet above to the surface.

"This is identical to the NBL in the Johnson Space Center in Houston, Texas," said the Captain. "It holds over six million gallons of water."

She stopped in front of a huge metal door within the glass of the aquarium windowed hall. She opened the door, and there was a small room inside with another huge metal door on the other side.

"This is the airlock," she said. "Get inside. It will fill with water, then the other door will open and the scuba divers will help you into the X37 in the microgravity environment. I will be there soon, okay? Just wait for me patiently."

Yeshua and Mohammed nodded in their suits. They walked into the center of the airlock room; then the door closed behind them. Water started to pour into the space through four pipes on either side of the walls.

Yeshua pushed his communication button. "Mohammed, I never asked you this. When we went back in time in Jerusalem and you got the horned ram to come up the mountain to be sacrificed instead of Isaac. How did you do that?"

Mohammed pushed his talk button. "Let's just say... sometimes we need to selflessly sacrifice ourselves for the greater good."

"But you mind controlled the ram, didn't you? You changed his free will. He didn't want to die," said Yeshua.

"Of course, he didn't want to die," said Mohammed. "No one wants to die. But the soul is eternal. We keep coming back. What we do in this lifetime will effect the next, and so on. Wouldn't you sacrifice yourself if you knew that it would help make the world a better place for everyone?"

"Yes. I would. Yes..." said Yeshua.

The small room filled completely with water; then airlock door unlocked and opened. The massive Neutral Buoyancy Pool was completed exposed in front of them. Six scuba divers swam into the airlock room and grabbed

Yeshua and Mohammed and brought them into the huge swimming pool and slowly moved them towards the X37.

Mohammed pushed his talk button again. "The past, present and future have all already happened. In the future, we've already done this. And everything in the past has led up to this point. We've all just actors in a cosmic play, without a beginning or an end. It's infinite. Contraction and expansion. Yin and Yang. That's what eternity is. The heart of the Universe beats on forever..."

The exterior doors of the X37 were open. There were four seats inside, two pilot chairs by the front controls and two passenger seats in the back. The scuba divers put them in the passenger seats in the back. The mocked up satellite was on the other side of the pool, about one hundred feet away.

"I wonder who the fourth seat is for?" asked Yeshua.

"Okay, I'm on the way!" said Captain Smith on the telecom system. She was in the airlock with her suit on. The room was filling with water. The door then opened and the scuba divers brought her over to the X37 sitting at the bottom of the pool. She got into the pilot's seat and pushed a button that closed the cargo doors. The three of them were sealed in the ship. There was a small glass window in the front of the X37, and they could see the black Satellite with a blue and white Israeli Star emblem on the far other side of the pool.

The Captain pushed her talk button. "I know this sounds stupid, but please put on your seatbelts even though the cabin is full of water," she said. "We are going to try to make this simulation as close as possible to the real thing.

We don't have a lot of time to train. You need to wear your seatbelts, because if in reality if the cargo doors opened unexpectedly you would be sucked out into space."

Yeshua and Mohammed put on their seatbelts. Captain Smith grabbed the controls of the ship and it lifted up off the floor of the pool. She pulled the throttle and it moved forward and she stopped it in the middle of the pool.

"Yeshua, are you ready?" she asked on the telecom. "You know how to defuse the bomb on the satellite? They told me you know what you are doing."

Yeshua pushed his talk button. "I'll be able to figure it out once I get there. But how am I going to get there from here? I'm not the best at flying through space just yet."

"We are working on a plan for that," said Smith. "Now I'm going to open the cargo doors and the scuba divers are going to take you over there."

"Check," said Yeshua.

The cargo doors opened and three scuba divers helped Yeshua out after he released his seatbelt. They helped him swim towards the satellite.

"Mohammed. Can you hear me?" said the Captain in her telecom.

"Yes, Captain. I can hear you," said Mohammed.

"I don't entirely understand this," said Smith. "They told me to tell you to go into Yeshua's mind and go with him to the satellite. That you have some kind of psychic powers."

"Yes. I can do that," said Mohammed. "Although I need total concentration. Any stimulus will interrupt me. I need radio silence."

"Don't you remember?" said Smith. "There's a volume control on the bottom of your DCM on your chest."

"Yes Captain! Found it," said Mohammed. "I'm jumping into my meditation now. See you on the other side."

"Roger that," said the Captain.

The scuba divers had brought Yeshua to the satellite and let him go. He clung to the Satellite with both hands and looked back at the X37 in the middle of the pool. He pushed his talk button. "Captain, can you hear me? I'm at the satellite. I'm going to look for the bomb now."

"Check," said Smith. "Keep me updated on your progress."

"Yeshua. I got your back," said Mohammed in Yeshua's mind.

"Mohammed! I've got you on my mind," responded Yeshua telepathically. "Can you see what I see?"

"Yes. Is your ear buzzing at all?" asked Mohammed.

"It's not," said Yeshua in his mind. "I don't think a fake bomb will cause my ears to buzz since it's not real danger. Ahhh... I think I found the fake bomb."

There was a large circular drone looking device hooked to the far side of the satellite. It appeared to have some strong magnets keeping it locked in place, and there was a metal case covering the center of the middle of the structure.

Yeshua pushed his talk button. "I found the bomb, Captain. It seems to be stuck to the satellite with magnets. There's a metal case on the front. I don't have any tools to open it."

"On your left arm is a compartment full of tools, including a screwdriver," said the Captain. "See what you can do," she said.

"Roger that," said Yeshua. He took his right hand in his glove and unzipped the compartment on his left arm. He held onto the satellite with his left hand. He found a screwdriver and pulled it out.

"Yeshua!" said Mohammed in his mind. "I see some screws on the edge of the case. You have to move your body around the satellite to see them better."

Yeshua was holding the screwdriver in his right hand and tried to move around to see the edge of the bomb better. He lost grip with his left hand while trying to move and he floated away from the satellite in the water.

"Damn it!" said the Captain. "You just lost the satellite. If this were real it would be game over. You would be floating out into space, and we would have to try to rescue you by flying the ship dangerously close to that satellite traveling at almost seven thousand miles per hour."

"I understand Captain," said Yeshua. "I'm sorry and will do better. However in the real mission, won't I have a cable or cord to secure myself to the satellite? If I lost grip I'd just tether myself back?"

"Yes, but if you did a maneuver like that, you might slightly knock the satellite off its orbit and the end result would be the same if the bomb blew up," said the Captain.

"Well, don't you have some kinda jetpack I can wear?" asked Yeshua, somewhat aggravated. "I've seen enough science fiction movies. And how am I supposed to get back to the ship once I deactivate the bomb?

"Yeshua, calm down," said Mohammed. "We're all on the same team here."

"Okay, the simulation is over," said Smith. "This isn't a suicide mission. You've got a lot to learn before we are ready to do this for real. The scuba drivers will help you back to the surface."

Mohammed came out of meditation and pushed his talk button. "That's my best friend out there. He's not perfect. He's just a human. But he will be able to stop that bomb, whatever it takes. Although how is he going to get to and from the satellite from the ship?"

"Like I said. We are working on it," said Smith. "Have some faith. I'm being hard on the kid on purpose. We all want to come back alive, right?"

Captain Smith opened the cargo doors and six scuba drivers were there to lift them back to the surface.

Chapter 22

The Shema

Kennedy Space Station, Cape Canaveral Florida
Three days later

General Geller, Moshe Katz, Elijah Spencer and Lieutenant Colonel Eliora greeted Mohammed, Yeshua and Captain Smith as they walked out of the NASA pre-launch preparation building near the Vehicle Assembly Plant. The three of them had their full spacesuits on except for their helmets. In the distance was the Atlas V rocket on the launch pad. It was midnight, as this was a secret military launch and the local and national press had not been notified.

"Good luck," said Moshe Katz. "May God be with you. May you return back safely, Baruch Hashem."

Yeshua hadn't seen Eliora since the violent encounter with the Iranian kidnappers inside the parking garage in Saudi Arabia. She was supporting her weight with a wooden cane due to the gunshot she had sustained in her leg a few weeks prior. As Yeshua shook her hand during the procession, he whispered, "I'm so glad you are okay." to her. She smiled back.

The astronauts entered the shuttle bus and left for Space Launch Complex thirty-nine. After sitting down in the vehicle, they sealed their helmets into their EMU suits. As they left, the entire greeting party of diplomats, politicians and military personal headed to the nearby command and control center to watch and monitor the launch.

The massive Atlas V rocket stood next to the huge service tower on the launch pad. Overnight, the space engineers have secretly installed a connecter bridge to the payload module at the top of the 205 foot spacecraft. The astronauts arrived at the base of the tower and took the elevator to the top. The night sky was clear and full of millions of stars. The half moon shone down directly above the Space Center.

Once at the top of the launch tower, the three astronauts crossed over into the modified payload fairing containing the X37. The cargo doors were open, and someone was already sitting in the co-pilot's seat.

"Gurion!" said Yeshua after pushing his talk button on his suit. "The robot is going with us?" Gurion turned his head and looked at the three astronauts and almost seemed to smile.

"We've been keeping him a secret," said Captain Smith. "He's been retrofitting with a special jetpack and will be transporting you to and from the X37 and the IDF Satellite. Consider him a very expensive celestial scuba diver." Captain Smith chuckled a little.

"Ahhh. She finally has a sense of humor," said Mohammed. "Is he being remote controlled or does he have autonomous artificial intelligence?" he asked.

"I am told both," responded Smith. "Every movement will be coordinated by the command center; however, if we lose connection, or in event of a data lag or glitch, his AI is designed to override and complete the mission."

"Brilliant!" said Yeshua as he maneuvered into back passenger seat of the X37. He clicked in his seatbelt and then was followed by Mohammed and Captain Smith as they boarded the ship. The cargo doors of the X37 closed, followed by the closing of the doors to the outer payload fairing off the top of the ship. Finally, the connecter bridge retracted into the tall service structure, and the rocket was ready for launch.

Captain Smith turned on the control module to the X37 and clicked on several switches, turned a lot of knobs and activated the touch screen in front of her. The countdown started.

"Report range status," said the launch commander on the intercom.

"Range green," responded Captain Smith.

"Status check," said another voice in the intercom. "Go Atlas! Go Centaur!" said the launch commander.

"Five..."

Mohammed turned to Yeshua and gave him a thumbs up.

"Four..."

"Three..."

"We have ignition," said the launch commander. The whole ship shook and rumbled.

"Two..."

"One..."

The Atlas V vibrated tremendously as the massive booster activated and shot flames and smoke out of its RD-180 engine at the base of the rocket.

"And lift off of the Atlas V Rocket and orbital space Mission Shofar One," said command control.

The main engine functioned perfectly and provided over 800,000 pounds of thrust as the first stage rocket burned through its liquid oxygen liquid kerosene fuel mixture.

The astronauts felt the intense G-force as the rocket blasted upwards. They could hear mission control on the intercom talking about the performance of the lift off.

"Continuous C good and pump speed and injector pressure on the RD180 looking perfect. Now approaching Mach one and one minute eighteen seconds into flight. All good on the Shofar One? Copy," asked the launch commander.

Captain Smith responded. "All good. We have confirmed perfect jettison of all flight SRBs. Copy."

"Beginning second stage burn," said command control.

"Confirmed. Flight path on course. Main booster jettisoned," said Captain Smith.

"Fairing speed at 10,000 miles per hour," said the launch commander. "Approaching seventy nine miles altitude. All green! All good!"

The astronauts could hear cheering in the background of the launch commander's microphone.

"Payload fairing separation commencing," said the launch commander. "Confirm separation."

Yeshua and Mohammed looked at the small front window of the X37. The huge protective casing of the nose of the ship split in two and disappeared from view. Through the window, they could see the curvature of the Earth and ahead the sun was coming over the horizon. It was the most beautiful sunrise they had ever seen.

"Approaching thirteen minutes and cutoff of the first Centaur boosting phase. Confirm," said the launch commander. More cheers could be heard on the intercom.

"Confirmed," said Captain Smith. "Commencing coasting phase."

"Okay boys, now we get to relax as we coast into sub orbit for a little bit," said Captain Smith after she pressed her talk button on her suit. "And just so you know, there hasn't been a single failure of an Atlas V launch since its introduction in 2002."

Mohammed pushed his talk button. "I know. I looked that up on the Internet. I've been repeating that fact over and over in my head since we got into the ship."

Yeshua pushed his talk button. "I know this sounds cliché, but I've always dreamed about being an astronaut since I was a little boy. I've always wanted to fly in space."

"Dreams are very interesting," said Captain Smith. "Do you know that some of Albert Einstein's most famous equations and theories are based on dreams he had as a child?"

Yeshua responded, "I didn't know that. I've always had vivid, lucid dreams. Just wondering, do you think dreams come solely from our own imagination, or is the dream state is like an alternate universe where the past, present and future can flow freely? And what happened exactly in Einstein's dream?"

"I'm not sure about all that Freudian dream stuff," said Smith. "But I do remember reading that Albert dreamed he was sledding down a tall mountain at night in the Alps. His sled went faster and faster and started to approach the speed of light. He looked up into the sky and the colors of the stars refracted and bent differently as he went faster. Apparently that dream became one his inspirations to help form his theory of relativity. There's also a dream he had about cows and an electrical fence that led to a huge epiphany although I can't remember all the details. Later in his life Einstein was quoted as saying something like 'My entire scientific career has been a meditation on my dream.'"

Yeshua had one of those déjà vu feelings. He remembered his dream about all the cows he rescued from the slaughterhouse and the fence. How very similar it was to Albert's dream he thought, more than just a mere random coincidence. He made a mental note to research Einstein's dream later after they returned to Earth.

"Yeshua has some very interesting dreams too," said Mohammed. "I think he's some kind of modern day prophet."

"How so?" said Captain Smith.

"Let's just say he has some special gifts," said Mohammed. "For example, he is about the save the world by stopping the bomb on the satellite."

"Let's not count the chickens before they're hatched," said Captain Smith. "We still have to accomplish our mission and get back safely. There are still a million things that could go wrong."

"That's not how I like to think," said Mohammed. "I focus on the million things that need to go right, rather than go wrong. I call it the law of attraction. Although I prepare myself for any possible outcome, I put most of my energy into positive and optimistic thoughts... and that often attracts the best outcomes. Positive thoughts attract more positive, and negative thoughts almost always seem to attract more negativity. That's the law of the Universe."

"I'd love to discuss more metaphysical mumbo jumbo with you later, seriously I could talk about that subject for hours and hours," said Captain Smith. "However it's time to focus back on the mission. I'll do my best to keep a positive attitude and make the Universe happy, okay?"

"Yes, Captain!" said Mohammed.

The launch commander came back on the intercom. "The Centaur main engine is about to be restarted for the second and final burn. Do you copy Shofar One?"

"Copy," responded Captain Smith. "Spacecraft separation protocol commenced."

The ship accelerated up into higher orbit for five minutes as the engine fired and burned through the rest of its fuel. The Earth became much smaller in the window and the half moon became significantly larger. Yeshua could see the Middle East and Israel on the surface of the planet passing under them.

Yeshua looked down at the Earth in a way he had never seen it before. The big giant orb rotated at approximately one thousand miles per hour hundreds of miles below. The green, beige and brown colored landmasses of the continents were partially covered with incredible patterns of white clouds. He thought to himself, "There are no borders. We are all one."

"Centaur has released the X37. Separation complete. You are a free bird. Do you copy?" asked the launch commander on the telecom. More cheers and clapping could be heard in the background.

"Copy that command control," said Captain Smith. "Please calculate geostationary orbit coordinates and trajectory."

"The IDF Satellite is orbiting at 22,236 miles above the equator with a velocity of 6,858 miles per hour," said command control. We have your flight path tracking perfectly with arrival in five hours eighteen minutes. Copy."

"Copy that," said Captain Smith. "I forgot my cell phone with my favorite playlist. You got some tunes for us?"

"Never thought you would ask," said the launch commander. "We couldn't find any good Shofar music, although we think we found the next best thing. Enjoy The Magic Flute Overture by Wolfgang Amadeus Mozart."

The wonderful resonant sounds of the horns section emanated from the astronaut's headphones into their airtight helmets, followed by gentle harmonious string sections. Then, the tempo sped up and the extraordinary genius of Mozart's back and forth question and answer style chamber music played into full effect as the X37 hurled through space.

After a few minutes of listening to the music, Captain Smith pushed her talk button. "Do you know that this song, and about thirty others including Beethoven, Bach and even Johnny B. Goode were printed on an audio-visual time capsule called the Golden Record and it was placed onto the Voyager One spacecraft and sent into deep space in 1977? It's now over thirteen billion miles away from the Sun and is the first manmade object ever to leave our Solar System. It's actually now in interstellar space travelling out into the Milky Way"

"Wow. That's just epic," said Mohammed. "So someday, space aliens might find the ship with the Golden Record? How will they play it? I hope they have one of those old record players."

"Actually, they did include a record player turntable stylus needle and printed instructions on how to do the binary playback," said Captain Smith. "It's like a galactic message in a bottle. The late Carl Sagan said something like the Voyager spacecraft will be encountered and the record played only if there are advanced space-faring civilizations in interstellar space, and that the launching of that bottle into the cosmic ocean says something very hopeful about life on Earth."

"Binary. You said binary. That's the mathematical system of ones and zeros, correct?" asked Mohammed.

"Yes Sir," said Smith. "It's how almost all modern computers and digital devices work. Binary is the computer language of recognizing the difference between ones and zeros."

Yeshua was literally spacing out as he listen to the music while looking at the vast cosmos outside the X37's front window. "Wait, what did you just say?" he asked.

"Binary code. It's the difference between one and zero," replied Captain Smith. "In the code, it's multitudes of repetitive patterns and combinations of all zeros or ones, kind of like digital DNA. Each sum value is like a switch... it's on or off, something or nothing. The computer sees the difference of the two values and the patterns and that is the basis of all information."

"Ahhh yes," said Yeshua. "I've heard that before. Someone once told be the meaning of life is the difference between one and zero."

"That's the meaning of life?" asked Captain Smith. "Wow, that's deep. It's the difference, huh? The value of the two opposites. Something and nothing. One and zero. Like duality... two opposites. So, basically, you can't have one without the other. You can't have love without hate. You can't have hot without cold. So life is then experiencing all the values... the difference of the opposites. You can't really know and understand the full value and significance of happiness without knowing what true and complete sadness is. That makes so much sense! Who told you that?"

"God," said Yeshua.

"God?" asked Captain Smith.

"Yes," said Yeshua.

Smith paused for a moment. "Well, be careful who you tell that too. Some people might think you are certifiably crazy."

Back down on Earth, at NASA… the entire command center was listening to their conversation on the telecom. As Yeshua said "God" on the overhead speakers in the huge control station room, almost everyone paused what they were doing and seemed to reflect deeply on the astronaut's spiritual conversation.

Mohammed pulled himself slightly forward from his passenger seat and looked at Gurion. The robot was sitting quietly and still in the copilot's chair.

"So, Gurion… do you have any cool stories about the mysteries of the Universe? Or maybe even a joke or two?"

Gurion turned his head and looked at Mohammed, and then he shook his head back and forth a few times to communicate "No."

"Wow, I just noticed the zero gravity!" said Mohammed. "I'm kinda floating. The only thing that's holding me back is my seatbelt."

"Don't take your seatbelt off, please." said Captain Smith.

"Okay. So here's the plan," she said. "When we get within one hundred yards of the IDF Satellite, I'm going to open the cargo doors. Right before the doors open, the ship's auxiliary oxygen will turn off and we will switch to our EMU oxygen supply. As we shift from our climate controlled cabin atmosphere and the enter the outside space vacuum, the temperature will drop to minus 454 Fahrenheit and your EMU thermal systems will activate. Yeshua and Gurion will tether themselves with this harness and then jetpack over to the Satellite." She held a fancy looking bungee cord in her hands.

"Easy peasy," said Yeshua. "We got this."

"Gurion will stand up and jump up out of the ship and pull Yeshua outside with him on the tether cord," said Smith. "Then Gurion will grab Yeshua like the scuba divers did in the training tank and both of them will jetpack over to the IDF Satellite. Once Yeshua deactivates the bomb, Gurion will fly back here and we will start the process of descending and re-entry back to Earth. Yeshua, your EMU has over eight hours of oxygen, so that should give you more than ample time to accomplish the task. You are instructed to keep updating mission control via the telecom link about your status, okay?"

"Yes Captain," responded Yeshua.

"And Mohammed..." said Captain Smith "You will do that telepathic meditation thingy you do and go with Yeshua over to the Satellite and help him get the job done, okay?

"Yes. Captain," said Mohammed.

A voice came over the telecom system. "This is command control. Shofar One, do you copy?"

"Roger that," said Captain Smith. "We copy. My tracking system shows the IDF Satellite in range. Are we on track or do we need to engage manual controls towards the final rendezvous point?"

"You are on a perfect bull's-eye flight path Shofar One," said command control. "Estimated arrival is eight minutes twenty seconds. You should be able to see the IDF Satellite now in front of you."

Just then, approximately 93 million miles away... a huge series of solar flares erupted from the Sun's surface near some massive dark sunspots. An enormous coronal mass ejection of plasma, cosmic rays and electromagnetic radiation surged from the Sun in the direction of the Earth.

"I see it!" said Mohammed pointing into the corner of the X37's window. "There's the IDF Satellite."

Yeshua looked into the widow. It was a tiny dot in the distance. He looked at the video display in front of Captain Smith and saw the tracking images of the X37's proximity to the satellite.

"Approaching 22,236 miles elevation and speed 6,858 miles per hour," said command control. "Activating final destination maneuvers. Copy, Shofar One."

Captain Smith pushed several buttons and turned a few more knobs on the control panel. She zoomed in on the satellite on her touch screen video monitor and tapped on a few more buttons.

"Copy. Course confirmed command control. Autopilot Engaged," said Captain Smith.

The X37 glided much closer to the Satellite. It looked just like the replica satellite model that was at the bottom of the pool at the Neutral Buoyancy Laboratory. When the spaceship reached approximately 100 yards away, the reverse thrusters fired and the X37 stopped its forward velocity and came to a halt.

"Command Control. We have reached our destination. Copy," said Captain Smith.

There was a moment of silence.

"Command Control. We have reached our destination. Copy," repeated Captain Smith.

Yeshua heard some faint buzzing in his right ear. He started to have an anxiety attack, and his heart starting beating faster as he looked outside the ship for signs of danger. He chose not to say anything to the others, just yet.

"Copy Shofar One," said command control through the intercom. "Proceed as planned. Initiate the open cargo door protocol. Copy."

"Copy. Okay, it's show time gentlemen!" said Smith. She tapped the OPEN button on her touch screen and the exterior doors slowly opened. The vastness of space thoroughly saturated the ship's passengers as the X37 doors unfolded fully.

"This is the best convertible car ever!" said Mohammed jokingly. "Look at that view!"

The most spectacular perspective of the Earth, the Moon, the Sun, the Stars and Milky Way galaxy expanded in front of them. It was beyond breathtaking.

Captain Smith hooked the tether harness to Gurion and then turned around and helped Yeshua place it around his waist.

"Just relax and let Gurion pull you out of the ship when he jumps," she said to Yeshua as she smiled. "It's time to be a hero." Yeshua's right ear started buzzing louder.

Gurion unclicked his seatbelt and Yeshua undid his. He started to float in the zero gravity as Gurion stood up. The robot looked directly at the IDF Satellite and appeared to be calculating the physics of the space jump. Then he leaped into outer space out of the ship, pulling Yeshua behind him on the six-foot cord.

"Command Control. This is Shofar One. We have completed phase one. Do you copy?" said Captain Smith.

There was radio silence. Gurion paused for a few moments then pulled the tether cord and Yeshua towards him. He then grabbed the back of Yeshua's EMU suit and they both faced the IDF Satellite, one hundred yards away.

"Command Control. This is Shofar One. We have completed phase one. Do you copy?" repeated Captain Smith.

Some heavy static came through the intercom. "Shofar One, we have a problem," said command control in a barely perceptible voice. "There's some massive solar flare and storm activity. It's hitting you now, hard. The..." More heavy static came through the audio channel. "We're going to lose contact..."

The intercom audio went silent.

"Oh my God," said Captain Smith. She pushed her talk button. "Yeshua. Can you hear me?"

"Yes," said Yeshua. "Is that normal?" he said, pointing back down to the Earth floating in space with Gurion. "Look down there at the Arctic Circle. Check out the Aurora Borealis! It's covering the entire top of the Earth!"

Mohammed and Captain Smith looked back down at the Earth. Almost the entire upper half of the northern hemisphere was covered in spiraling, rippling and dancing waves of glowing green energy. The light show was thousands of miles wide, and all along the edge of the radiant display of cosmic waves and wisps were hundreds of intermittent flashes of electricity in the surrounding cloud formations. The solar storm and Aurora had triggered a massive surge of global lightning storms.

"I've seen a few a few major Aurora events while I was stationed on the International Space Station a few years ago, but never anything like this!" said Captain Smith. "Apparently the massive solar flare outburst is causing all of this, and we've now lost radio contact to mission control due to the interference from the electromagnetic radiation."

"So, we are on our own?" asked Yeshua.

"Yes," said Smith. "Hopefully the storm will pass soon and we re-establish radio contact with mission control. Is Gurion working? He's probably lost contact to his earthbound programmers and handlers as well."

Just as the Captain said that, Gurion's jetpack activated on his back and both he and Yeshua accelerated quickly in space towards the IDF Satellite.

"He's working! We are on our way!" said Yeshua.

"Thank God," said Captain Smith.

Mohammed turned off the volume on his EMU suit and he started to go into deep meditation in the back seat of the X37. As he cleared his mind, his consciousness left his body and he was looking down at himself in the X37. Below on Earth, the Aurora's green luminous streams of light seemed to magically dance as they ebbed and flowed almost as ghost-like apparitions. Mohammed thought he could see thousands spirits swimming in the energy of the Aurora, almost as one would observe a huge school of dolphins moving and jumping effortlessly in and out of the ocean's surface.

"Yeshua, can you hear me?" said Mohammed telepathically after he joined his spirit aura into his best friend's mind.

"Mohammed! Yes! I can hear you," said Yeshua in his mind. "We are almost at the IDF Satellite. Can you see it? Can you see through my eyes?"

"Yes. I see it!" said Mohammed. "We are flying through space together, how totally freaking epic is this?"

Gurion's jetpack thruster turned off and they glided closer to the Satellite, now just a few dozen yards away.

Yeshua's right ear stopped high pitch buzzing. He clicked on his talk button. "Captain Smith, we are approaching the Satellite. Very close now. I can see the Star of David emblem on it. Copy."

"Copy," said Captain Smith. "Gurion's artificial intelligence neural network should have switched on when we lost contact with ground control as a backup. He should be activating his reverse thrusters and have you right on that satellite any moment now."

Gurion's jetpack fired some thrust from its top and slowed their momentum down significantly. The huge Satellite was just a few feet away. After a few more moments, Yeshua gently pushed himself off of Gurion and grabbed the outer rim on the Satellite.

"Captain Smith! I made it!" said Yeshua. There was silence. "Captain Smith? You there?" More silence.

"Captain?"

"There must be some heavy duty interference from the solar storm," said Mohammed in Yeshua's mind. "I don't think she is picking up your signal."

"Well, I'm so glad you are here with me," said Yeshua. "Do see the bomb anywhere on this thing?"

"I don't," replied Mohammed. "I think you might have to make your way around the satellite onto the other side."

Yeshua started to navigate his way around the huge circular satellite. Gurion, still connected to him via the tether cord, almost appeared like a giant robot balloon floating in the air. After a few minutes, Yeshua made his way to the opposite side of the IDF Satellite. He could no longer see the X37, or the Earth as he view was now completely obstructed by the satellite.

"There it is." said Mohammed telepathically. "The bomb is right there. Do you see it?"

"Yes. It looks way different than the one in the pool simulation," responded Yeshua.

The bomb was about the size of a barrel. It had six encased arm like structures that looked like drone propellers. Another thick robotic arm was firmly attached to one of the metallic bars on the IDF Satellite.

"It looks like a spooky robot alien spider," thought Yeshua. "Gosh, I really, really don't like spiders." He pushed his talk button and said "Captain. Can you hear me? I found the bomb. Are you there? Captain?"

There was still no response.

"Yeshua, I see an exterior panel on the side of the bomb," said Mohammed. "There are some screws along its edge. Can you see it?"

"Yes. Gotcha," said Yeshua in his mind. He maneuvered himself as close as he could to the panel and placed his gloved hand over it. His left ear gently buzzed. "That's it. I'm going to undo the panel."

Yeshua pulled out a bungee rope from the side compartment of his EMU suit and clipped it onto an exposed area of the satellite casing. He then unzipped his left arm toolkit compartment and removed a Phillips head screwdriver.

"Yeshua to Shofar One. Copy?" said Yeshua.

Still, no response. Silence.

"Mohammed. I can't reach the Captain," said Yeshua in is mind. "Can you come out of your mediation there in the ship and check on her? I think the solar storm is blocking the all the radio signals. Tell her I found the bomb and I'm going to deactivate it."

"Yes, Sir!" said Mohammed. "I'll be back in a bit. Don't go anywhere."

"Haha. Where would I go?" responded Yeshua.

"Gurion. Come here," said Yeshua.

Gurion looked at Yeshua and nodded his head. He was about six feet away connected via the tether cord. Gurion fired his jetpack gently and floated over to Yeshua and the IDF Satellite.

"I'm going to get as close as I can to the outer panel of the bomb," said Yeshua through his telecom. "I'll need to use both my hands, and I want you to hold my suit still so I won't move, okay?"

Gurion nodded again. Yeshua maneuvered his body so the panel was right in front of his face. Gurion held one of his robotic hands on the IDF Satellite to steady himself and his other on the back of Yeshua's EMU suit. Yeshua started to unscrew the panel with his screwdriver. After each screw was removed, it just slowly floated into space. After the tenth screw was removed, the panel came off and the electrical circuit boards were exposed.

Yeshua pushed his talk button. "Captain Smith, Mohammed. Anyone there? I've removed the panel to the control system of the bomb and now will be commencing deactivation. Copy."

There was only silence.

"Helllloooo," said Yeshua. "Is there anyone out there?"

"Well, Gurion. Looks like it's just me and you."

Yeshua placed his left hand over the open panel of circuit boards on the bomb. His right ear started to high pitch buzz. A red light started to blink inside the open box containing the circuit boards and Yeshua's ear buzzed more loudly. He quickly placed his fingers over each individual board and with no result as the loud buzzing sound in his right ear became almost deafening.

"Oh snap," said Yeshua. "Gurion, I think this thing is about to blow up."

The bomb seemed to almost come alive as several exterior LED lights turned on and flashed as the device started to vibrate.

Yeshua's right ear started to bleed and he winced in worsening discomfort. He grabbed his helmet and started to go into the fetal position as he was moaning and groaning in agony and severe pain.

Gurion looked at Yeshua, then looked at the bomb. He let go of Yeshua's back and grabbed the thick metallic arm that connected the bomb to the satellite with both hands, and then ripped it apart. The bomb start to vibrate more intensely and all the exterior LED lights glowed brighter and flashed faster.

Gurion detached his tether cord from Yeshua, still incapacitated from pain and now almost unconscious. The robot grabbed the entire cylindrical bomb in both hands and turned away from the IDF Satellite. He fired his jetpack and started to fly in the opposite direction, away from both the satellite and the X37 that was approximately one hundred yards away.

Just as Gurion started to move, his foot inadvertently sliced through Yeshua's bungee cord that had been securing him to the satellite. Yeshua was flung helplessly out into space as he watched Gurion rapidly accelerate into the dark void of space.

After a few moments Gurion seemed to disappear into black vastness of the Universe. The bomb exploded, sending bright blue light and shockwaves with intense energy in a perfectly circular trajectory, like a supernova explosion. The center of the outburst looked like the pupil of a giant cosmic eyeball.

The outer eruption of the bomb expanded into a huge orb-like blue flare and as it hit Yeshua, he was bounced backwards and knocked out unconscious. Everything went black.

When Yeshua woke back up, he was still floating in space. In front of him was an enormously sized nebulous blue light energy that looked like the Aurora Borealis. It continually morphed and shape shifted like the reflections of bright sunlight at the bottom of a turquoise colored swimming pool. Yeshua looked around. The IDF Satellite and the X37 were gone. He was happy to still be alive.

The pattern of brilliant and luminous light in front of him was mesmerizing. It reminded him of the giant Orb that came to him when he thirteen, while in a coma after a terrorist's bomb blew up on the bus he was riding on after his Bar Mitzvah on Masada. He remembered that while he was in that coma, he had received the Shofar from Rabbi Yohanan.

The blue, green and turquoise light from the cosmic Aurora started to shimmer more brightly and oscillate between expansion and contraction, almost as it were breathing. Yeshua at first thought the light construct in front of him was just a remnant of the bomb explosion; however, now he felt like he was in presence of some kind of divine intelligence.

He felt like he was in the presence of God, again.

It was God, in the form of the shimmering Aurora. As soon as that thought came across Yeshua's consciousness, the energy of the Light amplified and wisps of energy seemed to flow and expand in every direction.

Yeshua started to pray... he recited the Shema, the pinnacle Hebrew invocation to the Creator of the Universe.

שְׁמַע יִשְׂרָאֵל, יְיָ אֱלֹהֵינוּ, יְיָ | אֶחָד:

Shema Yisrael Adonai Eloheinu Adonai Echad.

The Aurora transmuted and became even larger in response to Yeshua's prayer. He repeated the prayer, in English...

"Hear, O Israel, the Lord our God, the Lord is One."

A massive beam of light formed from the center of the Aurora and shot through Yeshua's body. He felt electricity surge through his body. He repeated again...

"Hear, O Israel, the Lord our God, the Lord is One!"

Yeshua felt supercharged. His entire body rippled with energy and power. Then, thousands of familiar multicolored orbs streamed from the Aurora along the beam of Light and swirled around his body, like a vortex.

"I am your humble servant," said/thought Yeshua to God. "What would you have of me?"

Yeshua's offer of self-service seemed to please God greatly. The Aurora glowed and scintillated even more in a wonderful and beautiful way. Suddenly, the gleaming beam of energy coming from the center of the Aurora and into Yeshua's body gradually dissipated and then completely stopped.

There was a moment of silence. The Aurora paused and stopped moving for some time and seemed to be in a state of contemplation.

Then, in a loud booming voice… the words came from the Aurora and into Yeshua's mind.

"THE EARTH IS SICK. YOU MUST HEAL THE WORLD. THE EARTH IS VERY SICK…"

The bright blue and turquoise massive Aurora started to fade away, and then it became translucent and then transparent and completely disappeared.

Yeshua's body slowly rotated 180 degrees, and then he was looking directly at the Earth from hundreds of miles up in space. It was an incredibly spectacular view as the big blue globe spun its way around the bright Sun at 67,000 miles per hour.

He looked down at his body. His spacesuit was gone. The celestial aurora like energy and the glowing orbs of light swirled around his body almost like a boa constrictor would serpentine around its prey. He put his hand in front of his face and he looked in amazement, as it seemed that the cosmic electricity had enveloped his entire being. It radiated, glowed and morphed up and down his arms, chest and lower torso and down into his legs.

Something shifted and Yeshua felt some movement. He looked down, and the Earth appeared to be getting larger and larger. He was being dragged back to the Earth!

The powerful gravitational field of the Earth took hold of Yeshua and pulled him hard. He started to accelerate faster and faster, his arms and legs spread wide out as if he were doing a parachute jump during his IDF military training. However, he had no parachute. The energy vortex continued to swirl around and within him.

The round Earth now filled almost his entire visual field. He would see clearly the continents and oceans below partially covered by massive collections of white clouds. It all looked so peaceful from space. There were no wars visible. There was no pollution that he could see. There was no hate, no suffering, no stress. There was only this beautiful gem of a planet, inhabited by millions of species of interconnected plants and animals.

"Nice job, God," said Yeshua out loud. "I'm sorry we are messing up this planet so badly, please forgive us."

Yeshua entered the upper atmosphere. Miraculously, he did not burn up like a shooting star. His cosmic energy cloak seemed to protect him, yet he continued to descend at hundreds of miles per hour. He could see the black of the void of space turn into the blue color of the sky as his speed of descent slowed down as his body interacted with the denser sub-stratosphere molecules. The front of his body glowed brightly from the heat from the friction of the higher density air atoms.

Below Yeshua could see the Mediterranean Ocean, Europe, Northern Africa and Western Asia. He fell through an upper layer of cirrostratus clouds at approximately forty thousand feet and felt a cold blast as he crossed into a band of diffuse ice crystals. As he continued to descend, the jet stream forced him towards the east and in the direction of the Middle East.

After a moment, Yeshua saw that he was going to land back in Israel. He was on a direct course downwards to Jerusalem. He could see the Dead Sea, and just to the south the town of Beersheba where he grew up. He was not scared, at all. He kept falling and the Old City of Jerusalem and the large rectangular Temple Mount came into view. The octahedron shaped Dome of the Rock was just below him, getting larger and larger. He was going to crash into the top of the Dome! It reminded him of so many of his recurrent dreams where he would be free falling.

"Yeshua, Yeshua! Are you okay?" said Mohammed loudly. There was a loud knocking sound.

Yeshua opened his eyes. He had his EMU spacesuit back on and Mohammed was inside the front of the X37 and grabbing him in space with one hand while tapping on his helmet with the other. Captain Smith sat in the pilot's chair and held onto Mohammed's leg so he wouldn't drift away.

What? What the heck just happened?" asked Yeshua as Mohammed pulled him back into the X37's back passenger seat. He reached over and clicked the seatbelt secure around Yeshua's waist.

"Yes, what happened?" asked Mohammed. "What the heck happened to you? You almost died out there! We found you floating in space. Where's Gurion?"

"Wait a sec," said a very groggy Yeshua. "What happened to the bomb?"

Yeshua looked down at his display and control module on his suit. It said he only had one hour of oxygen left. Had he been gone for seven hours?

"We thought you and Gurion removed the bomb and threw it out to space," said Mohammed. "Thankfully, it exploded far enough away the IDF Satellite. It still seems to be working perfectly."

"We are closing the cargo doors, okay?" said Captain Smith. "Where is Gurion?"

"He's dead," said Yeshua. "I mean he's gone. I couldn't deactivate the bomb and it was about to blow up. So, Gurion took it and flew out to space. He seems to have sacrificed himself."

The cargo doors closed and Captain Smith pushed some buttons and turned some knobs on the control panel. The touch screen was dark. As the cabin filled with breathable oxygen, the astronauts opened their helmets and breathed the air.

"Well, my friend. We have some bad news," said Mohammed. "Between the solar flare storm and the shockwaves from the bomb, we've lost all our communication capabilities and most of our navigation systems."

"Yeah. This is crazy. I'm basically going to have to glide this thing back to earth blind," said Captain Smith. "The whole NAV module is fried, and I can't contact mission control either."

"Yeshua, I'm so glad you are alive," said Mohammed. "I honestly thought you were lost in space. After the bomb blew up, we searched all over for you. You were a few miles away just floating and unconscious."

Yeshua considered telling Mohammed about the entire Aurora Borealis experience and falling back to Earth, but he decided to talk about it later in private.

"Thanks for saving my life, again!" said Yeshua. "And we successfully accomplished the mission, right? That's great news. So, what's next?"

"We fly this bird back down to Florida and go to Disney World!" said an excited Mohammed.

Captain Smith smiled. "I piloted the old space shuttle back down many times, although it's going to be a damn bumpy ride on this little wing with no NAV. And we spent most of our extra fuel finding Yeshua, so I give our difficulty scale on returning in one piece a solid 9.5"

"I'm not worried," said Mohammed. "I have total and complete trust and faith in you."

The Captain pushed a few more buttons and turned a couple of knobs. "Okay, here goes nothing." She grabbed the control wheel with one hand and pulled the throttle lever with the other. The ship turned and accelerated towards Earth, approximately 22,000 miles away.

"It's funny, that word faith," said Captain Smith. "It means belief in something for which there is no proof."

The Earth began to get larger and larger in the front window of the X37.

"Let me ask you a question. Do you believe in God?" asked Mohammed.

"Let me reply with a question," said Captain Smith. "Is there any proof of God? Like any scientific proof? Why should I believe in something just because it says I should in some books that are thousands of years old?"

"Well, at the most basic level... something created the Universe, right? That something is God," said Mohammed.

"I get it. Yes," said Smith. "Something did create the Universe. But with that logic... what then created God? Listen, there was definitely an act of Creation. But who knows, maybe we are in some kind of alien kids school science project. Like in a big test tube or something. Who knows for sure, really. And if there is some kind of Supreme Being that made this vast giant Universe, why would he, she or it really feel the need to come to Earth and intervene with us silly humans?"

"All good points," said Mohammed. "I tend to think that as we learn more about the scientific nature of the Universe, it only leads to appreciating more the absolute brilliance of the mind of God."

"How so?' asked Captain Smith. She turned the control wheel slightly to the right and started to move the ship more tangentially towards Earth's rotation.

"Look at all the patterns," said Mohammed. "They repeat infinitely. The spiral shape of a galaxy, the shape of a hurricane, the shape of a seashell. The fractals and fibonacci patterns. It's all an ingenious design, even the DNA spiral. There's just no way pure chance and random dumb luck got us here. I understand you can say there's no evidence; however, there's probably a very good reason why there's no obvious proof of God."

"And what is that?" asked Captain Smith.

"That God is self evident," said Mohammed.

"What?" said the Captain.

"Look at the Earth, the Moon, the Sun, the Stars… look at the all the Galaxies, the entire Universe. Isn't it obvious?" said Mohammed. "We were created in the Universe's image!"

"I know," said Smith. "I've just been messing with you. I was born and raised Unitarian. All is one my Muslim brotha!"

"Wait, wait did you just say?" asked Yeshua.

"All is One," responded Smith.

"Yes..." said Yeshua, now finally coming out from his extended post spacewalk somnolence. "All is One. Everything! We all exist within the mind of God. We are all God's children."

"I totally agree," said Captain Smith. "God the Father of the Christians, Allah of the Muslims, Adonai of the Jews... it's the same exact divine Creator Being. To know God is to know the Oneness, the perfect unity of the Universe."

"Wow. You totally get it, Captain," said Mohammed. "I wish more people would get it and that our religious and political leaders would get it too. I wish humanity would stop fighting and fight each other over perceived differences and interpretations of God."

"I wish too," said Captain Smith. "Okay, boys, we are about to start our reentry now. Please keep your arms and legs inside the vehicle at all times."

The X37 started to shake as it hit the upper atmosphere. The underbelly of the ship started to glow and heat up to three thousand degrees Fahrenheit as it travelled from west to east back towards the surface of Earth.

"The thermal protection system is working perfectly," said the Captain. "I think we are going to land somewhere out in the Pacific Ocean, although I'm not exactly sure where yet. The GPS and tracking systems are totally out. And still no communication to mission control. I can only imagine the mood at NASA right now, they probably have no idea where we are, or even know that we are still alive."

The Captain pulled up on her control wheel harder and pushed a few more buttons. The ship started to shake harder from the turbulence as it descended.

"I have an idea," said Mohammed. "I'll send a SOS signal."

"And how do you plan on doing that?" asked the Captain.

"On our first day of IDF training in Israel, they gave us these fancy watches," said Mohammed. He turned the two large emergency knobs on his shiny black timepiece on his left wrist. "I pop open these two antennas, and BOOM... they activate a dual frequency distress beacon signal."

"Nice watch!" said the Captain. "That just might do the trick."

"What's that down there?" asked Yeshua, looking out the window at the vast Pacific Ocean.

"What's what?" responded Smith.

"That trail of smoke way out there," said Yeshua.

Captain Smith squinted her eyes and looked out the window directly to the east. "Ah, I see it now," she said. "That's must be the Kilauea Volcano in Hawaii! Good eyes Yeshua."

The Captain turned her control wheel and steered in the direction of the volcano. She pushed a few more buttons and knobs. "I'll guide us there. Good ole USA. Perfect."

"Oh snap! Our freaking landing gear is out too," said Captain Smith. "This just gets more and more fun. Looks like we will be crash landing in the ocean today, gentlemen. You guys know how to swim, yes?"

Both Yeshua and Mohammed nodded.

"Ok, here's the plan. This ship isn't designed to float like an Apollo return capsule," said Smith. "As soon as we hit the water and slow down enough, I'm going to open the cargo doors and we need to get out of here ASAP before it sinks. I want you guys to take off your EMU suits now and when we crash land, help me out of here. I'm not going to have enough time to get my suit off while I'm flying this bird."

Yeshua and Mohammed immediately started taking off their helmets and EMU suits. Ahead, through the window… the islands of Hawaii became larger and larger as the X37 descended. The lava and smoke from the Kilauea Volcano reminded Yeshua of the many dreams and visions he had about a similar mountain of fire in Saudi Arabia. Yeshua and Mohammed stripped down to their last layer of clothing, which was the liquid cooling and ventilation garments. They put their seat belts back on.

"Looks like we will be making our water landing right next to Oahu," said Captain Smith. "In about one minute."

About one hundred miles further to the southeast, the Kilauea volcano made a huge eruption of lava and smoke. The explosion shot miles up into the air, clearly visible to the returning astronauts.

"Wow. It looks like Mother Nature is really pissed off," said Mohammed, looking out the window.

"Brace yourselves," said the Captain. "We're about to land on Mamala Bay, right next to Pearl Harbor."

The X37's drogue parachute deployed and the entire ship jolted hard as it de-accelerated rapidly just a couple hundred feet above the water. A few moments later, Captain Smith nailed the landing. The bottom of the ship hit on a perfect angle and huge splash of water radiated around the landing zone. Ripples of water circulated in every direction, like a rock that is thrown just right and skims the surface of the water multiple times.

Captain Smith opened the cargo doors of the X37 as the ship came to a full stop in the large bay off of the Island. Yeshua looked above and saw a large United States Coast Guard Jayhawk helicopter flying in their direction from Pearl Harbor. The 11,000 pound mini space shuttle immediately starting sinking in the water. Yeshua and Mohammed both grabbed Captain Smith by her EMU suit, and they all jumped into the cold Pacific water just as the ship disappeared into the depths of the ocean.

The orange and white helicopter arrived exactly on time and hovered just over the three astronauts in the frigid water. One of the Coast Guard crew dropped down a rescue rope ladder and Captain Smith grabbed it first and pulled herself out of the water and she climbed up into the bay of the helicopter. Mohammed climbed up the ladder next, followed by Yeshua. The helicopter flew back to Pearl Harbor. The sun was setting in the west, and Kilauea continued to violently erupt to the southeast.

Chapter 23

Carpe Diem

Palmachim Airbase, Israel
Two Days Later

Yeshua and Mohammed patiently waited in the conference room alone. It had been quite an adventure. They had literally travelled all around the world and back again.

General Geller and Lieutenant Colonel Eliora entered the room. Yeshua and Mohammed both immediately stood up in attention.

"At ease gentlemen," said the General. Yeshua and Mohammed sat back down in their chairs as soon as Geller and Eliora sat across from them at the conference table.

"I've read the full report," said the General. "You are both heroes for your bravery and selfless actions. Aside from losing a 100 million dollar spaceship and a 20 million dollar robot, I would consider your mission a complete success."

Mohammed and Yeshua glanced at each other and they both grimaced.

"Don't worry. We won't send you the bill," said the General. "All is well. The IDF Satellite is still functioning flawlessly. The Iranians are thwarted again and scrambling to find some other way to sabotage our missile defense systems. We are currently one step ahead of them thanks to you." He nodded and smiled at Mohammed and Yeshua.

"Thank you Sir," they both said in unison.

"Yeshua... I have a question for you," said Eliora. "It says here in the report you were knocked unconscious by the exploding bomb and floated in space for over six hours until you were rescued by Captain Smith and Mohammed in the X37. Is that true?"

"Yes, Lieutenant Colonel," said Yeshua.

"Wow. It's a miracle you survived," said Eliora. "Do you remember anything while you were out in space?"

"Only bits and pieces," said Yeshua. "I kept fading in and out of consciousness. At one point I thought I was talking to God."

"What? You were talking to God?" asked a surprised Eliora. "What did He say?"

"Well, first of all… I don't think God is a he," said Yeshua. "God doesn't seem to be male or female. It's more like pure energy… like Light."

"Okay, I completely understand what you are saying. I think we say 'he' instead of 'it', because saying God is an 'it' just sounds really weird. So while you were in floating in space, what did God say to you?"

"God said we must heal the Earth. That world is really sick and diseased. God wants us to heal it," said Yeshua.

"I think maybe that's why God made you Hebrews the Chosen people," said Mohammed. "You are here to help fix this very broken and shattered world."

"Mohammed… I also have a question for you," said Eliora. "How did you mind control Gurion and fly the bomb away from the Satellite?"

"Huh?" responded Mohammed. He looked very confused.

"Gurion. The robot. You mind controlled him, correct?" asked General Geller.

"What do you mean?" said Mohammed.

"Gurion's software glitched and malfunctioned when the solar storm hit him," said the General. "His neural network totally crashed. And we lost all communications with him as well. He should have just completely stopped functioning. We figured you mind controlled him and helped Yeshua over to the IDF Satellite and then flew away with the bomb and blew it up at a safe distance."

"Sir. No, I didn't mind control Gurion," said Mohammed. "I telepathically went into Yeshua's mind until he got to the IDF Satellite and then came back to my body to check on Captain Smith. By the time I got back to myself, Gurion had already flown off with the bomb."

"So you didn't mind control Gurion at all?" asked Eliora.

"No Sir. I didn't. I swear," replied Mohammed.

"Then who did?" asked General Geller.

EPILOGUE

August 2239
Trans-galactic Space Station, Earth Orbit

The civilian shuttle transport ship arrived from Earth exactly at noon. It docked smoothly at airlock eighteen of the enormous cylindrical shaped rotating space station. The ship's lone passenger left the shuttle and walked through the airlock and into the decontamination chamber. A smoky mist was sprayed into the small room and then his body was scanned up and down with some red lasers. A light turned green in the room and the door opened to the main transportation hanger.

The man wore a dark long robe with a hood. Slung around his back was the Shofar. He walked through the large room full of fantastic looking spaceships. There were several maintenance and support personal in the hanger attending to the ships.

He stopped in front of one of the larger ships that looked like the sleek bullet train with wings. The side door opened and a man walked down a short flight of stairs to greet the robed man. He looked just like Mohammed, but much older.

"How are you, my friend?"

The robed man pulled off his hood. He had wavy reddish hair, a long beard and moustache. He wore a turquoise colored Jewish yarmulke on the top of his head. He looked just like Yeshua, but much older.

"I am well. I've brought the Shofar," he said as he slung it from his back and into his hands.

"Let's roll," said the man that looked like Mohammed. He walked back up the stairs and the man who looked like Yeshua followed him. Inside the spaceship, they sat in the pilot and copilot seats.

The ship elevated off the floor and hovered over to a large adjacent antechamber room. A large door closed behind the ship and then another opened in front exposing the outside of the space station. The bullet ship took off into deep space and accelerated further away from the Earth towards the full Moon.

Inside the spacecraft, the two men were talking to each other.

"Your left ear is high pitch buzzing now?" said the man who looked like Mohammed.

"Yes, it just started to buzz in my left ear. It's a sign," said the man who looked like Yeshua.

"Okay. I will stop the ship right here."

They both grabbed the Shofar. The red bearded man placed the Shofar up to his lips and blew with all his might.

Ba-ba-baaaaaaaaaaaaaaa...

Ba-ba-baaaaaaaaaaaaaaaa...

Ba-ba-baaaaaaaaaaaaaaaa...

Everything went black.

Out of the darkness came an array of lights. First it was dim, and then a tunnel of repeating concentric circles formed. The lights became much brighter and then transformed into multicolored patterns of rotating circles, like a celestial cosmic wormhole. From the end of the tunnel a bright light rapidly approached, and then two images formed from the light and were surrounded by total darkness.

Yeshua was floating in space tethered next to a robot. Nearby was the X37 spaceship with Mohammed and Captain Smith inside. Down below on Earth, there was an enormous green Aurora Borealis surrounded by massive global lightning storms.

There was a white and yellow aura hovering near Yeshua.

"Those young men look just like us!" said a voice coming from the white aura.

"Look, at that satellite over there," said a voice coming from the yellow aura. "I think I know what I'm supposed to do here."

The yellow aura moved and went into the completely motionless robot. Gurion's jetpack thrusted forward and he and Yeshua flew towards the IDF Satellite 100 hundred yards away.

TO BE CONTINUED...

About the Author

Joshua Kreithen was born on a Sunday morning, October 18th, 1970 in Albert Einstein Hospital in Philadelphia, Pennsylvania to Leslie and Marvin Kreithen.

His parents are descendants of Eastern European Jews who escaped religious persecution and arrived in America as immigrants in the early 20th century. Joshua's Grandfather, 'Zayda' Jacob Kreithen came to Ellis Island as a teenager and spent most of his lifetime supporting his family as a 'cutter' in a men's clothing manufacturing warehouse in Philadelphia. His favorite hobbies were listening to opera and painting, and his artistic creative passion has been passed down to all of his descendants.

At the age of 13, Joshua became a Bar Mitzvah at Ohev Shalom of Bucks County in Richboro, PA. As a customary practice during this ancient rite of passage into adulthood, all Bar Mitzvas would choose a special project to share during their Bar Mitzvah service. Joshua's project was focused on Kabbalah, based on ancient Jewish Mysticism.

Joshua went on to go to medical school and become a surgeon; he completed a plastic surgery fellowship at the University of Florida. He chose to combine all of his artistic, medical and technical skills to become a plastic and reconstructive surgeon and In addition to being an accomplished physician... he is a painter, photographer, musician and published writer.

Dr. Kreithen currently lives in Sarasota, Florida with his beautiful wife, Melissa... who always serves as a source of inspiration and vision for his creative endeavors.

www.ingramcontent.com/pod-product-compliance
Lightning Source LLC
Chambersburg PA
CBHW060153260626
47160CB00001B/246